SMITH RAISED AN EYEBROW

"Is there something wrong with the Master of Sinanju?" he asked.

"Nothing wrong. He just wanted to ask you for something."

"A trifling item, O illustrious Emperor," Chiun called.

"If it is within my power to do so."

"Oh, it is," Remo said. "Chiun wants to know if he can have your autograph."

"I am not sure I understand..."

"He thinks since you've been on the news you're going to break into the big time. He wants to get your signature first. Especially since he heard that a lot of autographs fetch big bucks."

"How you like to apply your base motivations to another," squeaked Chiun.

"So, you willing to do it or what?" Remo spoke to Smith.

"I'll see what I can do."

"And, Smitty?" Remo said.

"Yes?"

"Don't forget us litt

Created by
WARREN MURPHY
and RICHARD SAPIR

THE

BRAIN STORM

A GOLD EAGLE BOOK FROM
WORLDWIDE.

TORONTO • NEW YORK • LONDON
AMSTERDAM • PARIS • SYDNEY • HAMBURG
STOCKHOLM • ATHENS • TOKYO • MILAN
MADRID • WARSAW • BUDAPEST • AUCKLAND

First edition August 1998

ISBN 0-373-63227-4

Special thanks and acknowledgment to James Mullaney and Daisy Snaggers for their contribution to this work.

BRAIN STORM

Printed in U.S.A.

For Mary and Red Power.

And the Glorious House of Sinanju.

1

The thing that scared Andy Frost most that day was the parking.

The crime rate didn't bother him. Everyone he knew had been mugged at one time or another. Among New Yorkers, it was sort of a twisted badge of honor. In fact, it wasn't uncommon for people to invent stories of violence for the daily water-cooler competition.

The people themselves didn't frighten him, though the Christmas crowds had a tendency to get on his nerves. Everyone had a touch of agoraphobia at one time or another, but not Gothamites. When you were raised in a ten-story walk-up like a nest of rabbits in a squalid hutch with a hundred other human dregs screaming and pounding through the walls and ceiling and floor all hours of the day and night, you learned to live with overcrowding. You complained about it, sure.

Constantly. But you lived with it.

Yes, the murder rate was high. So what? Everyone died in his or her time. Here people were killed over stuff as trivial as a pair of sneakers or a leather jacket. What, they didn't have murders in Wisconsin?

Facing down the business end of a gun didn't worry Andy. And it was a trade—a high per capita murder rate in exchange for all-night drugstores, fresh bagels on demand and the chance to see *Cats* or *Evita* or a dozen other shows seven nights a week.

The other fearful things of everyday life in the city were too numerous to mention. You had to deal with Con Edison, rabid rats, cockroaches the size of ashtrays, greedy landlords if you weren't lucky enough to benefit from rent control and about a million foreign cabbies who seemed to have learned their driving skills behind the wheel of a Kuwaiti bumper car.

All of these things he could shrug off as part of living in the most exciting city in the world. If you complained about them, you were a New Yorker. If you complained about them and meant it, you were a schlemiel.

No, none of these things bothered him anymore. But the one thing that still made Andy Frost shiver and whimper like a rain-drenched fox terrier was the parking in midtown Manhattan.

Parking condensed every fearful element of the city.

You got your ticket from an angry foreigner in a tiny booth. You drove into a drafty underground garage that stank of urine and housed more species of wildlife than the Bronx Zoo. Muggers and murderers were likely skulking behind every other parked car. And at Christmas? Forget it.

You'd be better off leaving your car in the middle of the Triborough Bridge and walking the rest of the way in.

Fortunately for Andy, the holidays were months away and so the crowds of people heading to work were no worse than usual. It was ridiculous, but negotiable, which was good for him since he was already running late.

The parking garage was less than a block away from the bank where he worked, and as he angled down into the musty bowels of Manhattan, Andy took a moment to quietly curse his parents. Not for the first time today, and it surely wouldn't be the last.

They were the reason he had the car. In fact, it was their car.

The biggest, ugliest conglomeration of metal and plastic Detroit could produce, slapped front and back with the telltale orange-and-green Florida license plates. There was no doubt about it—if the Big Three started making cars with shark fins again, Andy's father would be first in line to buy one.

His parents were up on a visit with his mother's sister and they were going to spend the day taking Andy's aunt around town to see all the sites they had neglected to visit during their fifty-odd years of living in the Big Apple. It was an irony he had pointed out at least a hundred times during the past two days.

They had made Andy promise he would pick them up at Rockefeller Center at five-thirty that afternoon—a feat he still had no idea how to accomplish—and his father had dropped the keys to the Buick in his hand as he went out to work that morning.

And so here he was, at 9:11 a.m. on a Monday morning, already more than ten minutes late for work, driving down into some subterranean nightmare and not knowing whether or not he was ever going to see a ray of sunlight again.

He did. In record time. Andy was up on the sidewalk and trotting along through the heavy pedestrian traffic three minutes later.

As he jogged along, he continually checked his watch at thirty-second intervals, each time stepping up the pace a little more. Plowing through the choking throng of people, he caught a few angry glares from other pedestrians but in spite of everything that could have gone wrong, he was at the bank by twenty minutes past nine.

In front of the massive building, Andy noticed that the gutter had been marked off with several strategically placed orange traffic cones. These were obviously set up to discourage anyone from slowing down or parking in front of the bank's double doors. The sounds of honking horns and angry shouts were proof that not everyone appreciated their careful placement.

At the center of the arrangement of cones, directly across from the glass foyer doors of the bank, a large white van sat soaking up the few feeble rays of diluted sunlight that managed to penetrate the smog and towering buildings. The van's engine hummed softly.

As he approached, Andy noted that the cab of the van was empty.

Not a very wise move in New York. It was an open invitation to thieves. As he drew closer, Andy noticed the name PlattDeutsche A.G. stenciled in small black script above the door handle on the passenger's side. That explained it. This was the new security company which for the past few weeks had been installing the bank's new high-tech camera and vault system. Probably the van was wired to explode the minute somebody touched the door handle.

Suddenly the door separating the cab from the rear opened, and Andy got a quick glimpse of a distinctly high-tech environment. A brief flash of computer monitors, blinking lights and men in white lab coats moving urgently around the cramped interior showed before the door was closed once more. A young man moved from the rear of the van to settle down in the vacant driver's seat behind the leather-wrapped steering wheel.

The man sported a mane of dirty blond hair swept

carefully back onto the broad shoulders of his expensive suit, and when his gaze settled on Andy, the young mortgage officer found himself staring into a pair of the angriest blue eyes he had ever encountered. Looking at them was like peering into the eyes of a feral jaguar.

Andy didn't know what it was with those Platt-Deutsche people, but ever since they'd shown up more than a month ago, they'd been giving everyone at the Butler Bank of New York a first-class case of the screaming-meamies.

Andy tore his gaze away from the feral eyes of the young man and hustled through the massive bank doors.

An hour later, Andy had settled down behind his desk on the main bank floor. He was a junior member of the bank's mortgage team, and even though his father referred to him as a "glorified teller," he still hoped that one day he would move into the upper offices of the Butler banking empire.

As a junior officer in the banking industry, Andy generally considered his greatest misfortune to be the placement of his work space so close to the bank's main entrance. His proximity to the front door invited gentle queries on every imaginable topic from a wide range of the Butler Bank's many patrons. He felt that his desk was the informal information booth for the whole bank, and though he complained about it many times in the past, his supervisor had so far managed to avoid taking corrective action.

Today Andy wasn't complaining. He had completed the bulk of his work after a mere forty-five minutes behind his desk and he was intent on frittering away the remainder of the day until it was time to retrieve his father's car and battle his way through the insane rush-hour traffic. Most days when Andy goofed off, he had little to occupy his time save the endless shuffle of papers and an occasional trip to the men's room, but today he had a floor show. Through the bank's hazy tempered-glass doors, he watched the activity around the white van.

The young blond man had remained behind the steering wheel for the better part of an hour, staring down pedestrians with his steely blue gaze. Only when another car pulled up into the cordoned area behind the van did the van driver exit the cab. He and the driver of the new vehicle stood together by the side of the large white truck. Their matching suits made them look like twins.

Andy tore his eyes away from the sidewalk and feigned interest in a document in his hand. The columns of numbers and dry words ran together in an incoherent jumble.

He looked back out the door. Several more men had joined the first two. They stood, glancing up and down the street nervously, as the man from the car spoke instructions to each of them in turn.

Every now and then, one of the newest arrivals would glance toward the bank entrance. Even though Andy was certain that the glare of the late-morning sun reflecting off the black-tinted main doors would be enough to shield him from view, he nonetheless felt himself growing more nervous with each subsequent glance.

What were those guys up to?

His hand began to snake toward the phone, ready to alert security to the suspicious activity on the sidewalk out front, when something suddenly popped into view. Walked into view, more accurately.

Somebody had come over from the main bank floor, positioning himself before Andy Frost's desk and blocking his view of the men on the sidewalk. Andy leaned to one side, trying to catch a glimpse of whatever was going on outside.

"Excuse me," said a precise voice that reminded Andy of his grammar-school English teacher, Mr. Henry.

He could no longer see the men on the sidewalk. Andy leaned the other way, but his line of sight was still blocked.

"Excuse me," the voice repeated. It was somewhat nasal and parched, as if the speaker's larynx had been soaked in a gallon of grapefruit juice and left to dry on a desert rock.

Andy looked up, exasperated. "Yes. What?" he demanded.

"There is an error in my account."

Andy rolled his eyes. Just another mindless questioner. He was going to kill his supervisor if he wasn't moved into a cubicle soon.

"This is the mortgage desk, sir," Andy said in an icy tone.

"I realize that. But there is a discrepancy in my personal account that I wish to correct, and the lines at the teller windows are intolerably long. You seemed not to be busy."

The group of men on the sidewalk were quickly forgotten. With as much agitation as decorum would allow, Andy stared up at the old man standing before his desk.

"Sir, I am certain that any of our tellers are more than qualified to help you with your little problem."

"Perhaps," said the older man, "and I ordinarily would not mind waiting in line. But I have left my car in a nearby garage and if I do not return within the next fifteen minutes, I will be charged the day rate. I am certain it will not take you long." The old man offered Andy one of the brand-new Butler bankbooks, first remembering to remove an ancient plastic cover that was yellowed from long use.

Andy sighed audibly. As if he didn't have enough to worry about, what with having to pick up his parents on the busiest street in the world at the busiest time of the day, he was now reduced to checking on some old codger's passbook. The guy had probably just forgotten to add the interest payment from the previous month. Andy didn't want to count how many times he had seen that particular mistake when he was a teller. He snatched the bankbook from the gentleman at his desk, noticing for the first time that the old man's skin was the color of a sickly fish belly, and started to rise from his seat.

Andy froze in midmovement.

"Nobody move," a too cheerful voice shouted from over near the main entrance.

Andy could see that the two men—the young blond man and the later arrival—were standing at the bank entrance. The others, a larger group, were circulating through the bank, sweeping in around the velvet-roped queue and up to the bulletproof teller windows.

A robbery!

Damn! Andy thought. I should have alerted the security guards.

He'd known something was up earlier. If he hadn't been distracted by the old man, Andy would have called the manager, maybe gotten the police involved. He would have been a hero, but instead he was going to become just another hostage if this thing played out the way most of these daylight robberies did.

Worse, if he was late tonight, his dad would slaughter him.

Andy started to sit back down, determined to remain as inconspicuous as possible and hopefully to get through this thing in one piece. That was when the sudden realization hit him. He couldn't move.

Andy tried forcing himself to sit down. His legs wouldn't budge. He tried pushing them into place with his arms. He realized with a sinking feeling that his upper torso was frozen in place, as well.

Andy was locked in an awkward squatting position just above the seat of his vinyl junior-executive's chair.

He tried harder but found that it was no use. He was a human rock.

And, he soon discovered, he wasn't alone.

As Andy's frightened eyes darted helplessly around the bank interior, he found that the only people who seemed to be moving were the thieves. Each member of the larger group had taken up a post at every teller window, most standing directly in front of bank patrons, who for some inexplicable reason remained as motionless as statues. Not only that, but all of the normal extraneous sounds of people talking, coughing, shifting from foot to foot—indeed, all sounds save those of the robbers themselves—had ceased at the precise instant the main thief had first spoken.

Everyone within the bank—employees and patrons alike—was as helpless as a mannequin.

At one window, an old woman was standing too close for a robber to access the teller window. The man simply picked the woman up as if she were nothing more than a piece of wicker furniture and set her down over near the head of the line. Though her eyes darted wildly in every direction, the rest of her might have been carved in stone.

"Of course, that was an unreasonable demand," the cheerful voice of the head robber said into the silence of the frozen bank lobby. As he spoke, he moved toward the center of the lobby. The blond man remained dutifully behind, a loyal sentry at the bank entrance. "For an operation of this kind to work, there has to be some movement, obviously."

As if his words were some sort of prearranged cue, the tellers began reaching into their cash drawers and stuffing bills into bags that were handed over by the thieves. They moved like automatons, with simultaneous motions. Hands entered cash drawers, money was removed, hands entered bags, repeat. It was a flawless series of movements, seemingly more precise than the most meticulously rehearsed Broadway dance number. When the tellers were finished, they shoved the bags through the narrow slots beneath the bulletproof partitions and snapped to attention behind the windows as if awaiting further instructions.

Watching the entire procedure from a squatting position behind his desk and unable to move a muscle, Andy, in some lucid part of his mind, was struck by the surrealism of the entire procedure. It was an eerie tableau, as if everyone inside the bank were some sort of dusty museum exhibit demonstrating modern banking techniques.

Andy caught a hint of movement before him and shifted his eyes—which seemed about all he could move—in that direction. He had forgotten about his customer. The old man was standing stock-still before his desk, frozen like everyone else.

Not entirely, it seemed.

Faintly, so much so that it was barely detectable, the old man was swaying from side to side. Also, as Andy watched, there seemed to be a slight trace of movement at the tips of the man's slender gray fingers.

Andy's attention was distracted in the next minute when his legs suddenly buckled. He fell roughly back into his chair, dropping the old man's passbook to his desk blotter.

All around the bank, patrons suddenly began to stir as if some huge unseen switch had been activated.

Tellers backed away from their windows. Bank patrons stood nervously in place, eyeing the robbers, who seemed themselves at a loss for what to do next. The men looked suddenly panicked, as if the thought that anyone in the bank would be able to move had never occurred to them.

For the first time, Andy noticed that none of them carried guns.

Andy looked beyond the old man in front of him

toward the street, where he fervently hoped that an NYPD SWAT team was positioned to take out the robbers. All he saw beyond the large white van was a pizza delivery truck stuck in late-morning traffic, a giant CB antenna bobbing impatiently from its roof.

Suddenly a command cracked through the air. "Okay, hold it right where you are!"

Bank security. There were three green-suited guards standing around the lobby, their guns drawn and trained toward the largest concentrations of thieves.

The leader held his hands high above his head. "I'm certain that this is just a misunderstanding, sir," he said tightly. He tried to force the cheerfulness of a moment before, but the words sounded terse. He glanced impatiently out toward the parked van. Andy noticed that he wore a hearing aid.

"Shut up!" the head of the Butler Bank security force ordered. "Down on the floor, hands behind your heads! Now!"

The man looked back from the door, eyeing the guard balefully. "Do you have any idea how much this suit cost?" he asked. He shot another glance toward the bank entrance. The traffic seemed to be picking up. The pizza truck had moved a car length down the street.

"Down! Now!"

The robbers were beginning to comply. They

dropped to their knees, all the while watching their leader expectantly. The man refused to move an inch.

The pizza truck drove away.

Andy felt an odd tingling sensation at the back of his head.

It was a sort of tickle, as if someone had brushed his neck with a feather. The sensation made his ears itch.

The robber turned victoriously back toward the guard. With a boldness that was surely suicidally motivated, the man strode purposefully up to the guard and, wrapping his fingers around the barrel of the gun, tugged the weapon from the guard's outstretched hand. The guard didn't react, didn't move an inch.

With obvious relish, the robber tucked the gun back into the guard's holster. Frozen once more, the other two security men watched helplessly as the same procedure was repeated with them.

Andy tried to move but realized that he, too, was immobile. All around the bank, patrons and employees alike were once again rooted to wherever they stood.

Bags of money in hand, the robbers clustered around their leader in the center of the lobby. Some people were staring stonily off in other directions, but most were looking in the general direction of the thieves, their eyes darting helplessly from side to side. Drool leaked from one man's parted lips.

The lead thief grinned triumphantly around the lobby of the bank.

"And now, with your kind assistance, gentlemen..." With a nod from their leader, the thieves began to circulate through the frozen crowd.

This was it. They were going to start killing people. Or worse.

All thoughts of his dreaded commute were banished from Andy's mind as one of the thieves—a sinister-looking man in his forties—approached his desk. He reached into the money bag he had taken from one of the teller windows and, stuffing his hand deep inside, proceeded to remove a handful of bills. As the young mortgage officer watched in disbelief, the thief stuffed the wad of bills into the pocket of the old man in front of Andy's desk. Moving on, he found a patron who was standing nearer the door and went through the same motions.

Eyes straining to catch every movement at the limits of his peripheral vision, Andy saw the other thieves stuffing money into satchels and jacket pockets.

While they seemed to carry out this task grudgingly, their leader performed it with unreserved joy. One bank patron was dressed in only jeans and a T-shirt, but the gang leader carefully wrapped up a tight roll of crisp new fifty-dollar bills and tucked it neatly into the pocket of the man's torn shirt.

Oddly the Butler Bank employees seemed to be

the only ones who were left out of this bizarre re-distribution of wealth.

When all was done and the bags were once more empty, the thieves clustered back around their leader.

There was something cultured, almost regal about him. He raised his hand in a casual gesture that would have made the Queen of England feel as if she'd just rolled off the back of a turnip truck.

"Ladies and gentlemen," he called happily to the crowd. "My name is Lothar Holz, and you have just been privileged to witness the premier nonlaboratory test of PlattDeutsche, America's Dynamic Interface System."

Andy felt the strange sensation at the back of his head return. He realized immediately that he could move. All around the bank, patrons and employees alike were coming to the same conclusion. The guards were in the process of unholstering their weapons once more, but Andy saw that the bank president, Clive Butler, trailed by a clutch of VPs, had entered the lobby from the rear elevator and was now circulating among the crowd, calming concerns and exhorting employees not to succumb to panic.

A smattering of applause went up around the man who identified himself as Lothar Holz, led by the blond man at the door and the rest of the robbers. They were joined in their enthusiasm by Clive Butler and the other executives. With the urging of the suits from upstairs, it wasn't long before all of the junior employees were applauding the man who moments before had brought terror to an otherwise ordinary day.

Amazingly most of the bank customers also joined in. It was a classic example of mob mentality, deduced Andy, though he suspected that their enthusiasm for the would-be robber was mostly motivated by the cash in their pockets.

Lothar Holz stood in the center of the crowd, soaking up the admiration as if such a display was his birthright.

Clive Butler moved to Holz's side, quieting the crowd with a raised hand. When he spoke, his words had the clipped intonation of an old-money New Englander. It was as if the sounds were produced in his sinuses and every word had a gasping, affected quality that suggested each syllable would be his last. As he spoke to his customers, his teeth never parted.

"I want to thank Mr. Holz on behalf of the entire Butler/Lippincott family of banks for the privilege of witnessing his remarkable new technology firsthand. And I am certain that we are all thankful that it is PlattDeutsche who has developed our new security system. I know my money sleeps better at night knowing PlattDeutsche is on the job."

Andy was about to call the paramedics until he realized the painful series of groans emanating from Clive Butler's throat was the man's version of laughter.

A brief round of fresh applause ensued.

"Thank you, thank you," Holz said to the now genuinely enthusiastic crowd. "You will all be relieved to know that the technology used to temporarily immobilize you is a harmless neural linkup that connects the human brain to a computer. And thanks to the kind cooperation of my good friends at the Butler Bank of New York, we are now ready to offer our invention to the government of the United States. All of you will surely agree that the scientific potential for such a device is limitless. As it happened, this test was necessary to prove to our government that this is a viable technology.

"And a very personal thanks to my good friend Mr. Clive Butler for the generous use of these facilities to introduce our product to the world. And to further thank each of you for your cooperation in this most successful enterprise, my company is going to deposit five thousand dollars in each of your accounts. I thank you for your invaluable assistance."

The ensuing applause was deafening. Whistles pierced the staid lobby. A call for the amount to be doubled was pointedly ignored.

Like a prince after a tour of a peasant village, Lothar Holz exited the building, surrounded on all sides by his coterie of thieves. The blond man pushed the door open and fell in respectfully behind him.

Outside, a gaggle of press descended, as if they, too, had been frozen off at some distant point and only now released. They circled around Holz like a swarm of buzzing flies.

Andy Frost watched all of this with a mixture of confusion and relief. The bosses were making the rounds now, gathering information for the Platt-Deutsche deposits and instructing employees to put the best possible face on this bizarre event.

Not wanting to appear either flustered or lax in his work habits, Andy turned back to his desk. Remembering the old man, Andy reached for the bankbook he had dropped in the confusion. It was gone. He glanced around and found that the old man was gone, as well.

On Andy's desk was a handful of crumpled twenty-dollar bills.

HOLZ CLIMBED UP into the back of the van half an hour later. His delicate fingers were wrapped around the neck of a chilled bottle of champagne, which he had retrieved from the trunk of his car once the crowd of expectant reporters had departed. His young assistant wordlessly passed out crystal stemware to the elated collection of scientists.

"It all worked flawlessly, Mr. Holz," a nervous man said.

"Let's not delude ourselves, Mervin, hmm? It worked out very well. That's why we celebrate now." Holz downed his glassful of champagne in one gulp. With giddy looks, like schoolchildren proud to have come in first in a spelling contest, the gathered scientists followed suit.

His assistant offered the bottle to him once more, but Holz declined. While the others still reveled in their success, he waved his empty glass around the cramped interior of the van, indicating the complicated machinery with the offhand gesture. "That moment when we lost contact—what went wrong?" he asked.

"A radio signal, Holz. There was a truck out here with a powerful CB transmitter. It garbled our signal."

Holz tipped his head boyishly. "Mervin, your garbled signal almost got me shot," he admonished the programmer.

Mervin Fischer looked nervously at the others. "It wasn't a fault in the program. It's a design flaw. I warned you this could happen, Mr. Holz. We should have done more lab testing."

"How long would you suggest we take, my friend? Ten years? Twenty? The Japanese will easily outstrip us by then."

"Germany is the only country we have to worry about right now. No one's deeper into interface technology than they are."

Holz gave the man a paternal slap on the back. "No one is ahead of us," he announced. A nod of his head, and his assistant returned with a fresh bottle of champagne, filling the programmer's glass.

One scientist sat far back in the van, still staring intently at a monitor screen. His hands were flying across a compact keyboard as he sifted through all of the raw data they had collected in the previous hours.

Holz left the others and stepped over to the man.

"I had hoped you would revel in your success, Curt. Aren't you going to join us for a drink?"

Dr. Curt Newton didn't tear his eyes away from the screen. "This is amazing," he said, shaking his head.

"What is?"

Newton pointed at the screen. "As you know, the Dynamic Interface System not only manipulates the human mind, but we are able to download information as if it was stored on a computer. Which, in effect, is what the human brain is."

"So?"

"There was one individual in the bank who wasn't affected by our immobilization program."

"That is impossible. No one moved but us."

"Yes, yes," Newton said impatiently. "But look." His hands moved in a flurry over the keyboard. In a matter of seconds, he had pulled up the CD recorder files from the bank's stationary cameras.

Displayed on the small screen was an unremarkable man in gray standing before one of the bank lobby desks.

"He's not moving," Holz said.

"Look more closely."

Setting his champagne glass on a console, Holz leaned closer to the monitor. The old man was as frozen as everyone else, staring blankly in the direction of the would-be robbers. Holz was about to tell the scientist that he saw nothing that wasn't expected from the man when all at once he noticed movement at the end of the man's hand.

As he watched more carefully, he saw that the old man was swaying from side to side. It was obvious from the footage that this man was somehow immune to the immobilizing effects of the interface system. He was only mimicking the rest of the bank patrons.

"Explain this," Lothar Holz demanded, indicating the monitor.

On the small screen, the drama continued to play out. The robbers were circulating among the crowd, passing out money.

"I don't understand it."

Holz's features were grim. "Did the rest of the interface work?"

"We downloaded his thought patterns into our system along with the others in the bank. And that's another remarkable thing. If I didn't see him with my own eyes, I would swear the patterns were a computer construct. This man interfaces with the computer better than any human I've ever seen. He's remarkable."

Lothar Holz stood. "Use him as a test subject."

Newton seemed delighted at the prospect. "Gladly," he said. He couldn't wait to download the hard-drive information into the mainframes back at PlattDeutsche America's headquarters in Edison, New Jersey. The man's thoughts were so precise, so logical, that they would be easier to read than those of any of the laboratory test subjects he had used up until now. He couldn't wait to use the revolutionary new interface program to tinker around in the old man's head and see what secrets were hidden up there.

He watched the small monitor screen excitedly. On it, Harold W. Smith, the man on whom the "revolutionary new interface program" had no immobilizing effect, hurriedly dropped the robbery money onto the desk of Andy Frost. Without so much as a glance in the direction of Lothar Holz, he tucked his bankbook into the torn plastic cover he had received when he opened his original account at the Butler Bank of New York thirty years before and ducked out the bank's side entrance.

2

His name was Remo, and the last thing he wanted was the first thing he got.

The waiter dropped the glass of water to the red-and-white-checkered tablecloth. He did this from at least one foot above the table's surface. Warm water spilled over the rim of the glass and spread in a widening stain across the ragged and faded checkerboard tablecloth. Remo inspected the translucent glass carefully. A brown-crusted residue clung to the lip of the glass. He doubted it was food.

"What is this?" he asked, pointing to the glass.

"What's this?" the waiter mocked in a thick Bronx accent. "What are you, a comedian? What's this? It's water."

"I wanted the rice first," Remo explained.

"You wanted the water, then rice," the waiter replied flatly.

Remo closed his eyes patiently. Though he had kept his breathing shallow since he had first walked through the door to the tiny Manhattan bistro, the fumes from the kitchen were already getting to him.

"Look, I don't care what you think you heard,"
Remo said. "I want my rice, *then* my water." He
pushed the glass away. "And would it be too much
trouble to put a little soap in the dishwasher next
time?"

The waiter's eyes were angry, but the man didn't
say a word.

Instead, he left the glass where it sat, spun on his
heel and returned to the kitchen through a battered
steel swinging door. A menacing red-printed sign beneath the filthy Plexiglas window warned that this
entry was for employees only.

Occasionally a head would pop into view behind
the grease-striped glass, and a pair of blurry eyes
would peer nervously in his direction.

Remo had been aware of the stares from the back
room ever since he had entered the restaurant. Although he was used to hard looks from potential tar-
gets when he was on assignment, this time the agitation among the kitchen staff had nothing to do with
him. They were staring beyond Remo, at a tiny table
set at the very back of the small room.

It looked as if it had been a booth in a previous
lifetime, for there was a high-backed parson's bench
with accompanying torn and faded vinyl seat cover
pressed firmly up against the rear wall. The table
seemed to match the restaurant's original decor, but
on the nearer side the bench had been replaced with
three uncomfortable-looking hard-back chairs. The

absence of the bench allowed the occupant on the far side of the table an unobstructed view of the entire interior.

Though the restaurant wasn't large, a generous amount of space had been cleared around this lone table.

Three burly men in ill-fitting suits packed the bench awkwardly, their amply padded elbows jostling their neighbors' hands with every forkful of spaghetti that traveled up from their overflowing plates.

As they slurped up generous quantities of sauce-freighted pasta, the men crowding around the table used their vantage point to keep their watchful eyes trained suspiciously on the other bistro patrons as they came and went.

Only one of the three chairs was occupied. One man sat across the table from the others, his back to the rest of the room. His shoulders were broad, though not as muscled as those of the watchers, and they were clad in sea blue fabric that shimmered like silk. The suit jacket was cut perfectly, the matching trousers seeming to have been tailored to his legs where he sat. The shoes were the finest cordovan leather and polished with a shine so fierce that it reflected and amplified the dull glow of the spotty overhead fluorescent lights so that it looked as if the dingy room were illuminated all around with halos of golden fire.

Remo knew the man from various television news programs and newspaper articles. His legal exploits in New York City were grist for all of the late-night comedians.

Don Anselmo Scubisci.

With his back to the room, he exuded a cool confidence that almost dared someone to try to take him on. Of course, it didn't hurt that he had a trio of gorillas in suits staring down every man, woman or child who got within fifty yards of their boss.

Remo had heard that since the death of old Don Pietro Scubisci a few years back, a vacuum had developed in the upper echelon of the Manhattan Mafia.

This was not so unusual. Organized-crime families were reeling nationwide, due to the combined efforts of various law-enforcement agencies. Things had gotten so bad for the Mob of late that no one was moving up in any family for fear that a long-trusted ally could turn out to be a high-level government plant. The dons became fewer and older, the money became scarcer and the power from the old days had just about disappeared.

After the death of the elder Scubisci, there had been a few bloody years when sparring families, intent on getting a piece of the Scubisci Family action, had participated in a violent turf war.

The killing had spread as far in the U.S. as Miami, San Francisco and Spokane. Outside of America, the silent war raged on into Mexico, Colombia and the

Cayman Islands. A few bodies even turned up in London and Moscow. But when the smoke cleared, it was the late Don Pietro Scubisci's eldest son, Anselmo, who finally stepped in to fill the void, aided by his ruthless younger brother Dominic.

Remo had identified young Dominic Scubisci as the middle spaghetti-slurping thug, and though he would have loved to finish off the new don right then and there, he was only sanctioned to take out Dominic. Those were direct orders from Upstairs.

Remo's table was closest in the room to the rear booth, and he had pitched an ear to the hushed conversation since he had entered the small restaurant.

"We gotta get the nigga's outta here," Dominic Scubisci was pleading with his older brother. Flecks of expelled tomato sauce speckled the tablecloth as he spoke, blending with the red squares and marking the already well-stained white.

"Your attitude is not progressive," Don Scubisci said. He spoke precisely, in barely accented English. But here, as on television, he created the impression that the hood who lurked beneath the flashily dressed veneer would slip to the surface.

"Forget that crappola," Dominic whined. "They're stealing us blind. They're killin' each other left and right. They ain't reliable."

"Aren't," Don Anselmo corrected. And by the way his brother cringed, he appeared to be used to such grammatical corrections. "They are as reliable

as we need them to be. The high mortality rate among our youngest employees is handily offset by the level of protection their ignorance affords us. With the system we have in place, we are virtually untouchable."

Though Remo couldn't see his face, he could tell by the confident set of the carefully tailored shoulders and the look of defeat on his brother's face that Don Anselmo considered the discussion closed.

"I just don't like them nigga's," his brother said, shaking his head. He attacked his plate more violently.

"*Those*," Don Anselmo corrected. "Those nigga's."

There was an awkward silence broken by the thug on Dominic's left. "Da gooks is da ones what scare me," he said with a wide-eyed nod not uncommon among those who would have a hard time spelling *IQ*. The others on the bench all nodded in wordless agreement at this particularly piquant observation.

Don Anselmo didn't even bother to correct the man's grammar.

Remo's attention was drawn from the rear table by the reappearance of his waiter. The squat man held a tray high above his balding head as he breezed up to Remo's table. Before he had even unloaded the contents, Remo knew that the rice was unacceptable.

The stench had preceded him.

The waiter dropped the steaming plate on the disposable paper place mat and stood back, awaiting approval. Remo suppressed an overwhelming urge to retch.

The rice was dripping with clumpy red tomato sauce. Bits of sliced mushroom and chopped peppers peeked out from between the pink-stained grains of rice, and the plate was garnished all around the edges with sprigs of parsley and a lone lemon wedge. Remo might have been able to eat the lemon slice if it hadn't been slathered with the sickly, oily, rancid-smelling sauce.

"What is this supposed to be?" he asked, indicating his plate.

The waiter seemed geared up for an argument. "Didn't we go troo dis already? You ordered rice," he replied tartly.

"Apparently we didn't go 'troo it' enough. I ordered plain white rice. This is not plain white rice."

"Dere's white rice in it."

Because Remo didn't want to get into a fight, he asked the waiter to put the rice in a doggie bag and bring him his water. Plate in hand, the man vanished once more through the scratched kitchen door.

Remo had hoped to have supper before he went to work. Lamentably it was not to be. Rather than wait for a glass of tepid water that probably wouldn't arrive for another half hour, if ever, Remo stood. Casting a mischievous glance at the trio of goons across

from Don Scubisci, he casually crossed the area separating his table from the don's.

This stretch of floor had remained vacant the entire
time Remo had been in the small restaurant, save for
the occasional waiter who brought complimentary
food and drinks to the great man. It was as if a hy-
pothetical line had been drawn and stepping across
it could only be accomplished on pain of death. Even
though the rest rooms were in the back near the lone
table, not one patron dared breach the danger zone.

Remo made as if he was heading for the bathroom,
but at the last minute a twist dropped him into one
of the vacant seats beside Don Anselmo.

There was another pair of Scubisci's men sitting
at a tiny table near the main entrance, who couldn't
have been more obvious if they had Thug 1
and Thug 2 tattooed to their broad foreheads. They
rose, looking to Dominic for guidance. The younger
Scubisci brother gestured ever so slightly to stay the
hands of the henchmen who were even now reaching
for their shoulder holsters. It was a surprisingly subtle warning from a man his size.

"Whadda you want?" Dominic asked. He ripped
a crunchy slice of fresh Italian bread with his yellow
incisors and attacked his plate once more.

Remo said only two words. "Guillermo Murietta."

Three forkfuls of coiled spaghetti paused halfway

between table and mouths. Six dull eyes stared menacingly at Remo.

Remo smiled. It wasn't a pleasant smile. It was the smile of a skull.

"Youse better get outta here," Dominic threatened.

"Why?" Remo asked. "Is it time for you to go in the bathroom and untape a gun from the toilet tank now?"

Dominic placed his meaty palms against the chipped and cigarette-scarred side of the table. He was about to shove his way upright—an evolutionary milestone for his entire family—when a ring-laden hand pressed firmly against his thick forearm.

"Don't do anything, Dominic," Don Anselmo, silent until now, instructed softly. As Dominic seethed, the don addressed Remo. "An unfortunate accident, this Murietta," Don Anselmo said, nodding his sad agreement.

Remo looked at him and didn't even attempt to mask his contempt. "That's not what I hear."

"What is dis?" Dominic interrupted. "We're eatin' here. Do you see us goin' over and buggin' you when you is eatin'?"

Remo ignored Dominic. He continued speaking to the don. "There was only one legitimate accident. Murietta wasn't to blame, the courts decided that. But you decided he was."

Don Anselmo shrugged. "It's a rough world," he

said vaguely. "There are many accidents. Some people are simply unlucky enough to be in the wrong place at the wrong time."

"You got that right," Remo said, turning back to Dominic.

For an instant their eyes locked, and Scubisci seemed to read the promise of death in the depths of Remo's cold, deep-set eyes. A fat tendril of sloppy pasta hovered immobile before his open mouth as his free hand snaked carefully beneath his jacket. His fingers had barely brushed the steel butt of his concealed weapon when a commotion broke out at the door of the restaurant.

There was a single shout of warning before the shooting started.

The table was immediately upended. A flurry of hands, Dominic Scubisci's included, grabbed Don Anselmo and yanked him to safety behind it.

Remo stood, peeved that his moment had been interrupted.

When he turned, he saw a half-dozen men had piled in through the main entrance to the restaurant. They were exchanging fire with the pair of Scubisci bodyguards who had taken refuge behind a battered steel dessert cart. Occasionally a few shots were directed to the rear of the restaurant, where they plowed into the ancient Formica surface of Don Anselmo's table.

Though bullets whizzed all around him, they somehow seemed to cut a wide swath around Remo.

Remo leaned over to where the four hoods cowered, guns at the ready. He saw that a thick sheet of steel had been fastened to the underside of the don's private table.

"Isn't that cheating?" he questioned. No one answered.

When the shooting started, the restaurant had erupted in screams. Those patrons not hunkered down behind their flimsy tables were fleeing for the tiny emergency exit at the rear of the building.

That was a mistake. Seconds after the initial gunfire began, the rusted metal door exploded inward and three more goons poured into the restaurant, shoving panicked diners aside as they swept the front of the restaurant with fire from their lightweight Ingram Model 11 subguns.

Remo wasn't sure whose side these three were on. All of these guys seemed to have picked their suits from the Cosa Nostra section of the nearest Salvation Army store. Briefly Remo wondered how wise guys were able to tell each other apart. Looking at all of them bunched together in that small space exchanging apparently random fire, Remo decided that all mobsters should be required to wear numbered and colored muscle shirts over their suits so different factions could be identified.

A moment later, it became clear that these were more of Don Anselmo's men.

"Let's get him outta here!" Dominic shouted from behind the table at the new arrivals. He waved his gun around his head like a cowboy getting ready to rope a calf.

One of the new arrivals nodded his understanding and proceeded to unload a steady stream of slugs into the area around the cashier's desk and into the chests of two of the six armed aggressors.

Chunks of the ancient, cheap plywood exploded in deadly shards around the door as a spray of blood splattered against the smoke-smeared front window. The men fell in crumpled heaps, one landing against the hostess's desk and collapsing the entire structure in an avalanche of stale mints and laminated menus.

The strategy proved to be a mistake. Until now the bulk of the fire had been directed at the cowering men in the front, but now three of the four remaining gunmen turned their attention to the back of the restaurant, where their ultimate target lay.

Bullets began rattling against the surface of the table with the ferocity of hard-driven rain spewed from the mouth of an angry typhoon. Remo dodged and swirled to avoid the incoming projectiles.

Some latent survival instinct appeared to have surfaced in the mind of Dominic Scubisci. During the thickest part of the firefight, Dominic signaled to his men to lead Don Anselmo from the protection of the table to the rear exit.

The three who had entered from the back provided cover while the three behind the table swarmed around their leader and trundled him toward the door, all the time returning fire themselves with their side arms.

They had made it as far as the rear exit when Don Anselmo made an alarming discovery. Two of his men had just been shot, one critically, and he had to shout over the burp of automatic-weapons fire to be heard.

"Hey, where's Dominic?" asked the capo of the Manhattan Mafia.

"YOUSE IS IN SHIT up to your neck."

Dominic tried to sound tough, but the words lacked their usual conviction. This was probably due to the fact that the skinny guy had plucked him from his brother's flank and carried him through a heavy cross fire as if he were dancing through a field of early-summer dandelions.

They were in the kitchen of the restaurant. The service staff had fled through their own exit, abandoning various boiling pots and flaming pans on the great gas stoves. The war continued to rage in the outer room. Remo had pushed a huge ice machine in front of the door to discourage any of the other mobsters from ducking for cover inside the kitchen.

When they entered, he had placed Dominic's Colt automatic on a nearby stainless-steel counter, agonizingly close to the mobster.

The hoodlum eyed the weapon as he sized up Remo's lean frame.

"Dominic Scubisci," Remo said with the dispassion of a teacher reading an attendance sheet. "You are in charge of enforcement for the Scubisci Family?"

Dominic scrunched up his face disdainfully. For a second, his eyes left the abandoned gun. "You a lawyer?"

Remo smiled tightly, ignoring the question.

"In your capacity as enforcement arm, you took it upon yourself to rid the world of one Guillermo Murietta."

"He had it comin'," Dominic growled.

"For crimes against the Scubisci Family," Remo prodded.

"Yeah," Dominic said, jutting out his chin. He edged closer to the gun.

"The specific crime involving Mr. Murietta resulted in the death of one Tony Scubisci, your son." Remo was putting on his best Perry Mason for Dominic Scubisci.

Dominic felt as if he was in a court of law. He tried to call up the appropriate paternal sadness that he had summoned at the Murietta trial. Now, as then, he didn't quite get it right. He was used to being a defendant not a witness for the prosecution.

"He killed my boy."

"Your boy, Mr. Scubisci, was twenty-five years old, a three-time loser who had just murdered a member of the Patriconne Family and had run out into traffic between two parked cars as he was attempting to elude the police. He ran in front of the car operated by Mr. Murietta."

"He shouldn'ta done what he done," Dominic insisted. He took another subtle sidestep toward his weapon. The gunfire in the outer room had dwindled by now to a few feeble bursts.

"He was only driving down the street," Remo argued.

"Maybe he shoulda picked another street." With a sudden movement, Dominic leaped toward the nearby counter. His meaty palm slapped victoriously down atop the gun. Scooping up the pebbled handle in his large hand, he wheeled on his interrogator.

The skinny guy was gone.

Dominic started to turn but felt a sudden pressure against his right forearm. A voice, so close it almost sounded as if it were coming from within his own head, whispered in his ear.

"Murietta had five kids."

Dominic couldn't move. His spine had gone stiff as a board, and it felt as if someone was manipulating him from behind like a ventriloquist's dummy. Gun still in hand, he felt himself being drawn to the stove.

"What? It's my fault he don't know where the drugstore is?" Dominic's words were brave, but his jaw clenched in pain as the pressure on his spine increased. They were at the stove now.

A huge cauldron of spaghetti boiled for customers who had long since fled.

"Dominic Scubisci, you have been found guilty of murder in the first degree. Do you have anything to say in your defense before this court passes sentence?"

"Eat shit," Dominic offered.

To hell with Perry Mason. Remo wrapped his fingers around Dominic's wrist. Though the man outweighed him by a good hundred pounds, he proceeded to force the hand into the pot of boiling pasta. It was a display of impossible strength, the impressiveness of which was completely lost on the mobster.

Dominic's shriek of pain was almost feminine. He immediately released his gun. It dropped to the bottom of the pot with a muted clang. After a second, Remo pulled the hand free. Dominic was horrified to see that his skin had gone as scarlet as a cooked lobster. Blisters had already formed all around the palm and back of the hairy hand.

He howled in pain and rage, ready to spin on the faggy little punk who had destroyed his gun hand, desperate to vent his horrific rage. But before he had time to react, he felt himself moving up in the air, very lightly. The pain in his hand was constant and fierce, but he couldn't help but watch in wonder as the filthy tiled ceiling of the kitchen grew closer. All at once, he felt himself turning in midair. Blinking in surprise, Dominic found a moment later that he was upside down and staring into the churning, roiling pot of pasta. Steam poured up around his ears, pasting his short black hair to his bullet head. He felt himself being lowered toward the pot.

Utter panic struck him.

"Hold it! Hold it! I know everythin'!" Dominic begged. He tried turning toward his assailant, but found that he couldn't move. Hot steam curled up into his nose and mouth.

"That seems unlikely," Remo ventured. "What's six times seven?"

"What?" Dominic asked. His thick nose hairs were curling.

"See? You don't know everything."

The bubbling water came closer.

"I'll turn state's evidence." Dominic screamed as the pot closed in. "I'll give you my brother Anselmo on a silver platter. Just let me go."

The downward movement arrested. Bubbles of boiling water burst against Dominic's hair.

"You *want* me to let you go?" The voice behind him sounded puzzled.

"Yeah, yeah. Please."

Behind Dominic, Remo shrugged. "Suit yourself."

None of the members of the Scubisci Family had ever been very well supplied in the brain department, but it had been agreed by the rest of the clan that they could all safely look down on Dominic's limited mental capacity with superior disdain. But in that infinitesimally brief instant before his scalp touched the water, Dominic Scubisci realized that he had misspoken.

Before he could speak, before he could shout, before he could take back his ill-chosen words, gravity plunged Dominic's wrinkled head below the boiling water.

He immediately tried to pull himself free. Strong hands were again upon him, holding him in place. Though he thrashed in place like a large fish in a small boat, his head didn't move an inch from below the burning water. He tried briefly to fight the brilliant pain, but it wasn't long before it proved too great. All at once, he let himself succumb to the exquisite torture, and in that instant it was as though the bottom had dropped from the pot and Dominic felt himself slipping through the boiling water and into a greater, more eternal flame.

The fire here burned brighter and more fiercely hot than anything Dominic had ever imagined, and long after his earthly shell returned to the dust from which it had come, the name of Guillermo Murietta and countless others tormented him in unending flaming anguish.

SETTING THE TIMER on the back of the stove, Remo held Dominic in place for a good five minutes. The mobster had stopped wiggling in under a minute. Just like a lobster.

Once he was satisfied the man was done, Remo pulled him out of the water and dropped him back atop the stainless-steel counter.

The skin on Dominic Scubisci's head and neck was so bright it was nearly orange. Stringy bits of flesh hung off in reddish white tatters.

"You look done to me," Remo commented happily.

Milky white eyes stared ceilingward with unseeing horror. For good measure, he pounded a large meat thermometer between Dominic's open white eyes.

"Ooh, mobster head's trickier than I thought." Remo frowned. "You could have stood another minute or two. I'll have to remember that when it's time to parboil your brother."

Remo found his bag of rice on a table near the door. Scooping it up in his thick-wristed hand, he ducked out the emergency exit.

The scent in the air gave promise of a beautiful day.

3

Harold W. Smith carefully scrutinized the information on PlattDeutsche America as it scrolled across his computer screen. The monitor was buried beneath the onyx surface of the desk and angled upward. Only the person seated behind the large high-tech desk could view the information as it passed silently across the screen and back into electronic limbo.

Hardly an hour had passed since he had fled the Butler Bank, and Smith was already firmly ensconced in his office at Folcroft Sanitarium in Rye, New York. This unassuming office was the nerve center of the secret government organization CURE.

It was here that Smith had spent the bulk of the past four decades of his life. He fully expected to die at his desk, alone and unheralded at the helm of the secret agency that identified, tracked and addressed crises both domestic and international. Created by a young president, himself the eventual victim of an assassin's bullet, CURE was always in demand to safeguard America, and was many times the last best hope of each man chosen to serve in the Oval Office.

Smith had heard of PlattDeutsche, and knew it to be a company on the cutting edge of information technology. Because of this, the breakthroughs made by PlattDeutsche America at its New Jersey plant were sought-after by the Pentagon, particularly during the military buildup of the 1980s. Though quieter than Lockheed or Raytheon or any of the other military giants, PlattDeutsche America had carved out a comfortable niche for itself supplying technology and hardware to all branches of the United States armed services. This comfortable arrangement had lasted until the determined gutting of the American armed forces in the early 1990s.

The company was hit hard by the drastic downsizing of the military. In spite of its quiet achievements in computer-related research, for some reason, PlattDeutsche had never quite forced itself into the spotlight of popular culture. It was therefore not equipped to reroute its efforts into post–Cold War endeavors. Smith suspected that with the morning's flamboyant introduction of its new Dynamic Interface System, PlattDeutsche America was now poised to make the great public-relations leap necessary to survive in the fast-changing business climate.

The information bubbling up from Smith's buried computer screen was vast and complex.

There were several articles culled from the leading science magazines in the country extolling the breakthroughs PDA had made for the government's Defense Advanced Research Projects Agency. In particular the company was singled out for a DARPA-sponsored neural-network chip they had developed. The microchip was so advanced its function outstripped its closest competitor in the market by a factor of five. With a processing capacity roughly fifty thousand times faster than its biological counterpart, the chip used electrons to transmit information instead of the sodium and potassium ions required by the human brain.

Again in a more esoteric scientific quarterly, the company was praised for its work—alongside the New York State Department of Health—training users to emit brain signals to command a computer to move a cursor around a screen.

A seemingly small program that had apparently netted great results for the relatively obscure company, if the events at the Butler Bank were any indication.

A few minor articles in some of the local Boston papers several years before mentioned that Dr. Curt Newton, a noted MUT researcher and lecturer in the fields of applied mathematics and cybernetics, had been lured away to PlattDeutsche. The scientist boasted in one article that the unlimited funding offered by the large corporation would, in less than a decade, allow him to become the world's first physical cryptologist.

Smith wrinkled his nose at the phrase. At its most

basic, cryptology was the science that dealt with enciphering and deciphering messages. He had known cryptographers since his OSS days during World War II. Indeed, it was a young Harold W. Smith who had worked alongside British and American cryptologists on the top secret Ultra project, which was one of the most successful counterespionage operations in modern history and broke the Nazi Enigma coding machine and contributed to the Allied victory in Europe. But Smith had never before heard of anyone referring to himself as a "physical cryptologist."

He input the phrase into the computer and stuck the Search key. The computer responded almost instantaneously. There was only one article on the subject other than the one Smith had already read.

It was in a European computer journal, and the phrase was highlighted seven times, all in reference to its cover interview subject, Dr. Curt Newton. He described physical cryptology as the science of deciphering the neural codes in a living subject and transferring them to an artificial host via an electronic uplink. Physical cryptology would break down the very codes that defined human thought.

Preliminary research, he claimed, had reaped great results with servomechanisms and electrode attachments, but his ultimate goal was to make wire connection between human subjects and computers obsolete.

In the article—dated five years previous—Dr.

Newton vowed that his process would eventually become simplified to the point that wires would be a thing of the past. Radio signals would take their place.

Using the CURE mainframes' massive search ability, Smith sifted through all Pentagon information concerning PlattDeutsche. The search proved unenlightening. There were files that concerned the company's dealings with the Air Force and Army, all inactive. Smith hit similar dead-ends with the NSC, NSA and CIA. All had had accounts with the corporation in years past, but all had either completed the specifications of their various contracts or pulled the plug on whatever arrangements they had with the company when the national-security funds dried up.

In all the government, only the FBI continued to divert a modest hundred thousand dollars to PlattDeutsche for research into a prototype crowd-control device using radio-enhanced ocular signals.

Smith returned to his computer's main menu. There were other articles, but none offered any great insight. Smith scanned them all carefully before finally snapping the computer off. The screen within the desk winked out dutifully.

He turned slowly in his cracked leather chair and stared through the one-way glass office window at the silent black waters of Long Island Sound.

PlattDeutsche was a virtual island in the field of technology. It had apparently earned enough in government contracts to sustain itself during the long dry period. Indeed, it had used its earlier wealth to buy up a few other small companies—not related to the computer industry—making it a miniconglomerate. It had also started up the PlattDeutsche America Security Systems Corporation.

All of this was cushion enough to allow it time to develop the technology Smith had witnessed at the bank that morning.

But the technology was imperfect. It seemed that of all the people in the bank, Smith was the only one besides the robbers themselves who wasn't affected by the new device. He didn't know why this was so, but it remained a problem with the system that its designers would have to discover for themselves. Smith's work was far too sensitive for him to have given himself away.

But that didn't mean the technology did not hold great promise.

Smith, an old hand at computers since a time when the simplest calculators were measured in tons, was impressed by what he had seen. It was apparent that the intricate computer system necessary to immobilize the entire population of the bank was also able to differentiate between individuals. This would explain why the robbers themselves had remained unaffected. Any computer program that was able to scan and eliminate individual brain-wave patterns had been developed by an unquestionable genius.

So the ultimate question was, did Smith need to worry?

He doubted it.

As a contributor to sensitive government agencies, PlattDeutsche had received many high-level security checks. They had passed all unfailingly. It was obvious that the strange event at the Butler Bank was a public-relations exercise by the company to announce its arrival in the commercial world.

This Curt Newton had achieved what he had set out to do; he had become the world's first physical cryptologist. He had, in part, broken the code of the human mind—to what extent Smith didn't know. But it was remarkable that this man had, in such a small amount of time, identified and neutralized the structures in the brain involving conscious movement. In effect, he had learned how to rewrite at least part of the program of the human brain.

But fully integrating a human being with a computer was still many years off, Smith was certain.

He spun back around to his desk and clicked his computer back on.

As his hands reached for the edge of the desk, a capacitor-style keyboard appeared beneath his fingertips, its orderly rows of letters and numbers lined like patient soldiers waiting to do his bidding.

Smith paused before he began work. He pursed his lips, considering an idle thought.

After a moment of hesitation, he typed a few brief

commands into the computer that would track PlattDeutsche America activities, as well as the media's take on the events of that morning.

As a participant in the event and a proponent of technology, Smith had more than just a passing interest in seeing how such a development panned out.

That task accomplished, Harold W. Smith returned to the more mundane work of safeguarding America.

4

Remo took a shuttle flight from LaGuardia to Boston's Logan International Airport. He hired a taxi outside the airline terminal and settled into the back seat, arriving at his Quincy, Massachusetts, home late in the afternoon.

If Remo had owned a suitcase, he would have spent the better part of his adult life living out of it as he shuffled back and forth across the country from hotel room to hotel room on his business as enforcement arm for the secret agency CURE. It was only within the past few years that he had finally gotten what most people took for granted. A home.

Unfortunately home for Remo Williams was a garish condominium complex that had been foisted on Remo and his aged Korean mentor, Chiun, by their employer, Harold W. Smith. The place was an eyesore.

A former church, converted to its current state in a fever of real-estate-boom-inspired optimism, it combined several of the most unpleasant styles of architecture under one roof.

He sighed inwardly as the cab pulled up to the curb in front of the large building. It was true what they said. There was no place like home. But Remo doubted that most people thought of the phrase in quite the same way he did.

This day, unlike most other times when his eyes alighted on the building Chiun insisted on referring to as "Castle Sinanju," Remo's spirits were light. He paid the taxi driver and, grabbing the bag of rice he had brought with him from New York, bounded up the front staircase into the building.

His finely tuned senses told him that Chiun was in one of the rear rooms on the lower floor. Remo deliberately steered in the opposite direction. He'd let Chiun find him.

In the kitchen, Remo dropped the brown canvas bag on a low taboret and scooped the phone up. Moving to a safe spot across the room, Remo sat up on the counter and stabbed out the 1 button repeatedly, activating the simplified code system that automatically rerouted his call through various dummy repeater accounts along the East Coast before leading finally to a small office in Rye, New York.

"Yes," the lemony voice of Harold W. Smith said crisply over the secure phone line.

"You know, you never say hello or ask me how I'm doing, Smitty," Remo remarked.

Nor did Smith now. "Dominic Scubisci?" he asked.

Remo sighed. "His goose is cooked," he said, proud of his private little joke. His acute, Sinanju-trained hearing detected nearly silent footsteps in the hallway. He held the phone closer to his ear and pretended not to be looking at the door.

"May I take that to mean the assignment was carried out successfully?" Smith inquired dryly.

"Didn't you see it on the news?" Remo asked, disappointed.

Smith suddenly sounded vague. "No," he admitted, "I was...otherwise occupied."

"Counting beans again, eh, Smitty?"

Chiun chose that moment to enter the kitchen. He was a frail figure in a bright green kimono. His skin and bones were seemingly as delicate as those of a newly hatched bird. He regarded Remo with a look that one would generally reserve for a persistent sidewalk beggar.

Wordlessly he padded across the kitchen floor. He was very old, his face tracked with wise wrinkles, his eyes like the seams of walnut shells and his wrinkle-webbed mouth thin with thought. No hair sat on his shiny head. Wispy cloud puffs hovered over the tops of his ears, and something like the remnant of a beard clung to his chin. Despite his advanced years, his hazel eyes looked as youthful and mischievous as a child's.

"I was actually not far from you," Smith said. "I was in Manhattan on personal business."

"That's a bit daring for you, isn't it?" Remo said, watching Chiun from the corner of his eye. "You usually don't want to get within a country mile of me when I'm working. And sneaking away from the office on a school day to boot. Naughty naughty."

The Master of Sinanju was sniffing around the bag on the squat table like a dog on a scent and, like a canine, he seemed fearful of close contact with the alien item. He hovered a safe distance from the bag.

"Your assignment was far enough away from my location," Smith explained.

"Yeah, well, about that. Dominic seemed like small potatoes," Remo said. "Especially with his brother sitting right there next to him. I could have taken the two of them out, no questions asked."

Smith didn't agree and had had a difficult time explaining this to Remo the previous day. "The gears of justice are working against Don Anselmo," Smith said. "Better to let the American people know their justice system works by convicting him in a court of law."

"He'll beat any rap they hang on him, Smitty," Remo complained. "Scubisci'll just go on *Horrendo* and claim he was molested as a kid or something. Not only will America forgive him, he'll probably get his own sitcom out of the deal."

"Unlikely."

Remo watched Chiun's back as the old man circled the taboret once more. "Listen, Smitty, if Dominic Scubisci was the only thing on the front burner right now, I'm going to get a little R&R.''

Smith agreed. ''I will contact you if anything else comes up.''

With that, Remo replaced the receiver in the cradle.

''What is this?'' The Master of Sinanju demanded the instant the connection was severed. He pointed a long-nailed finger at the bag Remo had brought from New York.

''Dinner,'' Remo explained. ''It's my turn, remember?''

With the sharpened nail of his index finger, Chiun harpooned the bag, splitting it from stem to stern with a delicate flip of his bony hand. The white foam container within the bag burst open beneath the razor-sharp fingernail. The gooey red contents poured out across the gleaming surface like the bloody innards of some eviscerated marsupial.

''Aiyeee!'' Chiun screeched. ''What is this refuse?''

Remo took up a haughty tone. ''I'll have you know that is what passes for white rice at one of the most talked-about restaurants in New York City.''

The tip of his index finger quivered as Chiun extended it toward the mess on the table. ''If this is what these talkers consume, then they are either dead or deranged.''

''Actually a little of both,'' Remo admitted, with

a shrug. "I'll get the plates." He began rooting through the cupboards for their place settings.

"This reeks of the pummeled-tomato concoction the Romans once brewed to make food that is already unpalatable even less so."

"Them's good eatin's," Remo agreed. He placed their plates carefully on the taboret and scooped out a healthy portion from the large pile. He dropped the goo into the center of each stoneware dish.

Chiun raised a curious eyebrow and sank to the floor in a kneeling position across from Remo. He didn't speak another word.

Ordinarily Remo didn't use a fork, but he had retrieved one from a drawer near the sink. He scooped up a large forkful of the tomato-rice glop. He raised it to his lips.

Chiun watched, his face etched in stone.

Remo brought the fork to his lips. He opened his mouth. He paused, waiting for Chiun to speak.

As placid as a spring leaf on an early-morning pond, the Master of Sinanju regarded his pupil.

Inwardly Remo frowned. He moved the fork closer, nearly in his mouth.

All at once, he caught a green blur of Chiun's kimono sleeve and felt the pressure of four bony fingers against his forearm. Quick as a flash, the forkful of rice was in his mouth.

Remo gagged at the taste. His throat clenched reflexively, and he sprang from the floor, running to the sink. He spit out every repellent morsel, then rinsed his mouth under the running faucet and picked grains of slimy rice from around his teeth with the tip of his tongue. "Dammit, Chiun, that wasn't funny."

Chiun, looking as innocent as a newborn child, watched Remo as he continued to spit bits of food into the sink. "It was my impression that a moment ago it was the pinnacle of hilarity."

"C'mon, Chiun, it was just a joke."

"You would like the Borgias, Remo. They, too, found humor in poisons." Chiun rose. "And if we have dispensed with this evening's comedy, I believe it is your turn to make dinner."

"Okay, I'll order out," Remo said glumly. His cheery mood had all but evaporated.

"That is of no concern to me," Chiun declared, breezing from the room.

"White or brown?" Remo called after him.

Chiun's squeaky voice floated back from the hallway. "Brown rice. And carp."

"We had carp last night," Remo countered. "How about duck?"

"Carp," Chiun repeated. "And if the offensive odor from that offal on the table still clings to your garments when my meal arrives, you may eat out by the garbage pail." And to punctuate the ultimatum, a distant door slammed shut.

AN HOUR LATER, showered and fed, Remo sat back with Chiun to watch the evening news.

Though as a rule the Master of Sinanju didn't enjoy watching the nightly news, he did so on occasion to monitor—as he put it—the "daily degeneration of so-called Western society." There was a time in his life when an evening wouldn't pass without Chiun seated squarely in front of the broadcast image of news anchor Bev Woo, for whom the Master of Sinanju had developed a particular fondness. He had cooled to her of late, and those moments when he stumbled upon the anchorwoman he became almost plaintive. Woo was off tonight, and there was a substitute anchorman in her chair, a man with a consoling baritone and all the range of expression of a Ken doll.

"No one is claiming responsibility for the gruesome death of Dominic 'Grips' Scubisci, but the firefight that took the lives of two of Anselmo Scubisci's right-hand men was clearly the work of a rival organized-crime faction. Most likely, insiders say, the Patriconne Syndicate. No word from Don Anselmo on the death of his brother, but we have learned that the Manhattan godfather is holding Bernardo Patriconne personally responsible for the brutal murder."

Chiun listened to the report from a lotus position in the center of the living room. He tipped his birdlike head pensively. "First they say there is no news, and then they report the no news. If no one is speaking, then to whom are these idiots talking?"

"To each other mostly," said Remo from his spot on the room's only chair. He had eschewed the floor tonight. "They make up the news and usually attribute it to some unnamed source. It's some sort of First Amendment dodge. I guess it protects them from lawsuits or something."

"Incredible," Chiun said, shaking his hairless head in disgust. "I did not hear your name mentioned once in the report. Is there not one of these numbered amendments that requires these cretins to speak the truth?"

"If there was, it'd put most of these guys out of business," Remo said.

Chiun listened for another minute with growing anger while a flawless Sinanju assassination was credited to a group of rank amateurs with guns. At last his patience was exhausted.

"I will have no more of it," he announced.

The Master of Sinanju rose like a puff of angry green steam and crossed over to the television. He was about to slap the Off button with a furious palm when Remo suddenly sat up at attention.

"Hold it, Chiun," he said, raising an impatient hand.

The news anchor had segued into the next story. Remo saw the image of a crowded bank interior, taken from above, as if from stationary security cameras.

Chiun looked at the screen and then back to Remo. "Have you developed an even greater taste for inanity?" he asked blandly.

Remo was sitting forward in his chair, his brow furrowed in concern. "That's Smitty," Remo said, pointing to the screen.

At the back of the still image, through the stationary bank crowd, the profile of Dr. Harold W. Smith could be clearly discerned. He was standing before a desk at which a man was squatting inexplicably over a chair.

"No, you are not watching still images," the anchorman said with cloying playfulness. His producer had told the anchorman to use a light touch with the viewers during the next fluff piece. He managed to be both condescending and overbearing at the same time. "This was the scene at the Butler Bank of New York today as over one hundred patrons and startled bank employees had their assets, quite literally, frozen."

The camera began panning. Remo was surprised to see that it wasn't a stationary picture, frozen on a single image. Instead, it was the scene below that seemed locked in space. The camera stopped, completing its programmed arc, but Remo could still make out the pinched features of the CURE director. Even with the imperfect clarity of the television screen—which was limited by the number of pixels—Remo's sharp eyes spotted that of all the people, Smith alone wasn't completely immobile. Though it wasn't enough to attract attention. A second later, a few normally moving figures came into camera range.

The anchor continued. "A daring daylight robbery turned into a payday to those lucky enough to be caught in the cross hairs of a band of modern-day Robin Hoods. No, these robbers didn't steal from the rich and give to the poor. They stole from themselves. Network correspondent Gallic Uckbridge in New York has more."

The reporter on the scene described the Dynamic Interface System as the screen showed the robbers stuffing cash into people's pockets.

Videotaped footage followed, featuring an impromptu interview held on the sidewalk in front of the bank with PlattDeutsche America vice president for research and development, Lothar Holz.

Holz claimed that the interactive device would revolutionize home-entertainment systems, as well as increase automobile safety, eliminate the need for computer keyboards and physically connect the home of the future to the rest of the palpable world. With DIS technology, he said, eventually a surgeon would be able to operate from halfway around the globe.

In the wrap-up, the reporter disclosed how the

press corps had been kept at bay on the sidewalk while the experiment in the bank was going on. This was done, the reporter said, with the aid of the Dynamic Interface System. It was an application of the device, he noted wryly, that the White House was certainly already looking into.

When the story had finished and Remo seemed satisfied, Chiun slapped his hand against the small round button at the base of the console. The screen winked out.

"That's the business Smith was on today," Remo mused.

"I do not know how you even recognized him. In that crowd, he was as a single grain of sand on a beach. A white beach."

With a movement that was a flawless mixture of economy and delicacy, Chiun sank back to his woven-reed mat in the center of the floor.

The skirts of his emerald green kimono slowly settled around his bony knees like air escaping from a gently settling parachute.

"The way he is about security," Remo grunted, "I'm surprised he's not going nuts."

"Smith is already insane, Remo. The sky is seen in many shades of blue, but it is never striped."

"What is that supposed to mean?"

"It means that Smith is a lunatic, Smith was a lunatic and Smith will always be a lunatic. If there is a day he is more lunatic than another, it is only a matter of degree.''

''Just remember he's the lunatic who keeps us in rice and skittles.''

''And if his madness ever tells him to stop, the House of Sinanju will be better served to find an emperor who is not deranged. Leave me now, Remo.'' And with that, Chiun closed his eyes in meditation.

Remo got up slowly from his seat. The frail old Asian sat in the center of his tatami mat—seemingly as motionless as the people in the Butler Bank. Remo knew that Chiun was breathing rhythmically, a Sinanju technique that aligned him with the natural forces of the universe.

Walking quietly toward the door, Remo pondered the newscast.

He knew that Smith valued the secrecy of CURE over everything else. Nothing, except perhaps America itself, was more sacred to him than avoiding exposure. Even though it was a minor crowd scene and no one would possibly have picked him out, Remo couldn't help but think of his boss and what kind of reaction he'd have when he found out. If his past was any indication, a guest spot on the national news would probably make him lose his mind.

5

"See if it'll fire on 0010010. Okay, perfect. Now patch that across on LISP. There, that's it."

Dr. Curt Newton was like a gleeful child turning pages in a favorite book. And with every turned page, he came closer to unlocking the secrets of the gray old man in the bank. For motivation, as well as to increase the sense of mystery among his assistants, he had printed several copies of the man's face and had taped them up around the lab. A picture of the man with the features of a squeezed lemon stared vacantly from above the computer screen at which Newton now worked.

Lothar Holz looked at the image of the bland old man with as little interest as was humanly possible for him to generate. This was a calculated indifference that he used in all sorts of business and social situations to show that he, the great Lothar Holz, was above being interested in anything. And if Lothar Holz wasn't interested in something, then it wasn't worthy of interest.

He found, in short order, that it was he in whom

the scientists in this large room weren't interested. Dr. Curt Newton, their leader, was shouting something at a group of them about proper algorithmic treatment on the neural net. It sounded like just another load of gibberish. This was common to Holz. Since he had stolen Newton away from MIT a few years earlier to spearhead the interface project, he had been subjected to the worst kind of scientific lingo.

He had a nagging suspicion that these scientific types were just blowing smoke with a bunch of trumped-up terms. In fact, when this jargon seemed to have gotten completely out of hand early on, Holz decided to put Dr. Newton on the spot. The scientist wanted to conduct something called PET research as an adjunct to his interface study. Holz had demanded to know what the equipment was for.

"It's used for diagnostic imaging," Newton had explained.

Lothar Holz had nodded as if he understood.

"PET stands for Positron Emission Tomography," Newton had said patiently. "It gives us the chemical physiology, as well as structure of the brain." He could see that he wasn't getting through to Holz. He spoke very slowly. "A patient is injected with a glucoselike substance which emits positrons. The positrons then collide with electrons to form photons. We can then detect and record the speed and path of the photons through the brain."

Completely lost, Holz had asked gruffly, "Is it necessary for your research?"

"Crucial."

Newton had the PET imaging scanner the next morning.

Holz felt the same way now as he had then. Everyone in the interface R&D complex in Edison, New Jersey, was running around as if preparing for a coronation. And they were acting as if the nondescript old man whose brain patterns they had downloaded were their new king.

Holz tugged the picture down from above Dr. Newton's screen.

The image was in color, but Holz would have argued that fact with anyone. The old man still looked as if he were in black-and-white.

Or shades of gray, anyway.

"What's so special about him?" he inquired blandly.

The technician who was monitoring the rate the information was flowing into the smaller computers had just gone to the back of the room to check the mainframe.

"Only the culmination of years of research," Newton said. He snatched the picture away and replaced it above his screen.

Feigning boredom with the entire procedure, Holz asked, "Is he really worth all this effort?"

Curt Newton actually stopped typing and stared at

him in disbelief. "Are you kidding?" he asked, shocked. "This guy is like nothing I've ever seen. His mind is so orderly, if we can figure out how it works, we could work backward from him. His brain would be a flawless pattern for reverse interface engineering. Years of work could literally take only weeks."

Holz laughed derisively. "I doubt that."

"Lothar," Curt Newton said icily, "if you were impressed by the demonstration at the bank this morning, I can assure you that you will be stunned by what we can do with what we learn from this man."

Holz paused to consider. The truth was, he had been impressed by the demonstration. PlattDeutsche America had become complacent in the marketplace of late and had accepted the downsizing of the military without much of a battle. Though he hadn't exactly lied at the press conference when he listed all of the peaceful applications of the interface technology, the truth was, he was hoping to make the United States government realize what it was missing out on if it didn't sign on with PlattDeutsche. A big, fat government contract would help finance further development.

It had been a gamble. The board hadn't been pleased with the unauthorized test at the bank and the president of the company was screaming for his head. Holz had found that out through his own private channels. He smiled inwardly. If the president ever found out who really ran the company, he'd probably have a stroke. Holz was being called before the board for a meeting that afternoon. Maybe he'd drop the big secret on them then. He grinned at the thought.

"Have you learned anything about the old man so far?" he asked Newton.

The scientist continued typing at his workstation as he spoke. Monotonous sequences of zeros and ones flew by at breathtaking speed. "We know his name is Smith."

"How did you find that out?"

"We've programmed the computers here to recognize patterns of a certain type. Other information is more difficult to decipher, but the clearest patterns always start with numbers, which really govern people's lives in a lot of ways. In a literal sense—telephone, social security, addresses, birth dates. But also in a more esoteric sense. The basic alphabet can be seen in numerical terms. There's the finite number twenty-six, which in combination yields a virtually infinite number of possibilities. Infinite in terms of our capabilities, anyway," he added. "Computers read things in numbers. My theory is that the human brain does, too. I link up numerical sequences. It's that simple."

"And that told you his name was Smith?" Holz still sounded skeptical.

"Absolutely."

"So what's his first name?"

Newton was vague. "I'm not quite sure. In test subjects, that has generally been one of the easiest things to determine, the human ego being what it is. But this man has virtually no ego whatsoever. It seems that even in his own thoughts he hardly every refers to himself by his first name. And without many like references, it's going to be a while before we discern a pattern that our name file recognizes."

"So you've stalled." Holz seemed pleased that the brilliant Dr. Newton had stumbled.

"Only as far as that's concerned," Newton admitted. "But we've learned other stuff that tells us more about him."

"Like what?"

"Well, for starters, he's from New England originally. Right now I'm willing to bet Vermont. He had a strict upbringing. He lives somewhere in southeastern New York. And he's into computers... perhaps much more than he imagines."

Newton pushed against his desk. His chair rolled on its casters to a console several feet behind him, where two lab computer programmers were working on the background information on the test subject. "Stern and Geist have found a few interesting items," he said as he bumped to a stop against the new workstation.

The two men looked up at Holz, who had followed

Newton over. "There's a lot of morbid stuff in here, Lothar," the first technician, Ron Stern, said. "A lot of stuff about death, dying. It's a recurring pattern. Almost an obsession."

"But he's pretty old, so that probably makes sense," Geist, the youngest of the programmers, suggested.

"What's that?" Holz asked, pointing at the screen.

Stern shook his head. "It's a neural symbol that we can best match up to mean *destroyer*. We're finding it a lot."

"Maybe he was in the war," Geist said.

Holz raised an eyebrow.

Stern snickered. "Which one, the Revolution?"

Geist chuckled, and both men returned to their respective keyboards.

Newton tapped his balled fist in nervous excitement on the table a few times as he watched the raw neural data stream across Geist's green-tinted monitor. As if the endless lines of linked numbers were some sort of encouragement to his own work, he slid back over to his own workstation and attacked his keyboard.

He was doggedly followed by Holz. "I sincerely hope, Doctor, that all of the effort you're expending on this one man does not prove to be a waste of valuable PlattDeutsche time."

"I am saving PlattDeutsche more precious time

than you could possibly imagine.'' Newton didn't look up from his computer screen.

"I hope that you are. I've been called in front of the board this afternoon to justify the expense of this project. The higher-ups had a slight problem with our bank deal and decided to review the entire interface project.''

Newton stopped typing and spun his chair around, wild-eyed. "They're not thinking of cutting funding?'' he demanded.

"It's a possibility. I sold them on the project in the first place. If they've lost faith in me..."

"They can't,'' Newton pleaded. "Not now.''

Holz smiled reassuringly. "I'll do my best. But it would help if you could get the interface project further ahead of schedule.''

"I'll redouble my efforts.''

"That might help,'' Holz admitted. In his mind, he wondered how this would be possible. Newton already spent at least twenty hours a day at the lab. But that wasn't his concern. For all Holz cared, Newton could drop dead tomorrow. As long as he perfected his process today.

With an encouraging slap on the back that was devoid of anything resembling sincerity, Lothar Holz left the main R&D lab.

Once he was gone, Newton exhaled a nervous puff of air.

He hadn't told Holz that there was a snag. A huge snag.

Yes, the man named Smith had the most orderly mind the scientist had ever seen, but in that orderliness there was an area that was blocked off and had so far proved impenetrable to their best efforts. Its real-world counterpart would be a filing cabinet with many drawers. Most of them were wide open for inspection but there was one at the bottom that was locked securely. Why?

With renewed vigor, Dr. Curt Newton, P.C.— Physical Cryptologist—vowed that he wouldn't rest until he had broken into that mysterious bottom drawer.

6

"You have lied to me."

The man spoke English precisely. Carefully. He had obviously been educated in one of the finer universities in England. But the clipped words—seemingly sheared off at their consonants by the razor-thin lips—were imperfect. Captain Josef Menk preferred it that way.

The young man swinging from the bare beam in his small office on the island of Usedom was Menk's latest pupil, scheduled to learn the true horrors awaiting the young boys unlucky enough to land on the wrong side of this war.

An army corporal, not much younger than the dangling man, had just brought in a piece of paper that Josef Menk had taken officiously. Of course it was for show. To the Geheime Staatspolizei, much these days was show.

"You are not French," Menk commented absently at the exhausted, sweating man who dangled from the frayed ropes before him. He perused the paper in his hand a moment longer. When he was satisfied that sufficient time had elapsed to let the information sink in, he placed the square white sheet on the surface of his immaculate desk. He paused to stub out his cigarette in the spotless green glass ashtray.

He walked slowly over to the dangling man, who didn't cower at his approach. Menk bent at the waist, placing his gloved hands on the black woolen knees of his Gestapo uniform. He leaned in close. When he whispered, his mouth was no more than an inch away from the young man's ear.

"A man who lies under torture, hmm? You are very brave. What do you suppose I should do with you?" he asked softly, so that the man would have to strain to hear the words.

"Français," the man croaked.

Menk slapped the man sharply across the cheek. He had ordered his personal tailor to stitch a network of tiny ball bearings into the finger seams on the back of the glove. It increased the pain while simultaneously increasing Menk's pleasure. He smiled at the fresh trickles of blood that ran from three new gashes just above the man's jaw.

"American," Menk corrected. He leaned back against his desk and made a show of reading the information that he had already memorized before he had even entered the office. "Smith, Harold. Office of Strategic Services. You are a long way from Washington, Herr Smith."

The young man didn't react. He stared straight

ahead, at the concrete wall of the converted stone house.

There was a hint of black stubble across his normally clean-shaved jaw. His eyes were a watery, almost steel gray. His nondescript hair was cut short, too short to be totally disheveled by the five days he had so far spent suspended in Captain Josef Menk's torture chamber. His skin was pale, his clothing plain. But in his demeanor there was a certain precise dignity that hinted of the man he would grow to be.

"You are quite resistant, Smith," Menk said with more than a hint of approval in his voice. "One wonders why a man of your caliber would waste your time and, yes, your life, on these worthless, lost souls. The French." Menk spit on the cold granite floor as if he had just spoken a curse. "Dogs to a man. Europe will fall as easily. And a new order will be established that will allow mankind to achieve a greatness that you cannot possibly understand."

"You are insane," Smith said softly. For the first time in nearly a week, he spoke in English.

Menk grinned broadly. "A pragmatic man," he said. "I am liking you more and more every day, Herr Smith."

"My incarceration and treatment are in clear violation of the Geneva convention," Smith said.

Menk smiled. He waved his hand around the room. "There is no Geneva convention within the confines of these four walls," he said, laughing. "Have you not yet learned that?"

Smith said nothing. He was obviously in the hands of a lunatic.

The war in Europe was nearly over. Russian and U.S. troops were closing in even as Menk preened and threatened. The "glorious" Nazi Third Reich was at an end. Why did Captain Menk not seem to see that his brand of fascism was in its death throes?

Menk regarded Smith's silence with a curious tip of his head.

At last he crossed to his desk. Primly taking his seat, he called out an order on his office phone.

Seconds later the door opened, and a hulking man—whose broad shoulders nearly caught in the heavy oaken frame—entered the room.

Smith recognized the man. He was slightly overweight and, despite the coolness of the stone building, perspired profusely. He walked with a limp, probably from an injury in an earlier battle, which would explain why he was not off fighting now. Smith knew him only as Ernst. Menk's torturer.

Beneath his giant bicep, Ernst carried a tattered suitcase. The huge man set the package down on a wooden stool near Smith. Inwardly Smith cringed at the sight of the large valise. He knew what would come next.

As Ernst proceeded to pull a variety of gruesome and clumsy steel implements from the interior of the bag, Menk lazily pulled off his gloves. He examined his fingernails.

Beads of sweat formed on Smith's forehead. He had to bite down on his thin upper lip to keep it from quivering. Then Ernst seemed to find what he was looking for. In the wan light of the tiny room, he held up a metal rod much like a tire iron. At the end of the device, tiny metal prongs reflected the room's dull light.

Ernst would not be subtle today. With his clumsy fingers, he found the old bullet hole—the one that had been inflicted when Smith was first captured on this small island near the Peenemünde Army Experiment Station. They had given it some time to heal. But not too much time.

Ernst jammed the small end of the metal device into the scabbing wound. Smith knew it was coming, had braced himself for the incredible, searing pain. He grunted as the device was inserted. But he did not cry out. The sweat on his brow grew thicker. It was prickly and hot. The rivulets of perspiration that ran down his back were chilling. Smith felt the gooseflesh rise on his skin.

A mantra ran through his mind, the only help he had. Do not scream. Do not allow these madmen the satisfaction.

Ernst didn't seem disappointed. As Smith writhed on his ropes, the German gave the metal rod a full, harsh twist.

It was pain beyond pain. The metal spikes bit through the dead flesh. Living tissue tore away as the brutal man spun the metal rod in the other direction. The circuit completed, he jammed the rod farther into the newly bleeding wound.

Smith succumbed to the agony.

As the American OSS agent screamed in anguish, Captain Josef Menk noticed that one of the ball bearings stitched into the back of his gloves had become exposed. He could see the shiny silver orb peeking out between the splitting seams like the tiny hairless dome of an infant about to be born. He smiled at the simile. Captain Menk had always considered himself to be somewhat of a poet.

As he congratulated his own cleverness, Captain Menk made a mental note to have his tailor strengthen the seams in both of his pairs of uniform gloves.

SMITH MADE HIMSELF surface from his own thoughts.

Night had fallen.

A few weak stabs of light were streaked in shades of yellow and white across the gently undulating waters of Long Island Sound.

He checked his ticking Timex and was surprised to see that it was very nearly midnight.

Turning from the window, he checked his computer. The dull glow of the buried computer screen stared ominously up from the heart of the onyx desk.

Smith was mildly surprised at himself. He had been reminiscing.

This was not unusual for most people, but it was nearly unheard-of for Harold Winston Smith. There was much too much real work to do during the day without cluttering up the mind with errant thoughts. Reminiscing served no useful purpose; therefore Smith did not reminisce.

Yet he had.

Captain Menk. He hadn't thought of him in years. So why had he now?

The back of his head itched, and his immaculately groomed fingernails searched out the spot. It wasn't his scalp. It was an internal sensation. The remembered feeling of the Dynamic Interface System radio signal he had felt at the bank. He had been as helpless before Menk all those years ago as the bank patrons had been to the computer-controlled radio signal. That must be it. The reason for recalling those horrible events on Usedom.

But there was something more to it than that....

Smith was shaken from his reverie by a persistent blip of the cursor in the corner of his screen. Some new information had filtered into the PlattDeutsche file he had created earlier in the day.

Smith scanned the text quickly. The PlattDeutsche story had made it to the local 11:00 p.m. newscasts. It was a rehash of all of the earlier stories with one hitch. Apparently some of the bank's customers were not pleased by the demonstration. There was already talk of a number of lawsuits to be filed in connection with the incident.

Smith read the last line with a hint of sadness. More lawsuits. More wasted court time. More time for real criminals to exploit an overburdened system.

Exactly what America needs, Smith thought ruefully.

His own reliving the past was irrelevant, he decided. This was the world in which he lived. Where everyone, it seemed, had hopes of scoring big without expending any effort whatsoever.

There was no real connection between events of this day and those terrible events so long ago. It was odd, that was all. Just an old man allowing his past to cloud his present.

Smith was never a man given to wallowing in his own morbid past.

Menk was dead. As was the younger Harold W. Smith.

Smith shut his computer down. It was only midnight. Perhaps his wife was still awake. He'd surprise her by coming home early for a change.

Without another thought of his days in the OSS, Smith snapped off the dull overhead light and left his Spartan office.

NIGHT HAD TAKEN firm hold on the most exciting day of Dr. Curt Newton's professional life. It was remarkable. Simply remarkable. Who would have thought?

"Not me," Newton admitted to the dull pastel walls and carpeting of the empty office corridor.

That was it. He'd been working so long he'd started speaking to himself. He giggled as he strode through the half light. So he was speaking to himself?

"So what," he announced to any ghosts that might be loitering in the darkened recesses of Platt-Deutsche's R&D wing. "So I talk to myself. I'm a genius. I'm supposed to be eccentric." He giggled again as he stepped aboard the elevator at the center of the six-story structure.

He hardly wanted this day to end.

In the elevator, he checked his watch—12:26 a.m. It was already tomorrow. Oh, well. As someone once said, tomorrow is just another day.

And if it proved to be as eventful as this day, well then, Curt Newton, physical cryptologist extraordinaire, would sit back and enjoy the toboggan ride. Though he'd probably have to go on some of those new antidepressant drugs or something. What was that expression his father liked to use? High as a kite on goofballs? That's what Curt Newton felt like right now.

He got off the elevator on the top floor. This corridor, as well as all the others at the New Jersey complex, was deserted. Everyone not connected with the Dynamic Interface System program had gone home at five. They would, therefore, have to wait until eight o'clock the next morning to find out that the project was finished.

Successfully.

Well, not finished exactly. That was overstating it. It would take some time to work out all of the reverse-engineering procedures.

But they were already working on it, and Newton had already made more breakthroughs in a single day than he had in five years on this project.

And he owed it all to one remarkable, remarkable man.

There was a light coming from the foyer of one of the executive offices down the far end of the corridor. Newton steered for it.

Of course, there was one other man whom he would have to thank. Reluctantly. Lothar Holz was a rather dim bulb, not given much to understanding the complex nuances of scientific thought. Newton suspected it was because the man didn't much care for the whole endeavor in itself. But whatever his motivations, Holz had come through with the money. And without the money, Curt Newton wouldn't be poised on the verge of introducing a technology that would revolutionize the world for centuries to come.

When he rounded the corner into the foyer that was Holz's outer office, Newton was mildly surprised to find someone sitting in one of the aluminum-and-cloth chairs set against the inner wall. The man looked up with unblinking blue eyes when Newton entered from the corridor.

It was the young blond man who always seemed to hover near Holz. In the cafeteria. At the lab. In the bank this morning. And outside Holz's office at 12:30 a.m.

In spite of the lateness of the hour, he didn't appear to be tired.

Newton didn't even know the young man's name.

Some at the lab speculated that the young man, who had no discernible job at PlattDeutsche, was kept on retainer as a perpetual "escort." Newton had decided to quash any speculation of this nature early on. As long as Holz continued to funnel funds into the interface project, he could have buggered a rabid skunk for all Curt Newton cared.

The blond man rose wordlessly at Newton's approach. He swung open the office door labeled Lothar Holz: Vice President, Research And Development, and stepped back. Once Newton was ushered inside, the door was pulled closed behind him.

Holz was at his desk. The blinds were drawn behind him. A small lamp bathed his face in an eerie incandescent light. The distinct smell of fresh cigarette smoke clung to the interior of the office. This always surprised Newton. Holz was a man of meticulous habits, and Newton could not remember once seeing him with a cigarette in his hand. Yet it was common for his office to reek of smoke. It was strange in this day and age for a man to be so secretive about his smoking habit.

But Newton wasn't here to discuss the man's idiosyncrasies. He fell into the chair across from Holz, weary yet triumphant.

He dropped the computer printouts he had carried from the lab into his lap.

"This is an incredible piece of luck," he said, shaking his head. He couldn't refrain from beaming.

"As you've said."

"You can't begin to grasp the importance of this, Lothar."

Holz regarded Newton levelly. "It is just possible I can," he said, his words tinged with sarcasm.

"No reflection on you," Newton said, raising his hands, defensively. "It's just that…" He stopped and scooped up the papers. "With this I have so far been able to program the computers with a sixty-eight percent accuracy of response in the hypothalamus. The hypothalamus! I could only work the autonomous nervous system on the most rudimentary of levels this morning. Now I can make people perspire. I can raise or lower their blood pressure." He held up the papers triumphantly. "Thanks to our friend from the bank, I can now use the interface frequency to regulate hormones in human beings."

"I am certain every parent with an oversexed teenager will be lining up tomorrow for your invention,"

Holz droned in a bored tone. He stared beyond Newton at the reproduction of Toledo in a Storm that
hung on his office wall. The dark, grayish green hills
and the savage clouds of the El Greco painting
seemed to mirror his inner mood.

Newton raised an eyebrow. "Is there something
wrong?"

Holz drummed his fingers on his desk, still staring
at the painting. "There are those who question the
wisdom of our little demonstration."

There was only one thing the scientist could sur-
mise. "You went before the board."

Holz nodded. "This afternoon."

"And you didn't tell me the results?"

"I did not wish to disrupt your research."

Newton's voice shook with concern. "They're not
thinking of shutting us down?"

Holz shook his head. His gaze was distant, and his
voice soft as his eyes traversed the grim Spanish
landscape. "The board is nothing. I don't answer to
them."

"What do you mean?" Newton asked, puzzled.
The board was the ultimate authority at Platt-
Deutsche.

Holz allowed himself a wan half smile. He pulled
his eyes away from the painting. "Worry about your
test tubes and beakers, Curt. Let me worry about
other matters," he said. Newton shrugged. The last
test tube he had seen was on a TV show almost a

year before. He launched into his report. This was, after all, the reason both of them were putting in such late hours.

"We're working back from our subject's mind to program our computers. The work is going faster than I could have hoped for. But this guy is amazing. Truly an enigma. There was a whole section of his brain that was virtually walled off to all of my best efforts. Even Mervin had a hard time with it."

"Was the information damaged when it was downloaded?"

"No, it was perfectly copied. It's just that it was filed away in such a way that proved difficult to access."

"But not impossible."

Newton grinned as he placed his computer printouts on the large desk. "I haven't reached all of it yet, but I've scratched the surface. It's almost like a testament to triviality. This guy has locked away stuff on financial matters. That's always easiest to reach first because of the raw numbers. And I guess that it makes sense for him to lock it up. Prying eyes and all. But I haven't quite nailed down the proper ratios. The computer is probably multiplying everything by a factor of ten or something. It's saying that the amounts he's moving are in the millions, and that can't be right. We were stumped on the cash aspect, which has held us up on the rest of this area of his mind."

"Maybe his work requires him to move large sums of cash," Holz suggested.

"Please. He reminded me of my nickel-counting grandmother," Newton said. "I just wish so much of the initial data capture didn't revolve around raw numbers. It usually helps, but here it's hindered us." He pointed at the printout. "Look. A lot of this phantom cash goes to Korea, and a lot of it gets moved around here."

"Korea?"

"Yes. You're not going to believe this. The stuff this guy thinks is important enough to lock away is amazing. The money, according to our best guess, goes to a place called Sinanju."

Holz sat up. "Sinanju?" he said sharply. He snatched the computer papers from Newton but no matter how much he stared, could make neither head nor tail out of them.

"It's a small village in North Korea," Newton explained.

"I know where it is."

Newton looked surprised. "Really? I had to look it up. An interesting story. It seems that this small fishing village is listed in our files along with a bunch of other legends. For centuries, since the dawn of civilization, actually, the village of Sinanju has been the seat of the Master of Sinanju. The titular head of an ancient house of assassins. The story goes that the Master of Sinanju has rented his services out to the highest bidder for centuries. All myth, this Sinanju. I guess it's right up there with Robin Hood or Bigfoot. I'm just wondering how it found its way into our Dr. Smith's head.''

Holz had been frowning over the incoherent computer sheet until Newton's last words.

"Doctor?" he said.

Newton grinned proudly. "I've found him. He runs a sanitarium up in Rye. The first numbers to yield to our probe were his home and office. I looked him up in the phone book. He lives on the edge of the Westchester Golf Club.''

Holz considered. "The Master of Sinanju," he said softly.

Newton nodded and retrieved the computer sheets.

"He's probably just regurgitating stored memories. Neuron junk. He probably read about it years ago.''

"Millions of dollars in gold are shipped to Korea.''

"Only in his head." Newton was so tired he didn't even remember not mentioning the fact that the millions to Korea were in gold. "It is probably just a few thousand. Maybe he gets paper clips or other office supplies from there. I'm amazed by how much of his brain is filled up with that sort of minutiae. It seems half his occipital lobe is dedicated to comparing the prices of staples today as opposed to thirty years ago.''

Holz was no longer listening. He thought about the millions, about Korea. About the Master of Sinanju.

And about his superiors.

Newton cleared his throat. "Um, now that I know who he is, Lothar, I would like to get him down here, if you can arrange it. I'd love to do some laboratory study on him. It could step up the process."

Holz nodded slowly. "Yes," he said at long last. "Yes, I would love to meet this most fascinating individual."

Newton was beside himself with delight. "His full name," he said, "is Dr. Harold Winston Smith."

7

The phone rang bright and early at 7:00 a.m.

Maude Smith was in the kitchen preparing a batch of her famous pancakes—the ones that had the texture of dry wool and the color and tang of a block of charcoal. She left the wall phone dangling near the ancient linoleum floor and went to the bottom of the stairs to call up to her husband.

Harold Smith was in the process of knotting his striped Dartmouth tie around the severely starched collar of his plain white shirt. He sat on the edge of the bed and picked up the extension from the nightstand.

"Smith," he said crisply.

"Morning, Smitty," Remo's cheery voice announced.

"Remo?" Smith asked, shocked. The voice at the other end of the line gave a cheerful affirmative. Smith opened his mouth to speak but suddenly heard another voice on the line. It was female and matronly and somewhat distant. And familiar. The new voice was complaining quietly to no one in particular about something smoking far too much. Wordlessly Smith placed the phone on the lace doily that encircled the top of his nightstand and went to the top of the stairs.

"Maude, could you please hang up the phone," he called down the staircase. He heard his wife's muffled surprise at her own forgetfulness as she crossed the kitchen to replace the receiver.

This small act gave the already overdone pancake in the frying pan enough time to blacken to unrecognizability.

Smith shut the bedroom door and returned to the telephone.

"Your wife's burning breakfast, I gather," Remo said pleasantly.

"This is an open line."

"Open, shmopen, don't be such a girl's blouse, Smitty."

Smith crinkled his nose at the unfamiliar idiomatic expression.

"I will call you back," he informed Remo.

Smith hung up the phone. A minute later, once he had retrieved his special scrambled phone from his briefcase, he was once more speaking to CURE's enforcement arm.

"That was a foolish risk, Remo," he said.

"Oh, yeah, tell me about it, Smitty," Remo replied in a mock-serious tone. "No one ever gets a call at their house. You'll probably have the National

Guard and Ma Bell beating down your door by seven-thirty.''

"You have the special CURE line."

"I forgot the number."

"That hardly seems likely, even for you," Smith noted dryly.

Years before, Smith had been confounded by Remo's amazing inability to remember even the simplest phone codes. He had finally settled on the multiple series of 1s that was now in use, reasoning that Remo would be unlikely to forget the first digit. As it was, Remo had taken six weeks to fully get the hang of it.

"Yeah, well, you can shelve the cloak-and-dagger. This isn't a business call. It's personal."

"How so?" Smith said. Absently he checked the knot of his tie. As always, it was knotted to perfection in a four-in-hand knot.

"I wanted to congratulate you on your going public. Chiun says it was a mistake to go on when you did, though. The smaller stations are counterprogramming at the supper hour. He thinks *Family Matters* will trounce you in the overnights."

"I did not say 'trounce,' Emperor Smith," a squeaky voice called from the background.

"You said 'trounce,' Little Father," Remo said.

"I said that the other program has, in the past, been known to beat the emperor's program. But surely with the addition of Emperor Smith to the cast, the half hour of decadence will transcend its usual level of drollery and fecklessness and mount an effective attack against the sprite Urkel."

"You said 'trounce,'" Remo insisted.

"Did not."

"Did, too," Remo challenged.

"I will not argue with you."

"You should hear what he said about your acting," Remo confided to Smith.

Chiun raised his voice to a new pitch of squeak. "Do not listen to him, Emperor. Your skills as a thespian are matched only by your wisdom as a ruler."

"I rest my case."

This brought forth from Chiun a burst of Korean that Smith could not follow even if he were fluent in the language, which he was not.

"Is there a point to this phone call, Remo?" Smith asked wearily, once the tirade tapered off.

"I thought we covered that. I just wanted to tell you we caught you on the news last night."

"A masterful performance, O Emperor," Chiun called.

"Er, yes," Smith said, uncomfortably. "A neighbor informed my wife that I was in some of the background footage of the news story."

"You mean to tell me some of your neighbors actually know what you look like? I figured with those Dracula hours you keep they'd either have to be up after midnight or before five just to get a glimpse of you skulking through the bushes."

"I am as active in my community as our work allows."

"Yeah, right. From the house to the car to the office and back. You used to golf," Remo said. "When was the last time you were out on the links? Ten years ago? That neighbor lady probably dropped her colon when she saw you on the news. She must've thought you were dead."

"Remo, is there something I can do for you?"

"Not me, Smitty. It's Chiun."

Smith raised an eyebrow. "Is there something wrong with the Master of Sinanju?" he asked.

"Nothing wrong. He just wanted me to ask you for something."

"A trifling item, O illustrious Emperor," Chiun called.

"If it is within my power to do so."

"Oh, it is," Remo said. Smith could almost see the grin being beamed via satellite from the kitchen of Remo's Massachusetts home. "Chiun wants to know if he can have your autograph."

"I'm not sure I understand...."

"He thinks since you've been on the news that you're going to break into the big time. He wants to get your signature first. Especially since he heard that a lot of autographs fetch big bucks."

"How like you to apply your base motivations to

another," squeaked Chiun. "I would treasure the emperor's signature always, and hold it up for all to see. It would be witness to his munificent and generous nature."

"And you'll sell it as soon as you think you smell a buck."

"Visigoth," Chiun hissed.

"So, you willing to do it or what?" Remo spoke to Smith.

"I will see what I can do." Smith stood up from the bed, eager to end the phone call.

"And Smitty?" Remo said.

"Yes?"

"Don't forget us little people when you're a star."

THE KITCHEN REEKED of barbecued pot holders. The tiny hood fan above the stove was making a feeble attempt to clear the smoke-filled air as Smith took his seat at the kitchen table.

"I'm sorry the pancakes are a little dark," Maude Smith apologized as she placed a plate before him. It looked like a tarred stack of miniature manhole covers.

"They are fine, dear," he said. He picked up his knife and fork and began the laborious job of hacking his way through the pile of charred disks. His wife went over to the sink. With great care, she started to chisel the black grit off the still-smoking frying pan.

Smith considered the phone call from Remo as he

chewed languidly on a triangular sliver of carbonized pancake.

All things considered, he was holding up very well. Smith was a man to whom the security of CURE was paramount. For that secure shield to remain firmly in place, Smith could never move out into the limelight. The security of CURE and of Folcroft, and the possible compromise of both, had driven Smith into fits of terror for years.

It was, therefore, uncharacteristic for him to be so casual at getting his face plastered across the evening news.

But though it was normal for him to be upset as a general rule about such things, it was also just as normal for him to be pragmatic about any given situation. And the truth was, the news report meant very little.

Nothing of CURE's secret mission had been revealed. Smith's name had not been given out. The simple fact was, he had been just another face in the crowd, recognized only by a nosy neighbor.

But Maude Smith had been delighted.

She was waiting up for him when he got home the previous night and had treated him as if he were a real media celebrity. She had burbled on for an hour about how thrilled she was that Gert Higgins had called her after the six-o'clock news and how she wished Harold had allowed her to purchase a VCR machine so that she could have taped the later broadcast. She reminded him that she was going to visit their daughter, Vicki, at the end of the week and that Vicki would have gotten a real thrill out of the whole thing.

Maude was happier than he had seen her in years. In fact, he didn't generally eat breakfast at home—preferring instead to get a cup of coffee and a container of prune-whipped yogurt at Folcroft—but Maude had been so pleased at his brush with celebrity and so eager to do something special for him that he had agreed to eat a rare breakfast at home with his wife.

So here he was, home more than an hour later than normal, chewing in silence, lost in his own thoughts, while Maude Smith scrubbed diligently away at the blackened pans in the sink.

Smith was surprised at his own calm appraisal of the situation.

There was always risk of exposure. CURE had had several crises in the past. But this was nothing. Nothing at all.

Smith sliced away at a fresh sliver of blackened pancake, and raised it to his thin lips, first swallowing the wad of gritty, wet dough already in his mouth.

There was a timid knock at the kitchen door.

Maude went to answer it.

Probably the paperboy. Late, as usual.

Smith made a mental note to chastise the boy for

his tardiness. But all at once, a thought occurred to him. The paperboy collected his money on Friday. This was Tuesday.

"Mrs. Smith?" a man's voice asked from the door.

"Yes."

With worried eyes, Smith glanced up at the door...and nearly vomited his pancakes back up onto his plate.

He recognized the man from the bank. Lothar Holz.

Maude Smith recognized him, too. Before Smith could protest, she had ushered the man into the small kitchen and shut the door. With a quavering voice she announced him as "the man from the bank" to her seated husband.

"Am I disturbing you?" Holz asked politely, looking from Smith to his wife and back again.

"No, not at all." Mrs. Smith was clearly delighted to have the cause of her husband's celebrity in her own home. "Would you care for some breakfast?" she asked hopefully. When Holz accepted the offer, Maude restarted the burners and retrieved the damp, black pan from the sink. She moved around the stove excitedly, clucking like a proud mother hen.

"May I?" Holz asked. With a nod, he indicated the vacant chair across from Smith.

Through a colossal effort of will, Smith subdued

the urge to panic. He nodded stiffly, and Lothar Holz sat down at the tiny table.

"I'm certain you're wondering why I'm here," Holz began.

"The thought had crossed my mind," Smith said guardedly.

A slight smile passed across Holz's lips. "Indeed," he said with a look of satisfaction. He intertwined his fingers on the tablecloth and leaned closer to Smith. "I'm not sure if you realize this, Dr. Smith," he said conspiratorially, "but you are quite a unique individual."

Smith could see his wife grow more delighted as she fussed about the red-hot burners. He cleared his throat nervously. His mouth felt as dry as dust. "How so?" he said with a casualness he didn't feel.

"I'm not sure you realize the magnitude of the test you unwittingly participated in yesterday. Yes, the Dynamic Interface System is able to integrate with that part of the brain controlling voluntary movements..."

"The cerebellum," Smith offered.

Braun shrugged. "So my experts say. Truth be told, Dr. Smith, I know very little about the function of the brain or of the device that was demonstrated yesterday, for that matter. I am not a scientist. I am more of a research coordinator."

"I see," Smith said, nodding his understanding. Holz was the corporate front man. He probably had only the vaguest idea of the incredible technology PlattDeutsche America had developed.

"But there is something we did not reveal to the world. Our device is also able to duplicate the patterns within a human brain. As it was explained to me, the process we've come up with is now as simple as copying the contents of one computer floppy disk to another."

Smith began to get an odd ringing sensation in his ears. It was the increased flow of blood from his desperately beating heart. When he swallowed, his mouth was as dry as the dead center of a sack of flour. "Did you use this aspect of the interface system yesterday?" he asked. His voice sounded as if someone were strangling him with his narrow necktie.

Unblinking, Holz stared at Smith. "We did."

Smith flicked his glance away to his wife. Must keep the conversation going, the director of CURE thought. Must not allow Maude to become suspicious.

"It was my understanding that such technology was years away," Smith said weakly. His breathing was coming heavier. The more he attempted to quell it, the more urgent it became. His heart was pounding in his chest.

"It was, actually. Our scientists were able to duplicate all of the raw data. Everything from memories, both conscious and subconscious, to actual acquired learning, such as things learned in school and things long since forgotten. Even glimpses of synaptic images as far back as the prenatal state or as far forward as the last thoughts at the moment of transfer. But in spite of the fact that we were able to duplicate everything, we had a near impossible time *accessing* everything. That much was true even going into the demonstration at the bank.''

Smith allowed himself some cautious relief. He tried to will his heart rate to slow. ''So you are unable to crack all the codes.''

''*Were,* Dr. Smith. Were.'' Holz smiled warmly. ''And we have you to thank. Your mind is so remarkably orderly that we have been able to use it to access others. Our technology has taken a mighty leap forward in a single day. And we have you to thank.''

''Really.'' To Smith, his own voice sounded as if it were echoing up from the empty, dark bottom of a long-abandoned well. ''Will you excuse me a moment?'' He rose stiffly from the table and went down the hallway to the small half bathroom. Flushing the toilet to mask the sound, Smith proceeded to vomit the meager contents of his stomach into the white porcelain bowl.

When he returned to the table, his skin was drained of what little tinge of color it usually possessed. He had gone from sickly gray to ghostly white in a matter of minutes.

Holz was still seated at the table. He picked at a few syrup-smeared pancakes with the edge of his fork as Mrs. Smith watched him expectantly. He seemed relieved to see Smith.

"Is there something wrong, Harold?" Maude Smith asked as her husband retook his seat. She was wiping her damp hands on a sopping wet dish towel. Her brow furrowed in concern when she saw her husband's pallor.

"I am fine, dear," he assured her. "I believe I might be developing a slight head cold."

Maude Smith rolled her eyes. "Honestly," she said to her new confidant, "he works so hard it's a wonder he isn't always sick."

"Could I have my coffee now?" Smith interjected, lest she tell Holz any more than he might already know. With a tiny shrug, Maude went dutifully to a rear cupboard. The shoulders of her paisley frock rose precipitously as she dug in the back for the least-cracked mugs. Smith attempted a smile. "So, Mr. Holz, what is it you wish from me?"

It was a feeble, time-wasting question. But alone at the table, helpless in the face of an unknown enemy, Smith was at a loss for what else to do. His gun was at Folcroft. In a shoe box far back in his desk drawer. Remo and Chiun were too far up the coast to be of any help in an immediate crisis. And besides, he had no idea how much the man actually knew.

In another instant, his worst fears were realized. Maude Smith had pulled out a pair of almost matching mugs and was scrubbing the sticky coating of dust from their interiors when Lothar Holz leaned forward. His voice was low, so that Mrs. Smith would be unable to hear. The words he spoke sent a chill up Smith's spine.

"I know of Sinanju," he said softly.

The floor suddenly fell out from beneath Smith. He felt his empty stomach knot up like a rigor-mortis-clenched fist. His head swam with hundreds of amorphous, inchoate thoughts.

Only a few became fully formed.

CURE was doomed. America's most carefully guarded secret was an open book. And it was all his fault.

Maude Smith returned bearing a pair of steaming coffee mugs. Smith took his dully, automatically. Like a man who had just entered his last hour on death row.

Mrs. Smith and Holz chatted amicably. She told of her coming trip, of their daughter. Of her excitement at seeing Harold on television. Every now and again, Holz would glance knowingly at Smith. Smith merely sat there, his hands cupped around the steaming mug.

And though the heat from the scalding liquid burned his palms, Harold W. Smith didn't notice.

8

On the sixty-third ring, Remo picked up the phone.

"Joe's Taxidermy. You snuff 'em, we stuff 'em," he said in a bored tone.

There was a slight moment of hesitation from the other end of the line. Then Smith spoke, his voice tighter than usual. "Remo, report back to headquarters immediately."

Remo was mildly surprised that he wasn't chastised for making the CURE director wait. "Aw, Smitty, can't you just overnight-express the autograph?"

"Never mind that," snapped Smith. "Something important has come up."

"It's always important," Remo complained. "I was in the middle of something pretty important myself." In truth, Remo had been out in the large parking area beside the condominium complex that was his home watching some of the neighborhood children skateboarding. One of the kids had pretty good balance.

"Remo, please, just get down here as quickly as possible."

There was something odd about this call. Something much different than usual. Remo pressed on. "What's all that noise in the background?"

"I am, er—" there was a pause on the line "—not at the office."

"Well, where, er, are you?" Remo asked.

"At a nearby fast-food establishment."

"Outside?"

"There is an amusement area of some sort here."

There were children's voices shouting raucously in the background. Remo tried to picture Smith in his gray suit, rimless glasses, seated on a painted tin mushroom with his battered briefcase on his lap while dozens of children ran screaming around him. Try as he might, he couldn't summon up an image that could possibly do justice to the reality.

Remo sighed. "You could have told me about this earlier." Remo's internal clock—more accurate than any government-built atomic clock—told him it was only eighty-seven minutes and twelve seconds since he had gotten off the phone with Smith.

"This problem has just come up. Remo, please." There was a strange desperation in his voice.

"Okay," Remo said resignedly. "I'll be there as quick as I can."

He hung up the phone and went to inform the Master of Sinanju that he was leaving. He found the tiny Asian seated in the center of the glass-enclosed upper room of the building. Chiun's wizened face was pointed east and slightly upturned. The warming rays of the midmorning sun suffused his parchment skin and reflected brilliantly off the hand-embroidered gold piping of his fire-engine red kimono.

"That was Smith on the phone," Remo said upon entering the room. "He needs me back at Folcroft." He took a deep breath and stared out at the traffic on the street below. "He sounded strange."

Chiun didn't open his eyes. "And this struck you as odd?"

Remo shrugged. "No." His brow furrowed, unconvinced. "I don't know. He just didn't sound like himself."

Chiun's eyes instantly shot open. Hazel irises quickly flashed to shards of flinty concern.

"He did not hack?" the Master of Sinanju demanded.

Remo shook his head patiently. "It was nothing like that, Little Father," he insisted.

Only a few short weeks before, Remo had unknowingly charged headlong into an ancient Sinanju prophecy. An unholy band of false prophets had re-established the two-thousand-year-old Delphic Oracle in America's West. Those who breathed the smoke of the Pythia, as it was called, were possessed by the demon force. Remo had been unlucky enough to become the vessel of the Pythia for a time. His coughing spasms had been an early sign of possession to the Master of Sinanju.

"You are certain Smith has not been infected by Apollo's minion?" the old Korean pressed.

"Of course not," Remo said. "We blew Ranch Ragnarok to Kingdom Come, and the Pythia's urn along with it."

Chiun studied Remo's hard features. They had not discussed those events much. Something had happened to Remo while he was entrapped by the oracle. The old man suspected that it had something to do with yet another Sinanju legend—the one in which Remo was said to be the avatar of Shiva, the Hindu god of destruction.

Finally Chiun closed his eyes. "Do not be confident that we have seen the last of the Pythia," he said ominously.

"We smoked him once, we can do it again," Remo said, spinning to the window. His sure tone belied an inner concern. "And I was talking about Smith."

"Did he mention the autograph?"

Remo rolled his eyes heavenward. He turned back to the master of Sinanju. "Chiun, I told you. Smith's autograph is worth diddly."

"Now," Chiun said. "But it might not always be so."

"I guarantee you, a hundred years from now, Smith's autograph will still be worth diddly."

"But if it increases in value, I will be in a position to make a tidy sum. This with no personal investment, Remo."

"You plan to be around in a hundred years to sell it?"

Chiun opened his eyes. The ancient eyelids, as thin as rice paper and seemingly as delicate as a cluster of cobwebs, revealed a pair of surprisingly young-appearing hazel eyes. The Master of Sinanju regarded his pupil levelly. "I am not quite ready to climb into my grave." The eyes were cold.

"I didn't mean anything by it," Remo said. "It's just that one appearance on the evening news isn't going to make Smith a star."

"Robert Dedero had to start somewhere."

"De Niro," Remo corrected.

"A worthless currency," Chiun said. "Almost as worthless as the ruble. I will only sell Smith's signature for gold. But I will only sell it if you collect it, so make haste." Chiun closed his eyes once more.

And rather than attempt to explain to the Master of Sinanju that it was unlikely that Robert De Niro got his first big break on the evening news, Remo left.

REMO TOOK an afternoon flight and arrived by taxi at Folcroft by three that afternoon.

The security guard didn't even lift his eyes from his tiny portable television set as Remo strolled through the open wrought-iron gates and up the main driveway. He headed directly to the main sanitarium building.

Remo noticed a strange white van sitting in the no-parking zone in front of the large stone staircase to the main building. Its engine purred almost imperceptibly. He guessed it to be some kind of utilities truck, since his heightened senses detected a lot of electrical equipment inside the back.

Veering away from the main entrance, Remo took the narrow flight of stairs near the employee parking area up to Smith's office.

Smith's outer office was deserted. Remo considered that a stroke of good luck. Mrs. Mikulka, Smith's secretary, must have been away somewhere on an errand. Remo was pleased that he didn't have to contend with the older woman. She sometimes took her job as the personal secretary to the head of Folcroft Sanitarium far too seriously.

He moved across the outer office on silent, gliding feet.

Remo paused at the door to the office. There was someone else inside with Smith. He didn't know why his senses told him this; he just knew. Maybe this was the reason for Smith's urgency on the phone.

Without hesitation, Remo popped the heavy lock on the inner office door and slid stealthily inside. He hadn't passed more than a foot into the Spartan office before he felt a huge pressure on the back of his skull. The pain was intense and immediate. It was as if someone were compressing the fused bones of his skull in a vise. His ears itched. Remo reeled at the pain.

Smith sat behind his desk. The other man, a stranger Remo somehow found familiar, sat in a chair across from Smith. The stranger turned to Smith as Remo staggered in pain near the still-open doorway.

"This man is white."

"That is true, obviously." Smith's eyes darted over to Remo.

There was a hint of concern etched in the deep recesses of his flinty gray eyes.

"The Masters of Sinanju have always been Orientals. Koreans, specifically."

"Remo was able to absorb the training when no Asians could."

The man's tone became threatening. "It would be regrettable if I discovered you have been lying to me, Dr. Smith."

By the door, Remo was attempting to regain his equilibrium.

It felt as if someone had jammed two rusty ice picks in his ears.

The itching had moved inward. It now felt as

though a starving rat were trying to claw its way out of his skull.

With a colossal effort, Remo forced his jaw and larynx to work.

"What is going on, Smitty?" Though he was able to speak, the words were labored, sounding as though they were spoken by a stroke victim.

Dimly Remo recognized the man as the one he had seen on the news the previous evening. A look of mild surprise spread across the man's regal features.

"Unusual," he said. He nodded approvingly, as if Remo had just passed some private test.

Remo decided he didn't like him. The way he looked at Remo was maddeningly condescending. He wasn't going to wait for the order. He'd settle this guy's hash and then ask Smith what the hell was going on.

The look of surprise on the face of Lothar Holz became one of shock as Remo took a hesitant step toward him.

"Curt," the man said to no one in particular. "You don't have a lock yet." There seemed to be a nervous crack in his usually calm demeanor.

Remo took a second step. Though he moved like a marionette with hopelessly tangled wires, he was closer to Lothar Holz.

Holz stood. His face grew more concerned and he spoke urgently.

"Curt, he is moving."

For the first time, Remo noticed a small device pressed into the man's ear. It was no larger than a hearing aid. Apparently he was giving and receiving signals from some outside source.

A second later, Remo had forgotten about the transmitter-receiver. With no warning, Remo's left hand moved in a deadly arc.

It whipped up and around, slashing down solidly onto the back of an old oak office chair. The chair protested, but only for an instant.

All at once the legs buckled, the back and seat shattered apart and the entire chair collapsed into an unrecognizable pile of splinters.

The hand continued its vicious arc and slapped audibly against Remo's thigh. It rested there as Holz looked on, wide-eyed.

Holz wasn't the only one who was shocked. Remo looked at the pile of debris, a dumbfounded expression on his twitching face.

Something was profoundly wrong. He had been focused in on Smith's visitor. He hadn't told his body to shatter the chair. It had acted independently, exerting some foreign will over him.

The tingling at the base of his skull grew more intense.

"Mr. Holz, I have acceded to your demands. There is no need for random acts of violence," Smith said.

Holz. The man from the bank. The stunt with the interface system. And all at once, Remo knew. It was some sort of mind-control device. Smith had sold him out. To Holz. Remo fixed the man with a deadly glare.

"He is not under control," Holz snapped at Smith. He tapped the receiver in his ear. "Newton! Newton!" Frightened and cornered, he backed up against Smith's desk.

And though he moved with an uncertain, jerky motion, Remo still had his body partially under his control. With a look that would have inspired terror in hell's most stone-hearted demon, Remo took another step toward the cowering intruder.

"WHAT ON EARTH was that?"

"Autonomic response."

"From the peripheral system?"

"That's just it. This guy has no peripheral nervous system. It's all autonomic."

"That's impossible." In the back of the van, surrounded on all sides by various scientists, technicians and programmers, Dr. Curt Newton was having an impossible time figuring all this out.

He had been overjoyed to learn that Harold W. Smith had been contacted and even more delighted when he learned that Holz had set up a meeting with the doctor at Smith's place of business. But he didn't know why Holz wanted him to bring the interface van from the New Jersey complex.

"We have someone special I want you to download," Holz had said.

This was troublesome in and of itself.

There was a problem with the ethics of duplicating the contents of a person's mind when that person hadn't given prior consent. Indeed, Newton had learned earlier in the morning that some of the people at the bank were threatening PlattDeutsche with lawsuits—so Newton had assumed that they were going to put a hold on this aspect of the project. Curt Newton didn't have much of a problem with that. They had already demonstrated to the world that the process worked. Surely the government contracts would start rolling in now.

But Holz had been insistent, and so Dr. Curt Newton had loaded everything into the van and driven up to Rye to await the "someone special" he'd been promised.

The man had arrived at the building mere moments before. He had been a problem right from the start.

Not only did his synaptic and neural patterns not match anything the computers had on file, but something as simple as a cerebellum lock was proving to be near impossible. The man was going into some sort of nervous-system overload. Where they should have gotten control of him the moment the heat sensors picked him up in the rear office—which was where Holz had arranged for his meeting—the man was proving virtually impossible to detain. His acetylcholine levels were off the charts. Some rogue spark had just caused him to destroy a piece of furniture. Who knew what he'd go after next?

"Why haven't you gotten a lock yet?" Newton demanded of his panicking staff.

"He's resisting."

Newton shook his head. "Impossible." Newton, who had been acting in a supervisory capacity, pushed one of the technicians away from his terminal and dropped into the vacant seat. And immediately saw a problem. "Your readings are wrong," he said, indicating the neural monitors. "Your nervous-system model is shot," he said, waving toward the monitor. "These axons and dendrites aren't even from a human."

"Yes, they are," one of the scientists insisted. "I triple-checked. They've been reconfigured somehow. The interface program is having a hell of a time trying to adjust to the new system pattern."

"Afferent indicators are negative," a technician piped up.

"Shh! Shh!" one of the men hissed. He cocked an ear toward the speaker that connected the back of the van via a special radio signal to the headset of Lothar Holz. "He's still speaking!" the man said, incredulous.

Newton's face was severe. "He shouldn't have hypoglossal control at this point."

The scientists collectively shrugged or shook their heads in confusion. They redoubled their efforts.

An instant later, there was another crash from the office speaker.

In the back of the van, Dr. Curt Newton froze. He prayed that nothing had happened to his mentor. For without Holz, the money flow for the Dynamic Interface System would trickle to a stop. With wary eyes, he turned toward the heat-sensing apparatus.

THE CHAIR HOLZ HAD BEEN sitting in shuddered as if from some unseen inner force, then collapsed into a shattered lump on the threadbare carpeting. There was nothing left to indicate that the pile of splinters had been, until a few seconds before, a rather worn and uninviting office chair.

In a lightning-fast flash, Remo's hand returned to his side.

"Control your man, Smith!"

Holz looked clearly terrified. His unflappable facade had given way to a look of sheer horror as Remo, struggling to fight the interface signal, slowly advanced.

Smith kept his expression bland. He dared not allow Remo's unexpected resistance to raise any visible signs of hope. If Remo was able to battle the signal and take care of Lothar Holz, then perhaps this situation could be rectified quickly. But there was still the matter of the white van out in the parking lot.

"Master of Sinanju, I meant you no harm," Holz cried out as Remo closed in.

Remo managed a puzzled frown. Master of Sinanju? What was he talking about?

Remo wanted to ask, wanted to put the question to Smith.

But it had become too much of an effort to speak. He would take care of Holz first.

Remo's deep-set eyes were focused on his target, but he still moved in an awkward, stilted manner. He was battling a nervous system that had for years obeyed his every move and now felt sluggish and unresponsive. The itchiness inside his skull was a constant irritant.

His ears rang dully.

But he had Holz. The man cowered like a frightened, craven dog before him. He would finish him with a simple blow. Nothing fancy. Then he'd find out from Smith what the hell was going on.

But the blow he planned had a mind of its own.

To Remo's surprise, his hand slashed out automatically, his spear-sharp fingertips aimed directly at the sternum of the man who cringed before Smith's desk.

Sweating profusely, Holz cowered, petrified and utterly defenseless against the killer attack.

OUT IN THE VAN, Curt Newton was frantic.

"Boost the signal!"

"I can't."

"There's got to be interference coming from somewhere!"

"There's no interference. The signal's fine."

Newton shook his head. "This is impossible," he said again, desperately.

Information raced across the screen at a rate Newton had never before seen. The lightning-fast binary scroll was reflected in his owlish glasses.

"Master of Sinanju, I meant you no harm," the pleading voice of Lothar Holz hissed over the tinny speaker. Newton glanced at the speaker with a worried expression.

"Can you get the cerebellum lock yet?" Newton pleaded with one of his white-coated associates.

The man was bathed in sweat, red faced and pale in turns. He nodded sharply. "I could get it now, but we don't have the capacity."

"What do you mean?"

"His neural system is incredibly complex. There's not enough room for the file. That's why we've had a problem so far." The man wiped the sheen of perspiration from his forehead as he spoke.

"There's no way one man could fill the entire system."

"I don't think this guy is human," the technician

explained, shaking his head in awe. "It's almost like his neural codes have been entirely rewritten."

"But you're saying we don't have the capacity to duplicate the file?"

"Only if we destroy the other files in the system."

Newton's jaw was firmly set. "Copy over them."

"Are you sure?"

Newton nodded sharply. "Copy over everything we have. Get the cerebellum lock on him first."

"Yes, sir." The man immediately went to work, setting up the interface system to automatically delete old files as it copied the synaptic information from the individual in the rear office. The portable computers in the van whirred anxiously to life as the information flowed back over the radio signal from the rear office.

The massive databases rapidly began to fill with a wealth of new information.

"I've got cerebellum control," a tech announced after only a few seconds. He hunched over his screen excitedly.

Newton watched in fascination as new sets of binary codes—translated automatically by the preprogrammed interface system—began scrolling across the screen. The speed was far greater than before. Where they had first moved by in a flash, they were now a blur. When he blinked, the bands of white numbers seemed to congeal into single, static lines of washed-out white.

"Wow, this is great," said the technician who had informed the others of the cerebellum lock. He had isolated the information from that section of the brain and was now playing around at his keyboard.

"This guy's got some killer programming." He punched out a simple command on the cerebellum board.

"What did you do?" Newton asked. He was still nervous, still thinking about the funding that a major screwup could cost him. Still thinking about his place in future scientific textbooks.

The man shrugged. "I just ran a program this guy's brain had started. It was something that was already along the neural net. Pretty basic compared to the rest of this guy's programming."

"What was it?"

"It was a move."

Newton pressed. "What kind of move?"

Again the young man shrugged. "It was like a karate chop, sort of." He scrunched up his face at the inadequacy of the description.

Newton felt his heart turn to water and slide down into his stomach. This foolish little hacker in the van had no idea what he might have done. The man in the office was like no one he had ever downloaded before. He was something more than a man. And he had already been advancing on Lothar Holz.

Newton prayed that the blow had missed its mark.

FORTUNATELY for Lothar Holz, it had.

And fortunately for Remo, as well, it had been a simple stroke.

Any maneuver more complex might have ripped his arm from his shoulder.

His arm shot out, but the aim wasn't true. Holz had moved to one side. And while Remo's brain would have ordinarily compensated for the movement, he found to his supreme surprise that his brain was no longer his own. His hand breezed past Holz's shoulder. The powerful blow dissipated in the empty air above Smith's desk. His hand returned to his side, seemingly of its own volition.

Now, though Remo struggled against the mind control, he couldn't budge even a fraction of an inch.

Holz caught his breath. With grateful eyes, he watched Remo's hand slap back against his leg. It didn't move again.

Holz stood erect, straightening his tie. He tugged the cuffs of his suit jacket primly and, with a half turn of his neck, adjusted his Adam's apple against the collar of his white dress shirt.

"Well done, Curt," he said to the microphone. "Though a touch on the late side," he muttered under his breath. He walked over to Remo.

Smith looked deflated. Any hope that Remo could rebuff the interface signal was lost. His only hope now was the true Master of Sinanju. He prayed that Chiun would be strong enough to fight off the powerful radio signal. Hopefully, by lying about Remo's true identity, Smith had bought the organization a few hours.

Maybe, just maybe, Chiun would introduce a random element that Holz hadn't planned on. The element of surprise.

Smith took his seat. "You have what you came for. Could you please leave now?" he said.

"Not quite yet."

Smith's brow furrowed. "I do not understand."

Holz slipped his slender, perfectly manicured fingers around Smith's desk telephone. He lifted the receiver and extended it toward the lemony-faced man. His next words made Smith's already erratic heart muscle skip a beat.

"Call the other one."

And a Cheshire Cat smile displayed a row of gleaming, perfect teeth.

9

Chiun let the phone ring precisely one hundred times. He didn't wish to appear too eager to perform such a menial chore.

In any other kingdom, at any other time during the nearly five-thousand-year history of the House of Sinanju, an indentured servant would have been placed at the disposal of the Master of Sinanju. This servant's duties would have been varied. Among them would be drawing the Master's bath, laundering the Master's robes, and now—in the twentieth century, on the distant shores of the United States of America—answering the Master's telephone.

Since the crazed Emperor Smith, the true though secretive ruler of America, didn't wish for Chiun to have servants, the duty of answering the telephone generally fell to Remo.

But Remo wasn't there.

Remo had allowed the device to squawk more than sixty times earlier in the day. Chiun couldn't allow himself to appear more eager than his pupil, so he had decided that the perfect number, one hundred, would be the one on which he answered the ringing apparatus.

"I am Chiun," he announced into the phone.

"Chiun, I need you at Folcroft."

Smith was usually more formal on the telephone, electing to use Chiun's title rather than his name. Chiun preferred the formality.

"Remo is on his way, O Emperor," Chiun declared.

"There is a problem with Remo."

"He is missing?"

"No, no. He arrived here but...it would be better, perhaps, for me to show you rather than explain it over the telephone."

"You wish to show me something?"

"Yes."

Chiun tipped his head, considering. "You will hire me a conveyance?"

"A cab will be there to pick you up shortly. I have reserved you a seat on a 6:00 p.m. flight out of Logan."

"Very well."

Chiun hung up the phone.

Smith had something to show him. What could it be but the autograph? Doubtless the fool felt his name was too valuable to entrust the signature to Remo.

It had better be. Especially with all of the aggravation Chiun was going through to collect it.

Like a fussy hen, Chiun hurried around the house preparing for the trip.

TEN MINUTES LATER Chiun was in a cab on the way to the airport.

The driver was a sixtyish man with a crown of steel gray hair and a thick, wrinkled neck.

As they drove, Chiun complained loudly about Smith. He was upset at the CURE director's short-sightedness in not asking him to accompany Remo this morning. At least then he would have had some-one to complain to along the way. He also griped about Remo, a boy so dim he couldn't be trusted to carry out a simple errand.

"Tell me about it," the cabbie commiserated. "I got a kid. A son, too. Ten years out of college and still living at home. I tell the wife we should just toss him out on his ear. But, you know, he's his mama's boy. She says I'll go before he does."

"Pardon me," Chiun said. "Was someone speaking to you?"

The cabdriver shrugged. "I thought you were," he said. There wasn't a hint of malice in his voice. He was used to the rapid mood swings of fares.

"I am put through all of this for a simple auto-graph," Chiun said to the window. "A thing that could be sent to me by post."

"I wouldn't do that," the cabdriver cautioned. "My kid's got an autographed Willie Mays card.

You know, from back when he was playing. It's worth a bundle right about now. You tell me, is it normal for a thirty-year-old to pay a couple hundred bucks for a bubble-gum card?''

And because he didn't wish to hear someone griping all the way to the airport, Chiun touched the man lightly on the side of the neck.

Immediately the cabbie's vocal cords seized up.

The rest of the trip to the airport was blessedly quiet.

IT WAS DARK by the time Chiun arrived at Folcroft.

As he made his way across the tree-dotted lawns surrounding the sanitarium, he could see a few late-evening boaters chugging across the gently rippling waters of Long Island Sound. The lights on the craft bobbed hypnotically above the undulating black surface.

He spied a young blond man standing alertly beside a large white van parked at the apex of the long gravel driveway. He avoided the man, as well as the truck, and merged with the pervasive darkness surrounding the ivy-covered building, a shadow among shadows.

The side door was locked this late at night. Chiun wrapped his delicate fingers around the handle and wrenched. The hooked piece of shiny aluminum bent but stayed attached to the thick metal fire door.

The bolt dropped free of the latch and clanged into the damp inner stairwell.

Chiun entered the building.

The sanitarium was lightly staffed at this hour, and a cost-cutting measure instituted by Smith had dropped the ambient light within the corridors and stairwells to near nothing.

The Master of Sinanju became as one with the gloom as he moved through the empty administrative wing of the sanitarium.

He found Smith's office and, ignoring his supra-sensory data that told him there were three men inside—one obviously Remo, another obviously Smith—Chiun pushed open the doorway and entered the sparse room.

"Emperor Smith, the House of Sinanju expresses gratitude to you, its benefactor, for that which you are about to bestow. All hail—"

He was halfway through his speech when he noticed Lothar Holz beside Smith's desk. The man had been sitting, but stood when Chiun entered.

Chiun's eyes grew as wide as joyful saucers. "You have brought with you your costar," Chiun said delightedly.

"Master Chiun, you must dispatch this man at once," Smith ordered abruptly.

Surprised, Holz glanced from the aged Asian at the door back to Smith.

"Master?" he said. His eyes strayed to Remo,

who stood stock-still beside Smith's desk, a glint of impotent fury dancing in the depths of his deep-set eyes.

Chiun nodded sagely. "I have heard of such problems on television sets before. Do not fret, Emperor Smith, for this was merely the pilot episode. Surely your role will be expanded in the future."

Chiun suddenly felt something brush against the base of his skull. It was a slight tickle. The sensation intensified and moved around behind his ears. Chiun waved a long-nailed hand beside his head as if swatting away a pesky fly. Although he felt the unmistakable hum, he didn't sense the disruption of air an insect would cause.

"Chiun, quickly!" Smith called urgently.

"This is the true Master of Sinanju." It was a statement of fact. Holz unfurled a delicate finger in Chiun's direction. "Curt, get a lock on the old one."

Chiun was torn. Though his emperor was directly ordering him to destroy Lothar Holz, star of the evening news, he was momentarily distracted by the strange sensation creeping across the back of his eggshell skull.

But it was no more than that. A sensation.

And as quickly as the sensation had come, it passed.

Confusion clouded the cobweb wrinkles above his eyes.

Chiun took a step into the room…and was blocked by Remo.

The younger man had become suddenly animated. He had gone from being a motionless statue one moment to a springing tiger the next.

He leaped from his spot beside Smith's desk, landing softly in the center of the worn carpet.

Remo now stood protectively between the Master of Sinanju and Lothar Holz, barring Chiun's way.

Chiun's ancient eyes narrowed to curious slivers. "Remove yourself."

Remo said nothing. There was no malice in his deep-set eyes.

In fact, there was something closer to sadness. And fear.

"Remo is not himself," Smith insisted. "He is being manipulated."

"Do not be a fool, Smith," Chiun spat. He started to slide to Remo's left, but a thick-wristed hand shot out, blocking his path. It wasn't a threatening move, by any stretch of the imagination. But it was aggressive nonetheless. Remo was barring the Master of Sinanju from performing a duty to his emperor.

Chiun dodged right, but Remo's other arm shot out, faster than either Smith or Holz could follow. Both arms were stretched out now, like a Hollywood zombie's, with Chiun standing between them.

"Curt, what's going on?" Holz demanded of the

air. "Get the old man under control." He tapped the small receiver in his ear.

"Remo, step aside," Chiun said, under his breath.

And rather than move, Remo's hand lashed out viciously, in a direct line for Chiun's temple.

So shocked was Chiun by the unexpected attack that the blow very nearly registered.

The old man dropped low and feinted left, beneath Remo's deadly fist, and came up behind him, his back to Smith's desk. Remo spun a perfect pirouette in midair and landed facing Chiun.

To Smith and Holz, it appeared as if Remo's response were instantaneous, but Chiun saw that it was sluggish. It didn't have any of the normal fluidity or grace Chiun had come to expect from Remo's usual movements.

"Remo, what is this?" the Master of Sinanju demanded, his mouth a furious, questioning O.

He again saw the strange look buried deep within his pupil's usually expressionless eyes. Something that registered deep regret and deeper sorrow. Remo threw another blow at Chiun.

The Master of Sinanju swatted it aside as if it were nothing. But he could see that Remo was becoming more focused in his attacks. It was as if whatever was controlling his actions was growing more adept with each subsequent move.

"Chiun, Remo is under some kind of mind control. His actions are not his own," Smith cried pleadingly. "Holz is behind it." With a gnarled gray index finger, he indicated the man Chiun had seen on television with Smith the previous day.

Holz was tapping at the tiny object in his ear, not even paying attention to the battle being waged in the center of the office.

Remo attacked Chiun once more. It was more complex than his previous attempts and it very nearly worked. The Master of Sinanju had to duck away before he was able to join in the motion of the blow. He grabbed Remo by the wrist and, as the arm swung around, he moved the rest of the body along with it. They were like two dancers executing a simple routine, but when they were finished, Remo was facing away from the rear of the office, toward the open door.

Chiun swatted Remo on the back.

The contact of the flat of Chiun's bony hand against Remo's spine sent the young man sprawling across the floor. It wasn't a lethal blow, but one meant merely to stun. The most fundamental aspect of Sinanju was breathing, and Chiun had effectively robbed Remo's lungs of breath. It would be a moment before he would recover.

The itching at the base of his skull resumed, but Chiun ignored it.

He whirled up to Lothar Holz, a vengeful dervish, and plucked the small transceiver from his ear.

"Is this the device that robs my son's will?" He crushed the hearing aid in his wrinkled hand.

A movement. The press of rapid air. Too fast to move out of the way.

Chiun suddenly felt a great pressure against his back.

The blow was flawed. It didn't kill, nor did it rob him of air.

But it should not have landed.

Pipe-stem legs swung windmill fashion while arms fought for balance. Chiun felt himself going up and over Smith's desk.

Some air was lost. He opened his nose and mouth to pull in more oxygen even as he twisted in midair. He landed behind Smith's desk, catlike, on his sandaled feet.

Remo should not have recovered that quickly. The Master of Sinanju could see the strain on his pupil's face. As if his body was being forced to perform in spite of the damage it could cause him.

Smith stood beside Chiun, his gaunt face stunned. He hadn't even seen Remo move. The young man had gone from a prone position on the floor to an upright posture in a fraction of a second.

Holz had moved in behind Remo. Like a taunting third-grader protected by the shadow of a schoolyard bully.

And in the face of an unknown enemy that could rob a man of his spirit and force him to attack the one to whom he was most indebted, Chiun did the only thing he felt he could do.

Wordlessly the Master of Sinanju plucked Smith from behind his desk. He spirited the protesting CURE director past Remo, into the outer office. Seconds later they were across the lawns and over the walls of Folcroft, beyond the range of the Dynamic Interface System signal.

When they were gone, the engine of the white van with the fancy PlattDeutsche insignia continued to purr quietly into the warm late-spring night.

10

He called himself Heinrich Kolb.

He wasn't certain why. His real name wasn't a secret. At least, not here. But Kolb was the name he had chosen for himself more than fifty years ago, and he had been forced to hold on to it longer than he had wished. He was Kolb through the dark days in Europe and into North Africa. Still Kolb when he finally reached South America. He had spent the better part of his waning years as Heinrich Kolb.

And so when he at last settled here after more than thirty years of running from place to place, he came to a startling realization. He had been called Heinrich Kolb longer than he had been called his real name. He kept the newer name.

It was silly, really. There wasn't much point to subterfuge here, of all places. But by the time he was repatriated, he was an old man and it was hard for an old man to change.

He was a doctor of sorts, though he had not practiced seriously in nearly a decade. He was venerated by the others in the IV village. He liked the organization's name, too—a name that stood for an aspiration and a way of life, and nicely expressed in writing by the classic looking Roman numeral, and in ordinary speech as an ordinary number four.

This suited him. He felt it was his due. Especially since there were so few of the old ones left around these days. If the hunters didn't find them—unguarded, away from IV—old age inevitably took its toll.

Heinrich Kolb had tried for a long time to remedy mankind's ultimate malady—death—but after many years of trying, he had to at last admit defeat. Everything died. But that didn't mean a phoenix could not rise from the ashes.

It was an odd thought. Strangely eloquent. But it was the thought to which Heinrich Kolb awoke this morning.

He saw the bird. The phoenix. It perched atop a red disk, its wings spread majestically against the forces of man and nature. At the center of the red disk, a twisted black shape. Familiar to all.

Kolb knew that the image was recognized around the world. To most it was terrifying and hated. To Kolb it represented a freedom of expression he hadn't enjoyed in years.

He found his slippers at the foot of his bed. Putting on his heavy woolen dressing gown, he made his way to the bathroom.

There was still a web of early-morning frost clinging to the edges of the heavy window panes, but the warming yellow rays of the sun would soon send it scuttling for the shadows.

He ran a hot, hot bath and prepared himself for another day.

AN HOUR LATER, he was out in the village.

It was an amazing place.

It was as if some Titan had carved a piece from the rugged terrain of Bavaria and resettled it here into the cleft between three Argentinian mountain peaks.

The homes were adorable little chalets. Gaily painted shutters and flowering window boxes complemented the cobblestone drives. There were little shops from which the delectable smells of pastries and bread tempted passersby.

The roads were narrow and well traveled. The curbs were painted all around in a deep red. It was all very clean, very orderly.

There were many people out in the village. Some drove their tiny foreign cars, but these were either the young or those higher up in the movement. Most, like Kolb, preferred to walk.

The rarefied mountain air sometimes caused his breathing some difficulty, but today was such a beautiful day he refused to allow his aging lungs to hinder him. As he walked, he pulled a curved plastic device from his jacket pocket. At one end was a tube. Kolb placed this between his pale lips and inhaled deeply. He felt the prescribed medicine fill his tired lungs.

He breathed a few times, deeply and, thus invigorated, forged ahead, basking in the warmth of the bright morning sun.

He was at the door to a quaint little café where he often enjoyed breakfast when he was intercepted by an urgent young man who came running at him from the direction of the governing buildings.

The man had milky blue eyes and a crop of short blond hair. For a moment, Kolb thought that he was one of his own, but he realized that the age wasn't right. This boy couldn't be more than twenty.

"Herr Kolb, you are wanted at the main house."

Kolb made an unhappy face. "You have the wrong man." He attempted to slip through the doorway.

The boy was persistent. He shook his head. "It is you," he said. "Herr Kluge has requested your presence immediately. He insists it is quite urgent."

Kluge. The boy wasn't mistaken.

With all hope of a peaceful breakfast dashed, Kolb sighed. Nodding wearily, he followed the young boy to the main house.

IT WAS LESS A HOUSE than a fortress. It was an ancient temple that had been fortified in recent years to withstand a major ground assault. The walls were high stone, dark even in the bright sunlight.

Two armed soldiers snapped to attention as Kolb was ushered through the main entrance by his young escort. The man led him into a spacious office off the main corridor. A man he recognized as Adolf Kluge rose as Kolb entered. Kluge walked around the desk to shake the old man's hand as the young escort exited the office, tugging the heavy door closed quietly behind him.

"So, Doctor, are you up to a new mission?" Kluge asked, grinning.

"A mission?" Kolb made an unhappy face. "You were at my birthday celebration last month, Adolf. The number of candles nearly set the entire house ablaze."

Kluge chuckled. "You are in better shape than I am," he said in a self-deprecating tone.

"Then you are late to see your own physician. Very, very late," Kolb replied.

Kluge laughed once more, heartily. He crossed around behind his desk. "You are probably right about that," he said. "My doctor has to drag me into his office against my best protestations."

He reclaimed his seat.

"In that we are similar," Kolb admitted. He still stood by the door, suspicious of the motives of the man behind the desk.

"Come, come. Sit down." Kluge gestured to a large, comfortable chair beside the desk. "It will be your last rest for a while, I fear."

Kolb followed Kluge's extended hand, dropping silently into the overstuffed chair. "You are mistaken if you think I will leave the village," Kolb said, shaking his head. "I retired from my practice years ago. If you didn't know from the evidence around you, I failed in my experiments."

Kluge nodded, seriously. "There were limitations," he agreed. "Eugenics is not an exact science."

"Nor this laboratory genetics your predecessor forced me to dabble in," Kolb complained.

"Ancient history." Kluge waved dismissively. "You may live to see the fruit of your dreams after all, Doctor."

In spite of himself, Kolb was becoming interested. "What do you mean?" he asked.

Kluge leaned back in his seat. "Four has various stock holdings around the world. PlattDeutsche, as you know, is a company in which we are heavily involved."

"Yes," Kolb said impatiently. He was aware of all of this. Though only a doctor, he was allowed to attend the many meetings held during the formative years of the organization. He was one of the last founding members left alive.

"PlattDeutsche America is a very successful offshoot of the original company. At least, until the Americans decided to disband their military." Kluge leaned forward. "Our highest placement at the company is a man by the name of Lothar Holz. Do you know of him?''

Kolb shook his head.

''I am not surprised,'' Kluge said. ''He was educated in foreign universities. Of course, his primary education was here. The boy had a rather—'' Kluge searched for the correct word ''—circuitous path to us. But he is with us now and he has contacted us today with some remarkable news.''

''What is it?''

Kluge placed his palms flat on his desk. ''Prepare yourself, Doctor,'' he said, his voice serious.

When Kluge finished speaking ten minutes later, Heinrich Kolb was already mentally packing for his journey.

It was getter warmer in northeastern America now, but the nights would be cold. At his age, he was always cold. He would pack warmly and buy cooler clothes as necessity dictated.

Kluge rose to shake his hand, and Kolb left the large office, hurrying back down into the main village with its tiny little gingerbread houses and gleaming, spotless windowpanes. His missed breakfast was long forgotten.

An hour later, he was packed. The same young man who had led him to the main house was outside his cottage with a small Fiat, its engine running. He loaded the doctor's luggage into the trunk and helped the old man into the front seat.

A plane ticket to New York's JFK Airport was tucked into the sun visor above the passenger's seat.

The young man got in his own side and, revving the engine, made his way quickly and carefully through the clean cobblestone streets past the whitewashed buildings. They headed out to the mountain road.

And so it was that at eighty-nine years of age, Heinrich Kolb, best known as Dr. Erich von Breslau, history's notorious "Butcher of Treblinka," set forth from the tiny Argentine village to fulfill a dream he had thought was long dead.

11

Mervin Fischer quailed nervously in his seat before asking the question. "Is this ethical?"

Holz dismissed the possibility as irrelevant. "He's already agreed to it."

"I'm not sure it's right...."

"I am not interested in your opinion. You've seen Newton's data?"

"Yes."

"So you understand the possibilities? If we can download selectively?"

"Theoretically. But your host is a mess. He's not living in the real world. The delusions will be problematic. They'd be a real danger in practice."

"You'll weed them out."

Holz was very persuasive. But he should have understood that this wasn't exactly Mervin's area of expertise.

For the past hour, Mervin Fischer had examined the data as it streamed from the temple electrodes into the mainframe. The individual with the deep-set eyes that seemed to glare at everyone in the room at the same time had remained rigid beside the terminal throughout the entire procedure.

Mervin was glad the man couldn't move. There was something in those eyes—as cold and limitless as the far reaches of space—that the young programmer found unsettling.

Fortunately the signal from the mobile interface unit had been transferred to the lab when Holz had returned to the PlattDeutsche complex in Edison, New Jersey, and so the man was sustained in his immobile state. Good thing, too. If this subject was as dangerous as Holz said he was, it was a risk to even let him out of prison. Mervin wondered what kind of warden would allow a dangerous psychotic out without armed supervision. Of course, they had tested the interface on prisoners early in the developmental stage, but the experiments had always been on volunteers and always under strict supervision. And never, ever outside of prison walls.

Under ordinary circumstances, he would have doubted the veracity of the storyteller, but he had heard this from Mr. Holz himself.

Dr. Newton had gone to his own lab with a few information CDs and a single hard drive from the mobile lab. The driving force behind the entire interface project had been upset that he didn't have primary access to the volunteer. When Mervin had arrived, Newton had left, griping that he was being shut out of his own program. He hadn't even had time enough to download all of the subject's file from the van.

When the programmer requested the backup information to confirm what he had gotten from the subject, Newton had refused.

That didn't matter to Mervin. In fact, it was probably better this way. There were still problems with the radio interface hookup.

Sometimes the signal deteriorated due to background radio signals, atmospheric conditions or just a plain lousy signal. He couldn't count the number of times the tech people had to replace the little black signal antennae on the backs of all the computers.

No, in Mervin Fischer's view, whenever possible it was better to use a physical link. Hence, the electrodes on the volunteer's temples.

Mervin didn't really need the original files. He was just being anal. At least, that's what everyone always accused him of being.

Carefully he created his own backup file from the man's brain.

He had barely downloaded the information before Mr. Holz had stormed into the lab. A crew of technicians led by Ron Stern transferred the interface signal from the lab back to the van. They then trundled the test subject with the frightening eyes back outside on some kind of mysterious mission. Lothar Holz himself gave a few hushed last-minute instructions.

Mervin Fischer assumed his work was done once the information was downloaded. He was wrong.

Moments after the van had passed through the gates of PlattDeutsche America, Holz returned to Mervin's cramped office. What he asked from Mervin made the young man's forehead itch. It always itched when he was placed in a difficult moral situation. He could feel the large red blotches already forming.

"I'm uncomfortable with this, Mr. Holz."

His boss was asking him to do something that would push the interface technology further than it had ever gone before. And he wasn't quite certain if he was the right man to do it. But Holz didn't seem to have the same reservations.

"Fischer, I don't want your input. I want you to do it."

"Dr. Newton is probably best suited to perform this sort of test," the programmer said uncertainly.

"You know how to program a computer?" Holz asked testily.

"Yes, but—"

"You understand the interface programming?"

Mervin was sure that Mr. Holz knew he had written much of the interface programming himself. He nodded nonetheless.

"You're one of the ones who kept telling me that a computer was just a less complex version of the human brain. And if we can download human thought into one of these blasted machines, why can't we download the duplicated information into someone else's brain?''

''Theoretically…''

''Don't give me theoretically!'' Holz exploded. ''I've had it up to here with all of your theoretical garbage! Can you do it or not?''

Mervin was frightened. Barely twenty-two years of age, he was a brilliant computer hacker who had graduated from college three years early and moved swiftly into the work force. But he was hopelessly inept in most social situations. Mervin could remember being yelled at precisely twice in his life. Once by his father for breaking into his savings account and increasing the balance by eleven million dollars and once by a stranger when he had stepped in front of the man's car, his nose buried deep in the pages of *Star Trek* fan magazine. Both times he had responded to the shouting the same way. His bladder had burst like a mud-and-twig levee in a monsoon.

''I can, um… That is, um…'' Mervin looked at his computer screen. He nodded dumbly. A shiver pulsed through his body, and a flush rose to his cheeks.

''Is that a yes?'' Holz snapped. Mervin nodded again. Holz was mollified. ''Perfect. Great. That's the answer I expected after all the money we've dumped into this ridiculous program.'' He paused, sniffing the air. ''What's that smell?''

HOLZ FOUND A VOLUNTEER in Zach Pendrake, one of the white shirts from marketing who had been co-ordinating with the PR boys to put a positive spin on the bank fallout from the day before. Pendrake was a loudmouth, opinionated on any subject from politics to software to anything in between. He was the type who thought shouting down an opponent in a debate was the only way to win. Knowledge and experience be hanged.

Pendrake had taunted Mervin in the cafeteria for the past eight months to the point where the timid young man had taken to eating in the diagnostics lab.

Holz had moved Mervin into the large fourth-floor laboratory where the PET team and others connected with the early stages of the interface study had worked. The room was spacious and filled with equipment that had outlived its usefulness but had been stored here on the off chance that it might be needed once more. Nearly everything was covered with sheets of thick, translucent plastic.

Holz, accompanied by his young male assistant, led Zach Pendrake into the sterile room.

Mervin's stomach knotted when he saw whom Holz had tapped as a volunteer. Pendrake, on the other hand, seemed absolutely delighted.

"Mervin! Buddy! How ya doing, pal?" He slapped the nervous programmer on the shoulder.

Mervin winced. He bruised easily.

"Zach," he said with a timid nod.

"Mr. Holz didn't tell me you'd be testing me." Pendrake glanced at Holz. "Mervin and me are old buddies." He turned back to Mervin. "Why haven't I seen you at lunch, Merv? Got a little chippie stashed away somewhere?"

Mervin looked horrified at the idea. He glanced nervously to Lothar Holz and his silent assistant, stammering. "Mr. Holz, I... That is, I..." His eyes were watering.

Holz held up a hand. "Pendrake, calm down."

The marketing man smiled but grew silent.

He allowed Mervin to steer him to a wheeled table to one side of the lab, beneath the large bar-covered window. It was like a regular doctor's examining table. Right down to the sheet of disposable paper over the plastic-coated foam pad.

Mervin smeared a set of electrodes with a noxious-smelling gel and affixed them to Pendrake's temples. These led to the back of a small computer console that was hooked into the mainframe in the corner. Mervin had already transferred the information Holz was most interested in—the data on physical feats— into this larger computer.

He had Pendrake unbutton his shirt and proceeded to attach a second set of electrodes to his chest. These ran to a portable EKG monitor that had been shipped in from a subsidiary pharmaceutical company in New York. Mervin snapped on the machine, and instantly a steady green vertical line appeared across a small monitor in the face of the device. At regular intervals, a reassuring open-ended triangle spiked up from the solid line, accompanied by a familiar electronic beep.

Holz watched, anxiously wetting his lips, as Mervin slipped onto the rolling stool before his computer and began typing swiftly at the keyboard. He talked as he worked.

"I culled the stuff you told me to, Mr. Holz," he said. He avoided Pendrake's bemused look. "You wouldn't want anyone developing the psychoses your prisoner had. It's all about killing and stuff." He shuddered as he thought about the man with the deep-set eyes who was, at the moment, in the interface van somewhere on the Cross Bronx Expressway. "Anyway, what I concentrated on was the physical aspects of his nature. I tried to keep it pretty basic." He was no longer glancing at Pendrake but was becoming more engrossed in the data stream on the monitor before him.

The marketing man looked bored. He had volunteered for this latest experiment for the same reason he had volunteered for some of the earlier ones. To suck up to the boss. Plain and simple. And, as he had been with the earlier PET experiments, Pendrake was bored out of his skull in less than a minute. He exhaled deeply as the first bits of data began to download into his cerebellum.

All at once, he sucked in a sudden, unexpected lungful of air.

The EKG pinged once. It almost sounded questioning. As if the device were uncertain of the data it was collecting.

Mervin glanced up curiously. Lothar Holz watched, his face growing more expectant with each electronic spike of the EKG.

Pendrake felt the air pull down to the bottom of his lungs. It flowed into his heart and forced itself, fresher and fuller than ever before, into his bloodstream. The cleansing air coursed through his body, opening floodgates that someone who had dedicated his life to bar charts and smoke-filled rooms never knew were closed.

He felt suddenly invigorated. And light-headed.

For some reason, he found himself rotating his wrists absently. Holz was standing close, practically salivating.

"Is it working?" he asked Mervin. His eyes never strayed from Pendrake.

Mervin nodded. "He's absorbing it. Slowly, but it's working."

Pendrake knew what the little nerd meant. As he felt the power within him grow, he gripped the cold metal lip of the examining table in both hands. Still in a seated position, he twisted his hands. A simple action. He felt the strength of the metal beneath the pads of his greasy fingers. The strength of the metal was as nothing compared with what now flowed within him.

There was a loud wrenching noise, and when the others in the room looked they saw that Zach Pendrake had ripped a pair of foot-long sections of lead-enforced metal piping from the edge of the table.

He held the twin silver pipes in the air, a baffled expression on his face. It was as if he was wondering how they had gotten there.

Mervin looked on in wonder, Holz in slavering awe. Only Holz's assistant showed no sign of interest in the proceedings.

Pendrake no longer seemed to be aware of the others. In a crystalline moment of pure realization, he understood. Understood everything. The point of existence. The perfection that could be derived from the simple act of breathing. He knew that the limitations on the human body were placed there by men afraid to achieve. Terrified of true success.

The epiphany was short-lived.

Pendrake suddenly sat bolt upright on the examining table, as if jolted by a massive surge of electricity. The calm, soothing spikes of the EKG monitor stabbed sharply and held at a constant, dangerous peak.

Mervin frantically wheeled on his computer.

Holz took a few cautious steps back.

Pendrake was jolted again. His head snapped back and smashed against the painted cinder-block wall of the lab. They all heard the solid crack of bone. Pendrake snapped forward once more. A smear of hair-mottled blood stained the whitewashed wall.

"I think he's going into shock!" Mervin said desperately.

"Are you getting everything down?" Holz asked, his voice growing excited. He ignored Mervin, concentrating on the man on the table.

"I can't break the connection!" The information was being drawn into Pendrake too quickly. He was absorbing the new data like a sponge. The speed was frightening. As Mervin watched in horror, he understood what was happening. Pendrake's brain was overloading.

"Mr. Holz, we have to call someone!" But even as he pounded uselessly on his keyboard, Mervin knew there was no one he could call who could possibly help.

"Leave that alone," Holz ordered, pointing at the keyboard.

"Mr. Holz!"

"Leave it!" Holz yelled, wheeling on Mervin. He had a wild look in his eyes. He spun back to Zach Pendrake.

The marketing man was twitching spastically, as if someone had dumped a carton of red ants down the back of his shirt. His gaze was distant. When his neck twisted from side to side, a maroon patch of thick, coagulating blood on the back of his head was revealed. But no matter how hard he jerked in every direction, the electrodes didn't come loose. The EKG monitor continued to shriek a warning to those in the room, as if the pain Pendrake was feeling had somehow been transferred to the machine.

The steady high-pitched whine grew more intense inside Mervin's head. It rattled against his eardrums until he could nearly feel the power pouring through the electrodes himself. And when he couldn't bear the noise or the angry thrashing of the man on the gurney any longer, he did something totally uncharacteristic. He disobeyed a direct order.

Mervin stepped over to the examining table.

"Stop!" Holz barked.

But Mervin didn't listen.

Woodenly he reached for the pair of temple electrodes. His pudgy hand never got closer than a foot away.

Pendrake's hand shot out, faster than a cobra, faster than the pairs of binary numbers could be downloaded, faster than the human eye could perceive. It struck the young programmer squarely in the chest.

The fingers snapped like dried twigs against the solid sternum. No matter. The chest bone groaned in protest and collapsed inward.

A spray of blood erupted from the open chest cavity as shards of shattered bone pierced the heart. Several of Pendrake's own wrist bones shattered as the hand continued. Through the spine. Out the back, clutching air. Return.

Mervin looked down at his now open chest cavity as the arm withdrew. His mouth gulped, but no words came out. Only a small trickle of blood gurgled from between his parted lips.

With nearly no sound, he fell to the floor. He didn't move again.

Pendrake didn't feel the pain of his shattered forearm. It was as nothing compared with the symphony of exquisite torture in his own mind. Though science had determined that the brain had no true pain sensors, Zachary H. Pendrake would have disputed that theory with anyone. Except for the fact that the synapses in his own brain were popping like flashbulbs at an old-fashioned Washington news conference.

His thoughts were roiling into a supernova. His spine was acid dipped and on fire.

And all at once, his mind exploded in a flash of pure, searing energy.

Pendrake sat bolt upright one last time and then dropped like a sack of wet cement to the floor of the lab. He landed atop Mervin's prone body. The two electrodes on his forehead and one from his chest were wrenched free in the fall. The EKG monitor spiked one last time and then leveled out in a single, steady line. The keen of the electronic device buzzed quietly in the otherwise silent room.

After a moment, Lothar Holz stepped gingerly

over to the bodies. The marketing man continued to twitch occasionally. In one such move, the watch on his shattered wrist chipped a silver-dollar-sized chunk out of the concrete floor.

Holz glanced at his silent assistant, then at the EKG. Pendrake was still flatline. He was dead.

Holz placed his toe beneath the man's shoulders and flipped him over. Pendrake rolled off of Mervin and against the legs of the examining table. The last electrode popped loose.

His eyes were opened wide. Wider than they could have been if someone had grabbed onto both lids and pulled. The red-streaked white orbs bugged unnaturally from their sockets. What was also visible by its lack was that he had bitten his own tongue off in the excitement, his lips a red-ringed O of dismay and surprise.

"It's remarkable, wouldn't you agree?" Holz asked, grinning. He looked up at his assistant expectantly. His silent companion said not a word.

Holz sighed. "We are close. Closer than we have been in many years," he said quietly to himself. He straightened himself up.

"Von Breslau will be here soon. In the meantime, clean this mess up." He waved a manicured hand at the bodies on the floor. Picking his way carefully through the carnage, Lothar Holz left the room.

12

The world was sound and fury, narrowed down, telescoped to a sense that the world might end—in that very spot, unless something was done...

The bomb had blown out the rear wall of the office.

Ernst, the torturer, had been struck by a piece of flying rock. He crawled, dazed, across the rubble-strewn floor of the interrogation cell.

Smith had remained alert in spite of days of inhumane treatment. Though weakened, his mind raced.

The cross beams and plaster ceiling of the room had been new additions. Smith spied glimpses of the stone ceiling through the newly formed holes. The heavy beam from which Smith dangled had been jarred loose in the explosion. It was much lower than it had been, its end near the newly opened wall shattered by the blast. His toes now touched the floor.

Smith moved on tiptoe toward the open wall, sliding the rope along the beam as he moved. Every joint ached, every muscle protested.

From the floor, Ernst moaned.

The end of the beam was chewed, pulpy wood. Smith lifted the looped end of the rope from around the beam's end.

His arms ached. Fortunately they had taken him down not half an hour before to eat. It was the only time during the day he was freed from his bonds. If it had been another six hours later, it would have taken much more time to restore the circulation to his arms. As it was, they felt leaden and unresponsive.

Ernst grunted from behind. Smith turned.

The big man was pushing himself up, using the wall for support.

There wasn't much time.

Smith scrambled over the debris to the interior of the cell. His heart racing in his chest, he found the torturer's bag, which had overturned in the explosion. A heavy steel pipe had spilled out and rested beside the battered case.

Ernst grunted again. Smith glanced up.

The torturer was more alert. He realized what was happening. Groggily he pushed himself away from the wall, lumbering over toward the escaping prisoner.

Smith curled his fingers around the pipe. It was cold in his grip. Ernst was nearly upon him.

Smith stood, wheeling. He swung the pipe like a batter trying to put one out of the park.

The pipe struck Ernst in the temple. The big man stopped in his tracks, dazed.

Smith swung again. Another crack. Ernst blinked once, hard, and fell to his knees.

Smith lashed out once more. Ernst was too far gone by now to feel the blow register. Shattered skull fragments were already lodged in his brain. The final blow forced them in farther.

Like some great primal beast that knows when its time has come, Ernst's eyes rolled back in his head. The huge man fell forward onto his bag of torturer's tools. He didn't move again.

Smith quickly unholstered the man's side arm, tucking it in his belt. Captain Menk had left his great-coat on a hook in the corner of the room. Smith snatched it up, pulling it on over his grimy clothes as he ducked out through the opening.

From all around came the sound of shouting, panicked voices and frantic milling around.

Smith ducked into the shadows behind the building, hiding away.

Plotting his next move. He knew that Captain Menk wouldn't rest until he was dead.

Smith had become the madman's prey once more.

HAROLD SMITH AWOKE behind the wheel of the rented car.

For one frightening instant, he thought he was back on Usedom, but the thought soon fled. He was here, in the present. And the stakes were as high now as they had been then.

He checked his watch. He had slept for precisely eleven minutes.

Harold Smith removed his glasses and massaged his eyes with his fingertips. The same troubling thought that had passed through his mind for the past five hours resurfaced.

He should have shot Holz when he had the chance. His gun had been in the desk drawer the entire time. He could have ended this nightmare before it had even started.

It was a foolish recrimination, he knew. He had hoped that Remo would be able to take out Holz and his interface van quietly. That hope had vanished, along with Remo.

His organization was an open book to Lothar Holz, but Holz didn't seem interested in CURE. Only Sinanju. That had been the only piece of true luck in this entire ordeal.

Smith's only hope was to use the organization against Holz. But for that, he needed access to his office.

The passenger's door of the car suddenly opened. The Master of Sinanju slid in beside Smith. There was no rustling of leaves or clothing, not a single audible footfall to warn of his approach. These were the skills that had served the Korean Masters for cen-

turies and that had finally been rendered useless by
technology.

"The vehicle is not there." The old Korean's
voice was thin.

"You are certain of that?"

Chiun fixed Smith with an icy glare. "I am certain,
Smith."

Smith nodded curtly. He turned the ignition key.
"I'm sure Remo will be fine." He was embarrassed
the second the words passed his lips. Chiun didn't
respond. The wizened Asian stared stonily out the
windshield.

Without another word, they drove the last quarter
mile to the darkened gates of Folcroft.

THERE WAS A NOTE on Smith's desk.

> Your appointment informed me that you were
> feeling ill. Hope you are better today.
>
> E. Mikulka

Smith's secretary.

The note was neatly typed and perfectly centered
on the onyx slab. She must have suspected Smith
would return the next morning. In his entire time as
director of Folcroft, only dire circumstances had kept
him from his post for more than two days in a row.

He settled in behind his desk and booted up his
computer.

Chiun stood before the desk, tucking his bony hands into the voluminous folds of his brocaded kimono.

Smith ran a security check for any signs of tampering in the CURE system but found none.

It was a relief, though not entirely a surprise. He had been checking in at various intervals from pay phones around Rye. If someone other than himself had attempted to access any information, the entire memory core of the Folcroft mainframes would have self-destructed. However, it was still a relief to see with his own eyes that everything remained intact.

"You will use that device to locate Remo?" Chiun asked flatly.

He hadn't spoken much to Smith in the past few hours.

"It is my hope," Smith said. He stabbed out a few rapid commands, eyeing the results expectantly. He was surprised to find no listing of a Lothar Holz in any of the PlattDeutsche company records that were open to public scrutiny. "Odd," Smith said aloud.

He tried a different tack. Reasoning that they would have to bring Remo somewhere convenient to their research, he began checking real-estate holdings. He found that the PlattDeutsche Corporation and its subsidiary, PlattDeutsche America, had several smaller business concerns in the immediate vicinity. It was a well-diversified company, and as Smith ran through the various real-estate holdings, he eliminated most of them as possible destinations. There were only two research facilities in the area. One in upstate New York, the other in New Jersey.

But he needed to be certain.

He used his computer to gain access to Platt-Deutsche's vast database...and was instantly surprised at the complexity of the company's antitampering safeguards. Every time he tried to delve into the research material concerned with the Dynamic Interface System, he was rebuffed. Smith had little time to waste cracking the code. He couldn't even find a listing of Lothar Holz as vice president in charge of the operation. The entire R&D wing of PlattDeutsche seemed impossible to access.

And then it struck him. Lothar Holz. Vice president in charge of research and development.

Remembering the file he had created the previous day, he called up any information the computers had culled from a variety of media outlets. And there it was. An interview in a local New Jersey paper.

Glowing praise for Lothar Holz, rising star at PlattDeutsche. The computer offered a grainy newspaper photo of Holz donating a check to a local community center.

It was only then that Smith remembered. The van that had brought Holz to Smith's home had sported New Jersey license plates. They had taken Remo to their facility in Edison, New Jersey.

He stood.

"Master of Sinanju, Remo is in New Jersey."

Chiun didn't seem convinced. He held a slender index finger to his lips. He cocked a leathery ear toward the door. When he seemed at last convinced of some invisible certainty, he tucked his hands back inside his sleeves.

"That is where your machine tells you we will find my son?"

"That is correct."

"Then it is time to have it hauled over."

Smith frowned. "Overhauled? Why?"

"Because Remo is here."

And his voice was fraught with foreboding.

HE WOULD HAVE FELT more comfortable if Dr. Newton had come along. Or Mervin Fischer. But Mr. Holz had sent Ron Stern out in the interface van on a specific mission. A mission that he could not entrust to the others.

That Lothar Holz could trust Ron Stern to follow his orders to the letter was a certainty. Trust was the very foundation of their relationship.

Stern was a brilliant programmer who had come to computers late in life. He was nearly forty years old, but in spite of his advanced years—in terms of the computer field—Stern had worked alongside Fischer developing the earliest translation programs for the Dynamic Interface System.

His age made him a sort of father figure to the rest

of the men on the programming team, including the
real genius, Mervin Fischer.

But Stern and Fischer were polar opposites. Stern
was boisterous and outspoken. He was an avowed
sportsman and quite athletic. He watched his diet
more carefully than anyone else at the Edison complex. Even when the rest of the boys were eating
their fast-food burgers and pizzas, Stern always ate
nothing heavier than a salad. No dressing. Stern also
had one minor peccadillo that the others didn't know
about. He was somewhat more aggressive when it
came to the fairer sex than his friend Mervin. He was
just more persuasive, and though some people had
called it rape, Ron Stern knew that term was far too
strong.

Unfortunately for the computer programmer, the
authorities didn't think the term was strong enough
when applied to Ron Stern.

His world had begun to cave in shortly after an
incident concerning a PlattDeutsche executive secretary.

Luckily for Stern, when his darkest hour had been
upon him he had found an ally in the R&D vice
president. Holz put the entire muscle of the legal-
affairs division into defending the "poor innocent
man." The prosecution crumbled. In less time than
it took to bring the charges, Ron Stern was a free
man. And Lothar Holz had the programmer in his
back pocket. After that, the lines between right and

wrong further blurred to Ron Stern as Holz, his savior in his most desperate time of need, used him to deal with any niggling extralegal thing that came up.

Unbeknownst to Stern, most of these problems were manufactured, in a deliberate manipulation to train him to unquestioning obedience and make him feel more and more indebted to his boss.

And it had worked. Stern didn't question the motives of Mr. Holz when he was given his special instructions to return to the sanitarium in Rye with his "special cargo."

The others who had been sent along with him wouldn't be a problem. They had all had similar help at one time or another from Lothar Holz. The only thing that really worried Stern were the computers. He hoped they were up to the challenge.

They had parked outside the high walls of the sanitarium. One of the men had scrambled up to the roof and attached the rotating transmitter array to the coupling behind the cab. The curved black mesh looked like some kind of miniature Pentagon missile tracker. It would boost the signal so that they wouldn't have to enter the grounds of the sanitarium.

Ordinarily this wouldn't be necessary. The wide beam of the system was usually all it took. And the machines themselves were preprogrammed to handle hundreds of ordinary people automatically. It was virtually idiot proof. But this was a special case. They needed all the focus they could get just to hold on to one man. And Stern had permission to access the satellite if it became necessary.

In the rear of the van, three technicians operated the motion-coordinating terminals. Stern and two others worked the keyboards on the other side of the truck.

It was a go. Stern saw two people in the same rear office they had isolated earlier in the day. The thermal sensors outlined the men in red.

"One of them is that guy from the bank. We still can't get a lock on him."

"Doesn't matter," Stern said. "Mr. Holz wants them both dead."

He watched as another lone figure, also outlined in red, moved swiftly through the corridors of the administration building. And as the men behind him typed madly away, the spectral shape drew closer to the rear office.

THEY WOULD HAVE expected him to come in through the window. Or to explode in through the office door. Maybe to ambush them in the parking lot. What they wouldn't have expected was for Remo to saunter in through the doorway as if nothing was wrong. So that was exactly what they had programmed him to do.

"Hi, Smith. Hi, Chiun. How's it going?"

"Remo?" Smith asked, confused. Chiun raised a warning hand. "Do not trust your senses, Emperor."

"What's that supposed to mean?" Remo asked. His face scrunched up in a flawless computer re-creation of puzzlement.

"Come no closer."

"What? I waste half the night escaping from those goons you turned me over to and that's the welcome I get? Thanks a lot."

His words sounded sincere, but Chiun could see the look of anguish deep within his pupil's eyes. He knew that Remo still didn't control his own actions.

Smith looked at him, his staid features puzzled. He opened his mouth to ask for some enlightenment.

Unexpectedly, Remo sprang toward Chiun. His feet and hands lashed out like a manic windmill. The movements were much more fluid than they had been earlier in the day. Whoever controlled Remo had obviously been practicing.

Chiun blocked the arm blows with his forearms. In the move Remo used, the arms were not the primary means of assault. They were meant only as a distraction to the target. The real killing blows were focused in the legs.

Chiun dared not attempt to stop Remo's legs. He leaped up and over them, his skirts billowing as he landed to Remo's right.

The next attack was instantaneous, as if Remo had anticipated Chiun's first move. He whirled and struck out with the heel of his hand. Another millisecond, and he would have shattered the Master of Sinanju's windpipe.

Chiun no longer stood beside Remo. He was behind, then above him as his spindly legs flashed out, knocking Remo off balance. The instant Remo struck the carpet, Chiun was on him, his tapered fingers searching out the spot at the base of Remo's skull that would paralyze him.

When he was satisfied that Remo could no longer move, Chiun stood.

Amazingly Remo flipped over, thrashing out at Chiun once more. Chiun was stunned. This should not have been possible. Whatever this outside influence was that tampered with Remo's mind, they had no idea what their ham-fisted tinkering could do. They might irreparably damage Remo's delicate nervous system if they continued to override his body's instincts for preservation.

"Fiends," Chiun hissed, dodging Remo's lightning-fast hands.

Again he knocked Remo down and again he placed pressure on the top of the spine. On the floor, Remo grew rigid.

"Come here, Smith," Chiun said, beckoning to the CURE director.

Harold Smith stepped uncertainly from behind his desk and crossed over to the Master of Sinanju.

"Here." Chiun grabbed Smith by the wrist and pulled him down to Remo's prone form. "Place your fingers here, at the top of his spine." Smith did as he was instructed. Chiun rose, leaving Smith squatting on the floor beside Remo.

"What now?" Smith asked.

Heading for the door, Chiun called back over his shoulder, "Do not waver for an instant, or I fear Remo will kill you."

"Where are you going?"

"The vehicle that poisons Remo's mind is near."

"But you said the van was not here."

"It was not. Now it is. And in a moment, it will be no more."

And leaving Smith crouching uncomfortably on the office floor beside Remo, Chiun slipped out the door.

"WHERE DID the little guy go?" Stern demanded in the van.

The man beside him shrugged. "One minute the heat sensors had him, and the next minute he was gone. It was like he turned off his body heat."

"Maybe our guy killed him."

"And his body temperature switched off the minute he died? Not very bloody likely. He must've found a way to shield himself from the thermal sensors."

"Can't you use the interface signal to find him?"

The man smirked. "We can only focus the signal, Ron. And we need a target to focus it on."

"Can we use the satellite link to Edison? Maybe we can use the extra boost to widen the search area."

"We'd be searching for a ghost."

"Right, right," Stern said, shaking his head at the foolishness of his own question. He didn't like this. He was only a programmer. He shouldn't be in charge here. "Why haven't you gotten control of our guy yet?" Stern demanded of the row of hackers on the other side of the van.

"We've been locked out of the system," one of them complained.

"Manual override," said a second.

"Yeah," the first one agreed, nodding. "Manual override."

"This never happens when I play Riven," the first opined.

The man beside Ron Stern gave up tapping at his keyboard. Their operative wasn't responding to the interface lock, the other man in the office couldn't be controlled and the third—who might be somewhat controllable—had vanished. He crossed his arms and looked up at the leader of this expedition. "So, what do we do now, Ron?" he asked sarcastically, folding his arms across his chest.

His question was answered by a horrible wrenching of metal. The van rocked on its shocks.

"What the hell was that?" Stern demanded, grabbing at the wall-mounted table behind him for support.

"I just lost the interface signal."

Though they couldn't see out of the windowless back of the van, they heard something clatter to the ground outside.

"That's the booster," a technician said.

"We can't access the satellite," Stern said under his breath.

"Can you get a thermal reading now?" he demanded. "Someone on the roof?"

The man beside him clucked unhappily. "I'm getting something, but it's very faint...."

All at once, the rear door of the van was ripped from its hinges. The cab of the truck was lifted into the air by the incredible force exerted on the back door. The front tires remained several feet off the ground for a moment as the large white vehicle resembled nothing less than a wild animal rearing up on its hind legs.

The other five men in the back grabbed urgently at whatever they could, desperate to keep from falling through the open maw, but Ron Stern, who was still standing between them all, was tossed out the open door. He vanished into the night.

There was a painful screeching of protesting metal as the truck began to teeter in place. And then it fell. But even as the van crashed back to its four tires, bouncing wildly on its shocks, Ron Stern bounced back in through the door. At least part of him did.

Specifically, the part that had controlled the higher functions of the man who had been Ron Stern.

The head thudded against the closed door that led into the cab, then it came to a rolling stop at the feet of one of the computer operators.

The man instantly passed out.

Before the full impact of what had just occurred even registered in the minds of the others, the Master of Sinanju whirled into the cramped interior of the van.

The pudgy, pale faces of the two hackers still at their workstations grew shocked at the sight of the tiny Asian. On the computer screen, people were abstract. But here, in person, was one of the men they had been sent to kill. To them, he existed as a shadow in the strange electronic netherworld of bytes and binary.

They didn't have time to reconcile their computer-generated perceptions with reality.

Like an angry hissing typhoon, Chiun fell upon the two men. His movements duplicated those they had made Remo perform. But here, the execution was flawless.

Two palms flashed out, their long-nailed fingers folded neatly over like talons of some vicious bird of prey. Two windpipes collapsed beneath the pressure. The men dropped from their stools, joining their unconscious comrade and the head of Ron Stern on the floor. Chiun's foot lashed out in two neat jabs. A pair of holes erupted in their temples.

Chiun wheeled on the other two men. They remained in their seats, paralyzed with fear. Chiun's eyes narrowed as he saw on one of the screens the ghostly image of Smith bent over Remo.

"You will break the beam device that manipulates my son."

"It's severed," one of the men insisted. "You broke the signal when you derailed the satellite dish."

"The thing on the roof?"

"Yes. Yes, sir," they chorused obligingly, hoping that maybe there was still some chance to get out of this.

"That is what I thought," said Chiun. And grabbing the men by the scruffs of the neck, he steered their heads into their computer screens. A pair of muffled pops and a few sparks followed. The men didn't move again.

Chiun found the unconscious computer programmer and dragged the man out the rear of the vehicle. The evening was unseasonably warm. A faint breeze carried the scent of salt water in the air.

Chiun propped the man up against the side of the van and slapped him sharply across his blotchy white cheek. Immediately the young man's eyes sprang open.

"What? Where am...?" His words trailed off as

he spied the blood on his shirt. All at once, he remembered the head of Ron Stern rolling around on
the floor of the van. "Oooh..." He began to pass out
once again, but the Master of Sinanju struck him
roughly across the cheek, back and forth.

The pain revived him. He sucked in a deep lungful
of air.

"Remain alert, fat one," Chiun snapped, "for
though I would remove you now, my employer
doubtless has need for you." And with that, he
dragged the whimpering young man back toward the
gates of Folcroft.

"YOU MAY RELEASE REMO, O Emperor. He is once
more only a threat to himself." The Master of Sinanju swept into the room, propelling the computer
programmer before him. The young man glanced
around, frightened. To him, this was all still a giant
video game. This office was as unreal to him as a
Pac-Man maze.

Smith had grown weary squatting for so long. He
had dared not move a muscle. He rose stiffly from
the floor, releasing the pressure on Remo's spine.

"Thanks a heap," Remo complained. He tried to
climb to his feet, but found that he could barely control his legs. Smith helped him up.

"Why didn't you just hold me down there all
night?" Remo griped, rubbing the back of his neck
at the remembered sensation of the interface signal.

"You might have killed me," Smith responded blandly.

"Yeah, and I still might. You're the one who handed me over to them, remember?" Disgusted, Remo wobbled away from Harold Smith.

Smith ignored Remo. "Who is this person?" he asked Chiun.

"Hey, Chiun, that's one of them," Remo said.

"Hey, Chiun, that's one of them," Chiun repeated, in a mocking singsong. "I risk my life to rescue you from their evil clutches, and all you are able to do is state the obvious." To Smith, he said, "I have allowed this one to live so that you might question him, Emperor."

"I'm not certain I approve of doing this here," Smith said.

"It's the middle of the night, Smitty," Remo sighed. "Even the cleaning staff went home hours ago." He leaned back against Smith's desk, rubbing his neck, still trying to shake off the residual effects of the interface signal. It took much more of an effort of will for him to stand than he wanted the others to know.

Smith nodded his tense agreement. "Of course, you are correct, Chiun."

At a nod from Smith, the Master of Sinanju lifted the heavyset programmer into the air and tossed him back onto the worn office sofa.

The couch creaked in protest.

"You will answer my questions," Smith said to the man.

The programmer swallowed hard. He nodded.

"I am having difficulty accessing the Platt-Deutsche computers."

The young man watched Smith, wide-eyed. He nodded nervously. His double chin wobbled. "You tried to access a dummy system. We set it up for corporate spies. People waste hours and hours trying to access files that don't even exist."

Smith furrowed his brow. "It's all a ruse?"

"Everything that's public knowledge is buried in the modem-access system. That way, when someone finds something they think they're on the right track. But PlattDeutsche has a completely private internal system that is not hooked into the phone lines."

"It makes sense," Smith agreed.

"You can't get in?" Remo asked.

"I am not surprised," Smith said over his shoulder. "For a company that is involved in sensitive research, there is no telling what a diligent hacker could learn over an open line." He turned back to the young man. "Tell me about the security system at the Edison plant."

For the next half hour, Smith grilled the programmer about the various fences, guards and security codes that would gain them access to the Edison, New Jersey, facility.

When he learned everything he thought he needed

to know about the defenses and about the interface labs in particular, he nodded crisply to the Master of Sinanju. Chiun stepped over to the young man.

The programmer sensed what was coming. He held up two pudgy hands. "Wait, wait!" he begged. "There's more."

Chiun glanced at the CURE director, and Smith held up a staying hand. "What is it?" he asked.

"Holz is more than he seems," the hacker offered.

"Explain," Smith demanded.

The young man glanced nervously, first from Smith, then to Chiun.

"If I tell you, will you promise to let me go?" His eyes, nearly buried beneath layers of distended flesh, looked hopefully at the two men. At that moment, he seemed more like a lost and frightened little boy than a man.

"Perhaps," Smith answered vaguely.

The programmer seemed to take this as a solemn vow. "I guess maybe I ought to tell you that I was in a little trouble last year. Mr. Holz helped me out. But then he started making me do things...." The man cast his eyes down to the threadbare carpet.

"Go on," Smith prodded.

"I got to thinking that he was making me do this stuff for a reason. Sort of a control mechanism." The man smiled weakly. "Just because someone's socially maladjusted doesn't mean they're stupid. Anyway, I secretly broke into Mr. Holz's phone line. You know, just to see what he was up to. I figured maybe I could use it to get me out of my obligation to him."

"Blackmail," Remo offered from behind them.

"I don't know," the young man said. "It didn't seem that way at the time. It's just that the stuff I was doing wasn't right. I was looking for a way to stop."

"What did you learn?" Smith asked.

"Mr. Holz isn't exactly on the level," the programmer said with a sardonic laugh. "And neither is PlattDeutsche. The people who own it on paper aren't the real owners."

"What do you mean?"

"There were a lot of telephone calls—back and forth to Holz—from outside the country. They were scrambled, so I couldn't pinpoint from where, but the way Holz and this other guy talked, it was obvious the people who think they're running the company really aren't."

"That is not possible. There is a command structure in every organization. Someone always answers to someone else."

The man shrugged. "All I can tell you is what I heard. The people on the board of PlattDeutsche think they're running the show, but sometimes they get overridden by something outside. Particularly this week. Holz got himself in trouble for the stunt at the bank. The higher-ups at the company were talking about suspending him or worse. But then everything got dropped. I'm the only one who knows that it is because somebody somewhere else saved his job for him. The real owners. And even they chewed him out for putting the company at risk. They were real mad until yesterday. That's when he called and told them about your friend there.'' He nodded over to where Remo lounged against Smith's desk. ''I'm really sorry, by the way,'' he said.

''Don't mention it,'' Remo said sarcastically.

The young man looked chastened.

Smith was still thinking about containment. The contamination was spreading. There was no telling how much Holz actually knew or how many others shared his knowledge.

''Did he tell them of this place? Folcroft? About me?''

The young man shook his head. ''No. It was all just about the stuff he could do,'' he said, pointing to Remo. ''And about the master of something-or-other. And he asked the man on the other end to send someone up to examine him.''

Smith was feeling a wave of relief wash over him. There was still a chance to salvage this situation.

''Do you remember whom he sent for or when and where they would be arriving?'' Already he was thinking of intercepting the individual at the airport.

''Holz called him Breslau or something. He's a doctor. I guess he's pretty old by the sounds of things. They said no at first, but Mr. Holz said it was an emergency. Breslau is supposed to be some kind of expert or something.''

Smith sucked in a rapid hiss of air. "Breslau?" he demanded. "*Dr.* Erich von Breslau?"

The young programmer brightened. "That was it," he said with a happy nod. "Do you know him?"

Smith looked dazed. Woodenly he walked across the room and took his seat behind his desk.

"Von Breslau," Remo mused. "Why does that name sound familiar?"

The programmer glanced toward the open door. "May I go now?" he asked hopefully. He rubbed his sweaty palms on the knees of his jeans.

"Erich von Breslau," Smith said under his breath. He stared at the top of his desk.

The computer programmer stood. "I promise I won't tell anyone about this place." He began edging toward the door.

Smith was shaken from his reverie. "What? Oh, yes. Of course not. Thank you for your help."

The young man seemed greatly relieved and moved for the door. He didn't see Smith nod to the Master of Sinanju, nor did he feel the blow that stopped his heart muscle from working through his meaty back. He merely felt the sudden urge to take a long nap on the inviting floor of the sanitarium office. A wave of blackness washed over him, and he dropped to the floor. He didn't stir again.

"Smitty, why does that name von Breslau sound

so familiar?" Remo asked as the Master of Sinanju joined him before the desk.

"It has historical significance. Erich Von Breslau worked in three of the Nazi concentration camps during the Second World War. He was answerable directly to Mengele. Many reports have it that his brutality toward his victims was far worse than his superior's."

"Okay, that's right," Remo said. "I heard about him on a PBS documentary. But I thought he was dead."

"It would seem he is not," Smith said. "And someone obviously feels the lure of Sinanju knowledge outweighs the risk of exposing him to the world."

"But they don't have anything without me, right?" Remo queried.

Smith considered. "I am not certain." There was something larger going on. Why would they bring von Breslau here now? What purpose would it serve? He shook his head, trying to clear his thoughts. "Holz not only has a duplicate file of my brain but yours, as well. Either would be enough to compromise CURE. We must organize a plan of attack. But we must first find a location to store the Platt-Deutsche van. I presume it is nearby?"

"Beyond the walls of Fortress Folcroft," Chiun said.

"I will have to see inside, but I must check a few

things here first. Remo, could you make certain that there is nothing that will attract attention to the van?'' He was thinking of the Master of Sinanju's usual thorough work.

"I'm on it."

Remo and Chiun turned to go. Remo cast a glance at the programmer's body lying on the floor near the door.

"I'm not cleaning that up," he said, shaking his head.

"That is of no concern to me. Of course, if I am forced to carry this fat white thing, the strain might cause me to forget the secret method I have devised to shield myself from the demon signals. But that should not be a concern to you. You have done such a fine job representing your House in this matter so far."

"There's no secret method," Remo insisted.

Chiun didn't say a word. He smiled at Remo, his face a placid pool. When Remo glanced back at Smith, he saw that the CURE director was hard at work at his computer's buried keyboard. The light from the monitor screen cast an eerie, possessed glow on his pinched features.

Remo sighed.

"This better be worth it," he grumbled.

He hefted the body to his shoulders and carted it from the office.

13

The stewardesses all found him to be just darling.

He was so, so sweet. And polite? Everything was please and thank-you with him. He was positively the nicest little man they had had aboard the South American Air jet in a long time.

They just couldn't quite place his accent.

"Is it Swiss? It's Swiss, isn't it?" asked Bootsy. She was thirty-two, blond and as perky as an Osmond on uppers.

"You are very perceptive," the old man conceded.

"I *knew* it," Bootsy said. She turned to her fellow crew members and flashed a set of the most perfect caps her meager paycheck could afford. "I told you," she said with a superior tone.

Another stewardess, a twenty-eight-year-old molded-plastic beauty with lacquered hair and a nose that had been rhinoplastied nearly to extinction, put on a pouty expression. "I knew it was European," she complained, as if this somehow gave her extra points. Her name tag identified her as Mindy, and she turned to the steward behind her for verification of her claim.

He, like Bootsy, was in his early thirties and, continuing the similarities, shared her strong physical attraction to the plane's copilot. The tag on his starched white blouse announced him as Brion.

His carefully plucked eyebrows furrowed as he looked the old man in 21B up and down. "I never would have guessed Swiss. It's a little rougher than that, isn't it? No offense," he added hastily.

The passenger squirmed in his seat. "Please, I am very tired."

"Of course you are," Bootsy said in a motherly tone. She shooed Mindy and Brion away.

"It still sounds sort of German to me," Brion said as he and Mindy picked their way back up the aisle.

"I'm sorry about them," Bootsy said once they were gone. She sat in the vacant seat beside the darling little man and placed her hand on his jacket sleeve. "They're really awfully, awfully nice. Except sometimes." She laughed as if she had just said something terribly amusing.

"It is our burden to endure the imperfect," he agreed. "Tell me, how soon will we be arriving in New York?"

She checked her watch. "Oh, another hour. Can I get you anything? Coffee? Tea?"

He raised a hand. "I am fine."

"Then I won't bother you anymore." She patted

him on the arm and stood. She carefully smoothed the wrinkles from the front of her uniform skirt.

"You have lovely eyes," said Erich von Breslau. He considered himself an authority on eyes, having removed many sets of them from a large number of screaming, nonanesthetized patients.

"Why, thank you," Bootsy gushed. She batted her glued-on horsehair eyebrows.

"They are very beautiful. Very blue, aren't they?" He breathed deeply, considering. "Tell me," he said after a moment, "are you a religious person? If you don't mind my asking?" He tipped his head and stared into her beautiful blue eyes.

Bootsy sucked in a mock-guilty hiss of air. "Oooh, you got me. Not really in a strict sense. But my mom was a Baptist. My dad was Jewish."

"Oh." Though he tried to mask it, there was a strange coolness in his tone.

She wasn't sure what she had said to offend him. "Not Orthodox," Bootsy said quickly. "He was Reformed. He didn't run around with the curly sideburns or anything. We ate pork and everything. But with me and my brother, my folks didn't want to force us into anything—you know, they didn't want to upset either family—so they waited and let us decide what to do when we were eighteen. I guess I sort of decided on nothing really." She held up her hands. "That's not to say I'm not religious. I am. In my own way."

"How nice for you."

Bootsy beamed. "It is, isn't it? Look, I've got to make my rounds, but I'll be back. Don't you worry." She touched the darling little man on the arm once more, reassuringly, and headed up the narrow aisle.

Dr. Erich von Breslau looked down at his sleeve where the Jewess had placed her hand. Though no difference was visible to the naked eye, he knew there now was one. He made a mental note to burn the jacket he was wearing once he reached New York.

14

"Yuck, this is disgusting." Remo had already dumped the body of the young programmer into the back of the white van and he was searching the surroundings for anything Chiun might have left lying around in his usual earnestness. He found the headless body of Ron Stern sitting in some bushes on the side of the road. He hefted the body into the air, careful not to get any of the drying blood on his T-shirt.

"You might have done a neater job," he complained. He tossed the body into the back atop the others. "Where the heck did you throw the door?" He began picking his way through the nearby thicket.

Chiun stood at the side of the road. He seemed rooted to the asphalt. His face was etched in stone. "You might show some gratitude," he sniffed.

"For what? You know, if I'm not picking up after you, I'm traipsing off on some autograph expedition."

"And you do neither well. The door is in that direction." A slight upturn of his delicate chin indicated that Remo should search the thicket farther down the road.

Remo found the van door a hundred yards away wedged in between a cluster of maple trees. He trotted back up the road and jammed the door back into place. The hinges were ripped, gleaming metal shards. He used his fingers to twist and knead the steel into some kind of usable shape.

He stood back and placed his hands on his hips. The door was crooked. He shook his head. "I hope that holds."

Remo walked around front and climbed into the cab. Chiun slid in beside him.

"You are welcome," the Master of Sinanju declared softly.

Remo gripped the steering wheel and sighed deeply. There was only one way to silence the Master of Sinanju. "Thank you, Little Father," he said. He didn't glance right, but stared straight out the windshield at the midnight blackness.

"It was nothing," Chiun said.

"Give me strength," Remo muttered. He drove the van around to the front gates of Folcroft.

At this time of night, the guard on duty was generally either sound asleep in his shack or off somewhere else, probably chatting up one of the nightshift workers. Though Harold Smith would ordinarily not put up with such a lax attitude toward work as administrator of Folcroft, as head of CURE he occasionally found the man's incompetence useful.

Unchallenged, Remo drove the van around the back of the administrative building. He backed it up against one of the old, unused loading platforms.

He climbed down from the cab and stepped out from the small alcove in which the truck was nestled. The lawns behind Folcroft were moist with dew. They rolled downward to the edge of Long Island Sound. A decrepit boat dock rocked almost imperceptibly on the undulating surface of the water.

Chiun joined Remo at the front of the truck.

"Mission accomplished," Remo said. "Now, do you want to tell me the big secret on how to block out that interface signal?"

Chiun nodded. "I will tell you, Remo. But you must promise to adhere strictly to my words, for to ignore them surely invites death."

Remo agreed.

Chiun first glanced around the darkness of the loading-dock area, making certain there was no one near. Satisfied there were no eavesdroppers who might overhear his words, Chiun drew Remo down to him and leaned in close, so that his lips were a hairbreadth away from Remo's ear. When he spoke, Remo felt the warmth of his breath.

"The secret to avoiding the demon signal of the air. That is what you wish to know?"

"Yeah," Remo said.

Chiun pitched his voice even lower. Remo had to strain to hear.

"Do not be stupid."

Chiun straightened back up. There was a slight playfulness in his hazel eyes.

"Why doesn't that surprise me?"

"Ah, you anticipated my words. You who plucks phantom signals from the air like a great, lumbering television set. You are most wise, Remo."

"It didn't take a genius to know you were going to yank my chain about all this."

Chiun smiled condescendingly. "Then why did you ask of me the secret?"

"Because, Chiun, there was still a slim chance you wouldn't yank my chain. And if you really had a way to stop this thing, I wanted to know it." Remo shook his head. He stared helplessly out at the Sound, rotating his wrists absently—it was an old habit he had never broken. "They had me attack you, Little Father. I couldn't stop myself." When he looked up, his eyes were moist. "I'm sorry." And unlike the thank-you Chiun had cajoled out of him earlier, he spoke these words with feeling.

Chiun's usually harsh features grew softer.

"You were caught in a weak moment, my son," Chiun said with a knowing nod of his bald head. The wisps of white hair above his ears quivered at the movement. "Perhaps your recent experience with the Pythia is to blame. A frailty, if such is the case, that is not your fault. The attack made within your mind was not anticipated—therefore you had not properly prepared yourself for it."

"So why didn't they get you?" Remo said. "You didn't know about it, either."

Chiun straightened up to his full five feet. "I am the Reigning Master of Sinanju," he said.

Remo shook his head. "I wouldn't be so cocksure if I were you. When they had me in the van, they said they'd used up a lot of space to get me under control. Maybe they just didn't have enough room left to take you on, as well."

"Do not be foolish," Chiun said impatiently. "The Master of Sinanju cannot be switched on and off like a common household appliance."

Remo shrugged. "If you say so. I just don't want the same thing that happened to me to happen to you."

"Give the matter no more thought," Chiun directed with a wave of his hand. He looked over at the Sound, lapping gently at the shore.

Farther out, the murky black strip had taken on a few gray hues at its most distant edge.

"Come. It will be light soon. We will leave this vehicle to Smith."

THE PLANE TOUCHED DOWN just before dawn.

Von Breslau had the homosexual steward help him

with his luggage. He was disgusting, but at least he was a Lutheran.

At the door, he encountered the Jew woman who had dared touch him.

She smiled her perky smile when she saw him coming up the aisle.

"Hope you had a nice trip," she said cheerily.

There was no need for pretense any longer. He had arrived safely.

Staring straight ahead, he ignored her.

He crossed the enclosed ramp and was led by the steward through the bowels of the terminal building. The endless, windowless corridors had the look and feel of a subway. Though subways tended to be designed with a bit more imagination.

The steward even went so far as to help him through customs. When they were finished with him, he led the nice passenger out to meet his friend who was waiting just beyond the security gates. The airline attendant was delighted to see a delicious-looking blond hunk waiting with the friend. But though he tried to make a little friendly eye contact, the man merely stared sullenly at the passersby.

The steward shrugged a tiny shrug and smiled at his little old friend. Of course he didn't expect a tip. But he did expect a polite thank-you for going so far out of his way.

He got nothing.

Once a few pleasantries were exchanged, the old

man and his friend—along with the blond-haired dreamboat—fell in step, abandoning the young steward without so much as a backward glance. They passed through the automatic doors and slipped into the back of a waiting limousine. The car then sped off.

"DOCTOR, IT IS such a pleasure to meet you."

They had shut out the noise of the surrounding traffic when they had entered the limo. A row of parked yellow cabs slipped away to their right. Lothar Holz practically beamed with pleasure.

"I am sure," von Breslau said crisply. He nodded to the front seat of the car. On the other side of the tinted bulletproof glass, they could just barely make out the long blond hair of Holz's assistant. "He serves you well?"

"One of your many great successes, Doctor. And now that you are here, we will have yet another very soon."

Von Breslau didn't seem pleased by Holz's enthusiasm. He settled back in his seat, crossing his arms. "I hope for your sake that you have not dragged me away from the village on a fool's errand."

There was a cautionary edge to his voice.

"Hardly," Holz answered. "I am told you know of Sinanju."

The old man nodded. "There was a rumor that I

heard after the war concerning this Master of Sinanju,'' he said vaguely.

"I have heard the same rumor. You know, then, of their capabilities? The amazing physical feats they are able to perform?"

"That I do not know about," von Breslau stated. "All I know are rumors and conjecture. I warn you again—for your sake I hope you have not brought me out of retirement because of a fairy tale."

Holz shook his head.

"You will be amazed by what we can do. Do you understand anything at all about computers?"

"Yes, yes, yes. I know of this technology. I own a personal computer myself. Do not assume because a person is old that he is out of touch."

"Oh, no, I did not mean to insult," Holz hastened to reassure him.

Von Breslau drew his mouth up in an impatient grimace. "Yes, I know something of computers. Yes, I know something of your interface system. I am not an expert, but I understand the basic premise. You purport to have captured the Master of Sinanju with it?"

Holz seemed hesitant. "We believe it was his protégé."

"Was?"

"He has vanished. But we have everything we need," he added quickly, heading off an outburst.

"We have even tested downloading the information into a host."

Von Breslau's eyes narrowed. "Did you succeed?"

Holz shrugged. "A first test is rarely one hundred percent successful, Doctor," he said. "Let me just say that the results were…promising. With your assistance, I hope that we can refine the process so that there is no rejection." He grinned triumphantly.

Von Breslau studied his host for a long minute. "We will see," he said at last.

"You will be amazed," Holz assured him.

"Amazement is for the very young or very stupid," von Breslau countered. "Is it far to your facility?"

"It will take some time. The roads at this time of day are already quite crowded."

"Wake me when we arrive." And with that the Butcher of Treblinka closed his eyes and settled back comfortably in the seat.

Within moments he was snoring peacefully—a man with not a single care in the world.

THE MASTER OF SINANJU assured Smith there was nothing to worry about.

"We will vanquish this dastard and destroy his vile machines, Emperor Smith."

"I vote for a little caution, Smitty," Remo said,

glancing at Chiun. "I'm not convinced we have this interface signal licked yet."

"Then you do not have to come," Chiun sniffed.

"The van is safe?" Smith interjected. After the grueling night they had all spent, he didn't wish to mediate a shouting match between the two men.

"It's out back," Remo answered. He nodded toward the large plate-glass window. Past the trees, streaks of orange painted the sky above the rising sun.

Smith checked his watch. The night was gone. Even if they left now, Remo and Chiun wouldn't arrive in Edison before the PlattDeutsche plant was fully staffed. He would have preferred to send them in under cover of darkness, but he dared not give Holz another day with either the CURE or Sinanju information.

"You should go," he said to Remo.

"Smitty, I want to punch this guy's ticket more than anyone. I just don't think Chiun really understands what he's up against."

"Do not assume your failing will be mine," Chiun said to Remo. "I understand this innerfaze sigmoe implicitly," he announced boldly to Smith. "Send me to it, that I might break it in twain." Hands directed chopping blows to the invisible air before him.

Remo rolled his eyes. "I guess it was silly of me to be worried," he concluded with a sigh.

"You might not encounter a problem, Remo,"

Smith said, trying to sound reassuring. "If you can get to Holz first, the interface signal becomes a minor problem. If you can get to the apparatus that controls the interface signal first, you can handle Holz easily."

"And if Holz gets to us with the signal first, then what?"

"It will not happen," Chiun proclaimed.

Smith rubbed his eyes beneath his glasses and then replaced the rimless frames on his patrician nose. "I wish there was some alternative. My impulse, Master of Sinanju, is to err on the side of caution." He nodded toward Remo. "But we do not seem to have any viable alternatives. Holz remains the primary target. If you are able to get in and neutralize him, we might be able to clamp the lid tightly down on this affair. Once we have access to the Edison facility, I will hook into the PlattDeutsche system and destroy our respective files."

"What about that Nazi doctor?"

Smith shook his head. "I have had no luck checking the manifests of flights into either of the major airports. Of course, he would not be traveling under his own name, but the number of arrivals at La-Guardia and Kennedy International is prohibitive for an in-depth search. It would help if we knew where he was coming from."

"Don't all the old fascists retire to the sunny beaches of South America?"

"It is never that simple, Remo. There have been suspected or confirmed Nazi sightings on nearly every continent over the past fifty years. Of course the numbers have dwindled with the passing of time, but the Jewish Documentation Center in Vienna has had reports of suspected war criminals from Africa and Europe, as well as from South America. In spite of several hoaxes of late, some collaborators have even been discovered living in the United States and Canada. It is just too broad a search parameter."

"Well, cliché or not, I'd check South America first."

"I will continue to investigate," Smith said. "But we should not allow the presence of von Breslau to cloud our perspective. Holz is your primary target. If von Breslau is with him, you may eliminate him, as well."

"With pleasure," Remo said.

"My secretary will be here soon," Smith directed, indicating the door with a slight tip of his head.

Remo got the message. "We'll be back as quick as we can, Smitty. Hopefully," he added. He slipped out the door.

Chiun had been right behind him, but paused at the open doorway. He turned. "Do not concern yourself, Emperor. Remo is still young. The incidents of this past day have been disturbing to him. We will return with this villain's head on a rail." And bowing, he slipped from the office. He was so graceful, so swift, it was as if he had never been there at all.

Smith stared at the closed office door a long time after Chiun had gone. He hoped the old Korean was right. He and Remo had skills greater than anyone Smith had ever before encountered, but the CURE director feared the pair might have finally met their equal.

And as the early-morning sun stole up over the windowsill, its bright, warming rays heating the back of his worn leather chair, Smith's orderly mind began sorting through possible scenarios. In spite of the Master of Sinanju's assurances, Harold W. Smith found himself devising an alternate plan. On the chance that this would be the first time Remo and Chiun failed.

15

Dr. Curt Newton hadn't slept for two days. At first it had been the exhilaration at unexpectedly finding the key to perfecting the Dynamic Interface System in the mind of an unwitting bank patron. But that had only been the first night. Now there was another reason for his restlessness.

He wanted to take the matter up with Lothar Holz, wanted to discuss what he felt was totally unethical behavior on the man's part.

But Holz wasn't in.

It was 7:00 a.m., and many of the lab people were already at work.

Even some of the paper pushers were trudging off the elevators.

Lothar Holz was generally in his office at seven on the dot. The day before had been understandable—he had been meeting with Dr. Smith—but where could he be today?

When he couldn't find Holz, Newton decided to pass the nervous minutes until the confrontation by discussing some minor aspects of the interface program with the computer people. He was surprised to find that more than half of the programming staff weren't present.

Mervin Fischer, Ron Stern and several of their key people hadn't come in to work yet, either.

To make matters worse, the interface van was missing. Holz had sent Ron Stern out on some mysterious mission with nearly eight million dollars' worth of equipment, and the dumb ox hadn't even brought it back yet. It was probably parked outside some Jersey City brothel getting picked over by scientists from Japan's Nishitsu Corporation.

Years' worth of research could be lost because of one man's abundance of testosterone. He'd take that up with Stern when he finally staggered in. He only wished he had access to the van now.

Newton wandered aimlessly through the lower levels of the Edison facility. He could be on the verge of something miraculous, but the tools to complete his work had been taken from him.

Holz had ensured that a duplicate file was created of the results obtained in the prior day's interface exercise, but Newton had no idea where the computer information was. All he had gotten from the van when they returned from Rye were a couple of CDs and a few other things grabbed in haste. The original file was, by and large, still in the van's system and Newton was anxious to take a look at it.

That man was incredible. But he also posed a problem for Curt Newton.

While he didn't enjoy going on Holz's little outing yesterday, Newton himself wouldn't necessarily forgo the opportunity to rifle through the mind of yet another unwilling test subject. It was, after all, in the name of science.

And some good might as well come out of something that he found personally distasteful.

Newton felt justified with the argument. Even though the information was obtained under questionable circumstances, the scientific benefits far outweighed any moral qualms he might have in not obtaining the prior consent of his test subject.

And after all, who was he to say what was or wasn't moral? He was just a scientist. A man who, in his mind, was already preparing his words to the press for his inevitable Nobel prize.

It was the increasing recklessness of Lothar Holz that was agitating Dr. Curt Newton. Didn't the fool know what was at stake?

If, God forbid, some unwilling test subject successfully pressed charges against PlattDeutsche, the whole program could be shot.

Some other company would surely take up the research where he'd left off, and all the laurels would go to them. A man who was locked out of his own scientific research didn't win Nobels.

Newton had been meandering fecklessly through

the ground floor of the building and he was surprised when he looked up to find that he was in the main lobby, beneath the huge bronze plaque bearing the company logo.

When he turned, he almost ran into Lothar Holz, who was marching in through the main doors. He was in the company of his assistant and a cross-looking old man. The three of them swept past Newton as if he were a common secretary.

"Lothar?" Newton called after him. He hurried to catch up.

Holz and his entourage were standing at the elevator that the assistant had summoned. When Holz turned, he looked displeased. "Yes? Oh, Curt. What is it?"

Newton was somewhat taken aback by the sharpness of his tone. The old man hadn't even turned to face him.

"Um, this is really kind of private," the scientist said, nodding toward the old man. "I just need a minute."

The elevator doors opened, and the old man stepped aboard.

"Sorry, Curt, I don't have a minute. Tight schedule." Holz tapped his watch. He stepped on the elevator, followed by his assistant.

The doors slid closed on the three of them before Newton was able to voice an objection. Holz didn't even glance his way again.

Newton was stunned. He stood, staring at the closed elevator doors for several long seconds. Lothar Holz had just blown him off. Him. Dr. Curt Newton. Physical cryptologist. That hadn't happened once in the five years he had been here.

A bell chimed nearby, startling Newton. He glanced up. The light above the doors indicated that the elevator had stopped on 4. That wasn't right. That floor wasn't even in use anymore. It housed all the original interface experimental equipment. It was virtually abandoned. He was sure Holz had made a mistake, but when the elevator car returned a few seconds later it was empty.

What were they doing on the fourth floor? And more importantly, who was the old man?

A horrible thought suddenly occurred to Newton. What if that fossil was a scientist Holz had brought in to work on the final stages of the Dynamic Interface System?

Newton set his jaw firmly. One thing was certain. If that ancient geyser wanted his name on Curt Newton's hard-earned Nobel Prize, he'd better damned well be prepared to kill for it.

A look of determination in his eyes, Dr. Curt Newton stepped on the elevator and pressed the button for the fourth floor.

"I TOLD YOU to clean up in here," Lothar Holz snapped.

The bodies of Mervin Fischer and Zach Pendrake had been piled, one atop the other, against the wall near the door. There was a mop and bucket that had obviously been used to clean up Fischer's blood.

The water in the large bucket was a stained crimson.

The blond-haired man nodded his apology and wordlessly took the handle of the mop and steered the wheeled bucket into a small side room. A moment later, the sound of water being slopped into a deep basin echoed out into the vast room.

"These are the ones you told me about?" von Breslau asked, ignoring the noise. He indicated the corpses on the floor.

Holz nodded. "The one in the dress shirt was our test subject. He literally put his fist through the body of the other one," Holz said, his tone like that of a proud parent whose child had just won a spelling bee.

Von Breslau stooped and examined the bodies. He removed a pen from his pocket and prodded Pendrake's shattered hand. As he did so, the blond assistant reentered the room, having disposed of the matter of the cleanup.

"How long was it before this man exhibited an increase in strength?" von Breslau asked.

"A minute. Two, perhaps. It happened very quickly." He suppressed a giddy laugh.

"Yes," von Breslau said. "Perhaps too quickly."

Holz furrowed his brow. ''We pushed him too fast? Was that the problem?''

''I do not know. That is what I am here to find out.'' With difficulty he straightened up. ''I want to test this procedure of yours immediately,'' he added, walking back over to Holz, removing his jacket and throwing it to the floor. When the assistant moved to retrieve it, the old man told him not to bother.

''Wouldn't you like to review the data first? I can have one of the scientists explain the interface technique.''

''I cannot be bothered with that now. I understand this—'' he tapped Holz on the chest ''—what you can feel, what you can touch. My world is the physical. I need to see this incredible discovery for myself to judge whether or not my journey has been wasted.''

''Surely you want to review my report on this one?'' Holz indicated the body of Zach Pendrake. ''For background?''

''I trust my eyes. I do not trust reports.''

Holz nodded in understanding. ''You're right, of course. I'll see if I can find—'' He fell silent, a startled look on his face.

Curt Newton had just stormed through the door to the lab. The scientist's eyes were angry as he searched out Holz. When he found him over by a disused mainframe, he marched purposefully over.

"I don't appreciate being shut out of my own research," he said accusingly.

"Curt, this is not the time—"

"Don't tell me that. Don't you dare tell me that. Not when you're bringing in this...this *amateur*. I did all the work. It's only fair I get the credit."

"You will. Please, Curt." He was leaning and twisting, trying to interpose himself between Newton and the bodies on the floor. His gyrations weren't successful.

"Oh, my..." When he at last saw the bodies, Newton's voice was small.

"Who is this?" von Breslau demanded impatiently.

Newton had stepped past both of them, inching closer to the two corpses. "That's...oh, my. That's Mervin, isn't it? And that's, that's Pembrake. He's a company lawyer or something. What happened?"

He squatted on his haunches by the bodies, more curious than repelled.

"It is an internal problem, Curt."

"Not by the looks of it," Newton scoffed. He was looking at the hole in Mervin Fischer's chest through which some indistinguishable organs had slipped. "Did he impale himself on his keyboard?"

"We are looking into the matter," Holz assured him.

Still squatting, Newton turned. "I think it's safe

to assume he's not a cop," he said, indicating von Breslau.

"Who is this man?" von Breslau asked again.

"Dr. Curt Newton. He pioneered the interface technology."

"He is the inventor? Good, I have need of his expertise."

"Wait a minute there, Grampa," Newton said, standing.

Holz held up a staying hand. He seemed to consider something deeply. When he seemed to reach an internal decision, he beckoned Newton to him.

"You remember that difficulty you had three years ago?" Holz whispered. "The traffic accident?"

Newton felt as if he had just been punched in the stomach.

He remembered a Christmas party that had gotten a little out of hand. He also vaguely remembered a body lying in some snow. It was an indistinct memory, almost like a dream. He didn't know what Holz had done that horrible night. All he knew was after the phone call he had left his car at the scene and been driven home. The vehicle was in his driveway when he awoke the following morning, washed and waxed and gleaming as if nothing had happened. Newton had forced the incident from his consciousness. For his part, Holz had never breathed a word of the incident. Until now.

Newton gulped and nodded.

"It is good to remember some things, good to forget others," Holz remarked, nodding toward the bodies.

Again Newton silently indicated his understanding.

"You have made some remarkable advances here, Curt," Holz said approvingly. "With the aid of Dr. von Breslau, you will make even more."

Newton gulped. "Breslau? That wouldn't be *Erich* Von Breslau, would it?"

The old man ignored the question. Holz leaned in closer to Newton. He said crisply, "You will not tell anyone. The doctor is involved in the management structure of PlattDeutsche International. If this is discovered, there are forces who would argue that all of our research is tainted. Including your own."

Newton's mind was racing. His brain conjured up images, countless photographs he had seen over the years, depicting horrific scenes of a war that had ended three years before he was born. He saw London after the blitz; merchant vessels sinking, torpedo victims, orphans crying in the streets, wasted figures in tattered clothes lined up along barbed-wire fences, shallow mass graves stacked with rotting corpses.

Putting all of that on one end of a scale, he placed his own career on the other. His career won out.

He heard the voice of Lothar Holz, breaking through his thoughts.

"Curt? Do you have a problem with this?"

Newton blinked. He glanced at Holz, then at the small aged man standing impatiently next to him. He didn't look all that dangerous.

Newton extended his hand. "I'm certain I will enjoy working with you, Doctor." And the smile Curt Newton flashed was sincere.

16

Remo and Chiun took the interstate from New York onto the Jersey turnpike. On either side of the highway, industrialized New Jersey was a joyless, flat expanse of smoke-belching factories built in swamps. At night the ugly yellow glow of a million parking lot and chimney lights gave the flats the surreal tone of a depressing futuristic film. In the day, everything just looked squalid.

Chiun sniffed at the air, thick with chemicals and other pollutants. His face became a pucker of displeased wrinkles. "Why do they call this province 'new'?" he asked Remo.

"Because it was at one time," Remo replied.

"The newness has been eroded. It is time it was renamed Old Jersey."

"I think that's over in Europe. It's an island or something in the English Channel."

Chiun's eyes narrowed suspiciously. "Its history predates that of this malodorous place?"

"By centuries."

"Remind me never to visit there, Remo, for time

has surely allowed the vile Old Jersians to amass an even greater volume of filth than their descendants.''

''Not very bloody likely, but I'll make a note of it,'' Remo promised.

They got off the turnpike near Highland Park and threaded their way over to Edison.

The PlattDeutsche America complex occupied a separate corner of an industrial park near the edge of town. It had its own fence to cordon it off from the other buildings on the site. Several tin patches decorated in red, white and blue adorned the fence at regular intervals. They sported the logo of a private security company.

Remo parked his car in one of the nearer lots and he and Chiun walked the rest of the way over to the PlattDeutsche America compound.

It was nearly nine and the place was open for business. People hustled from building to building. Cars were continually passing back and forth through the main gate.

''I don't like this,'' Remo warned. ''Maybe we should wait until tonight.''

''I do not wish to prolong my exposure to this foul air. When you were last here, to which building were you brought?''

''That one,'' Remo said, pointing at one of two matching buildings at the front of the complex. It was a gleaming steel-and-glass structure. The early-morning sun reflected brilliantly off hundreds of huge, glistening black panes.

"Then that is where we begin."

Chiun's hand chopped down. The links of the high fence popped, one after the other, beneath the side of his razor nails. When there was a large enough gap in the fence, he wrapped his fingers around the serrated edge and drew it back.

Remo followed Chiun through the tear in the fence and the two of them made their way across a stretch of well-watered lawn for the main building.

"I don't think we should barge in through the front door," Remo said when they were on the sidewalk encircling the building. A vast parking area stretched out to their left.

"The Master of Sinanju does not use the servant's entrance," Chiun sniffed.

Remo paused on the sidewalk. Grudgingly Chiun stopped, as well.

"Look, Chiun. It doesn't make sense to announce we're here. You might not be worried about that gadget of theirs, but I am. If we go in the front door, their security is going to know something's up. We don't even have passes."

Chiun glanced at the entrance. Several employees were passing into the building at that moment, their laminated security tags attached to a lapel or hanging from the neck. An older woman had one clipped to her pocketbook.

"Wait here, O worrier," Chiun said with an annoyed sigh.

Stranding Remo on the sidewalk, Chiun flounced off toward the parking lot, disappearing behind a tall row of neatly trimmed shrubs. He returned a moment later, two plastic tags in his frail hand. He handed one to Remo. "You may stop worrying now."

Remo looked at his tag. It identified him as Louis Washington III. A charcoal black face was pasted in the corner of the pass.

"This doesn't fill me with much confidence," Remo said as he affixed the tag to the collar of his T-shirt.

"These will not even be necessary," Chiun insisted. He clipped his tag to the front of his kimono. "I am merely indulging you. Come."

As if he were master of the entire PlattDeutsche complex, Chiun marched boldly for the door. Reluctantly Remo trailed in his wake.

LESS THAN A MINUTE later, they were roaming the corridors of the company's research-and-development wing. The passes had gotten them beyond the main security desk and onto the elevator. The guard at the R&D level hadn't even looked up when they disembarked from the elevator.

A gold-embossed sign above the main corridor read Advanced Research Division, but it looked as though the research division had become fixated on a single item. Almost the entire floor had been turned over to the Dynamic Interface System. Down the hall were a few smaller signs announcing Computer Labs, DIS; Product Design, DIS; and Physical Cryptology. On the door of the last lab, a hand-written note was taped to the wall: "Dr. Curt Newton, resident genius."

Chiun sniffed the air. "I do not sense the vibrations of the innerfaze device," he said.

"They might not have the machine turned on," Remo suggested.

"Is this the correct floor?"

Remo glanced around, considering. "I'm not sure. All these rooms look alike."

Chiun nodded his understanding. "The banality of American architecture."

"Maybe we should split up," Remo suggested, thinking it would improve the odds that one of them would destroy either the interface equipment or Holz. It would eliminate the chance that they would both be taken at once.

"Agreed." Chiun spun on his heel and marched down the corridor.

As he watched him go, Remo noted that the old Korean looked very small, very frail. He wished he could have impressed upon his teacher the frustration he had felt at being manipulated so easily. It was a feeling of helplessness he wished the Master of Sinanju would never have to experience.

"Chiun?" Remo called.

"Yes?"

"Be careful."

Chiun did not turn. "I am never not."

NEWTON AFFIXED the electrodes carefully. His test subject—a program accountant—appeared disinterested in the procedure. Newton talked while he worked.

"I was surprised to find a lot of his abilities were stored in memory," he said over his shoulder.

Von Breslau, from his spot near the electrocardiogram machines, looked up for a minute. "That is consistent with my knowledge of Sinanju."

"Is it?" Newton sounded upset. "I wish Lothar had been more up front about everything earlier. I hate playing catch-up."

"I see in your notes something about 'co autono.' What is this?" Von Breslau was near the electrocardiogram. His thin lips pursed unhappily as he read some of the hasty notes Newton had scrawled to himself in the van the day before.

"Controlled autonomous," Newton explained. "That was the only way I could think to describe it. He is able to physically control every autonomic response. It's like one big motor nervous system."

"And the nervous system is altered, you say?"

Newton laughed. "It would have to be, wouldn't it? But I don't think it's been altered medically. It's more likely the result of an ongoing training. My people speculate the level our Subject A was at took at least a decade to achieve. Perhaps more." He finished with the electrodes and joined von Breslau near the monitoring equipment.

"Quite probably," von Breslau agreed.

Newton took a seat at the same monitor station Mervin Fischer had worked from the previous day. He absently hooked his feet around its metal legs.

"Fischer eliminated temporal junk from the program. All limbic stuff. What we're working with is a distillation of his physical attributes alone."

"Have you raised the dopamine level?"

"There's a precursor to the main file that will trick his basal ganglia into elevating the level of dopamine."

"You should monitor ATP, as well."

"I'm not taking any chances." Newton tapped away at the keyboard. "I'm pushing everything else up, too. ATP, serotonin, acetylcholine. Everything. Fischer didn't have sense enough there. Bright guy when it came to programming, but a bit of a neophyte with the rest of the interface system. His failure to chemically compensate might explain the reaction he got." He entered a final command. "I'm ready."

"Have you set your machines to deliver the information slowly?"

"I've increased the download time by a factor of

four. If it becomes necessary to slow it any further, I can break in manually.''

Von Breslau seemed satisfied. "Proceed," he said.

Newton glanced over to the spot where the bodies had been. They were gone. He had no idea where Holz's assistant had hidden them. The light brown patch on the floor where Fischer's blood had stained could have been caused by a spilled cup of coffee.

Newton took a deep breath and tapped out "Copy" on his keyboard.

Erich von Breslau stared at their test subject, an expectant, avaricious expression on his features.

Exhaling loudly, Newton hit the Enter key.

IN THE HALLWAY one floor above, the Master of Sinanju felt the electrical signal switch on.

It was different than it had been. Not as far-reaching. More concentrated. But though the signal was faint, it remained distinctive.

Chiun didn't hesitate. Black sandals slid in confident silence along the drab grey hallway carpeting. Moving swiftly, he headed back down the corridor to the elevators.

A guard intercepted him before he reached the end.

"Hold it, old-timer," the man said. A hand snaked cautiously to his hip holster.

"Out of my way, lout. I am on important innerfaze business."

"Are you?" the guard said skeptically. "Then you might be interested to know we've had a security breach. We found two of our people unconscious in the parking lot. Both of them were missing their security passes."

"That is not my concern," Chiun spit. "As you can see, I still possess my special identification."

"You're Stella Tresaloni?" the guard said. He indicated Chiun's laminated security tag. A woman's smiling face beamed out from the corner of the pass.

Chiun didn't have time to deal with niggling details. He left the unconscious guard behind an empty receptionist's desk and raced for the elevator.

"CUT THE SPEED IN HALF."

"Already?"

"Do as I say," von Breslau commanded. He watched their test subject carefully. "How do you feel?"

The man's shoulders lifted in a bored shrug. "I don't know. Kind of a little tingly, I guess. Is this going to take much longer?"

The two scientist ignored him.

"I've reduced the rate by half," Newton said. "Chemical production has adjusted accordingly."

"His heart rate is elevated. Skin tone flushed."

"That isn't unusual."

"No." The German thoughtfully steepled his fingers, then ordered, "Increase by a quarter. Slowly."

Newton made the adjustments. Fischer's program informed him on the computer screen that there was a slight dip in the level of adenosine triphosphate. In the time it took to relate the message, the computer had compensated for the change.

The computer downloaded through the interface program for nearly another minute. Von Breslau stood beside the test subject throughout.

At last he held up a hand. "Let us stop here for a moment."

"Already?" Newton asked. He sounded disappointed.

"Shut down your machine."

Reluctantly Newton did so. He went over to the man and removed the electrodes from his forehead. He had been so engrossed in his work he hadn't noticed the change in the EKG. The normal spikes that were present when he had begun monitoring had dropped. There were no more of the rough triangular shapes. There was now a serene waviness to the line. Like a gently rolling sea. He pulled the electrodes from the man's chest.

"Pick that up, please," von Breslau said to Newton.

There was a heavy steel crowbar lying on the floor near the gurney. Holz had borrowed it from the gardeners earlier. It was a five-foot-long rod they used for prying up rocks or stumps on the grounds.

The tool was much heavier than it looked. Newton grunted as he hefted it from the floor.

Von Breslau looked down at the man on the gurney. "I want you to bend this, if you would be so kind."

"Are you out of your mind?" the man said. He glanced at Newton. The scientist's face showed intense strain from holding the bar.

In return, von Breslau smiled tightly. "Please humor an old man."

The man shrugged. "This is crazy," he said. He reached out and took the bar from Newton. And almost bowled the scientist over. He wrenched the bar out of Newton's hands, lifting it high in the air. "What the—? This thing's light as a feather."

He lowered the heavy bar and took it in one hand, rolling it from palm to fingertips. The truth was, it felt lighter than a feather. It was as though the crowbar had substance, but no weight.

"Now, can you bend it?" von Breslau asked.

The man laughed. "Sure. No problem." He placed his hands approximately two feet apart on the bar and twisted. There was an angry cry of protesting metal, and when he was finished, the bar had a U-shaped bend.

There was a gasp from the room. But not from either von Breslau or Newton. An enraged voice cried out from near the door.

"Thieves!" it shrieked.

Newton turned. Von Breslau puckered his lips, his eyebrows rising in annoyance.

The Master of Sinanju stood in the doorway, his bony hands clenched in balls of white-hot rage. Tight hazel eyes shot charged streams of fury with laserlike intensity at the pair of men across the cold laboratory floor.

"Fiends! Barbarians! Plunderers of greatness! Prepare to pay for your venal pilfering in blood." And like the angry driving wind propelled at the fore of a furious tempest, the Master of Sinanju whirled dervishlike into the laboratory.

REMO HAD DECIDED his time might best be served trying to locate Lothar Holz.

Holz was a vice president, Remo knew, so it seemed logical he'd be wherever it was vice presidents hung out. Since the building didn't seem large enough to house an eighteen-hole golf course, Remo opted to check the executive office suite.

He abandoned the R&D level and took the stairwell at the end of the hallway up to the offices.

He found the place swarming with tanned, trim executives, just a hair or two on the younger side of middle age. Their expensive suits were tailored to perfection, and as they walked past Remo, he overheard them discussing everything from actuarial tables to market placement to on-line strategy. It was worse than any image of hell the nuns at Saint Theresa's Orphanage had tried to instill in him.

Remo assumed that someone along the way would try to stop him. He wore his usual black T-shirt, black chinos and loafers. In this sea of suits, Remo thought he stuck out like a sore thumb. What he didn't realize was that in a company used to many computer-related projects, he wasn't dressed unusually when compared to any of the computer programmers on staff. It was assumed by everyone that Remo was just another programming nerd. Everyone, that was, except for Lothar Holz's secretary.

"Hello, there," the girl purred when Remo entered the office at the end of the hall. She placed an emery board she had been drawing languidly across her index fingernail into the top drawer of her desk.

"This is Holz's office?" he asked.

"Uh-huh," she said. She leaned forward. "Can I do anything for you? Anything at all?"

"You can cool your jets. I'm here for Holz."

Remo headed for the door, but the girl was quick. She leaped from behind her desk and plastered herself against the inner-office door.

Her body was pressed between Remo and the door.

"Mr. Holz isn't in right now."

"I can hear his heart beating through the door."

"That's mine." She grabbed Remo's hand and

placed it on her chest. "Let's go someplace and talk," she urged.

Remo didn't have time for this. He tapped the woman lightly on the inside of her wrist. She gasped once loudly, her eyes rolled back in her head and she collapsed sideways onto the office sofa. A broad smile stretched across her overly made-up features.

Remo popped the flimsy door lock and entered the inner office.

THE PAIN from the Dynamic Interface System signal was immediate and intense. It was far more powerful than it had been the day before.

It felt as if someone were dragging his brain and spinal cord out of his body through a raw hole in the back of his neck.

Then all at once, the pain receded.

Lothar Holz was seated behind his desk. A row of tinted windows behind him overlooked a grassy courtyard. Beyond the courtyard was the matching PlattDeutsche building, reflecting its sister structure in its glassy facade.

Remo tried to lunge for Holz, but was rooted in place. He heard the door behind him close and saw Holz's male assistant step out from his peripheral vision and move across the office to stand behind his boss.

"Don't bother to struggle. You know how pointless that is."

Remo gritted his teeth. ''Not as pointless as you might think.''

He was surprised to find that, unlike the previous day, the impulses weren't arrested when he tried to speak.

''We've eliminated certain aspects of the program. Speech, most involuntary responses. The pickup time is greatly increased. You can thank Dr. Smith for that. His input—so to speak—has helped us a great deal. He delivered you over to us in every sense of the word.''

Holz grinned triumphantly.

Remo felt foolish. He wanted to say something like *You'll never get away with this,* but the fact was he had already experienced the futility of trying to battle the powerful radio signal. He had tried for hours the last time and had failed. He screwed his mouth tightly shut and stared stonily ahead.

Holz tapped a pen on his desk. ''When the interface van didn't check in, the entire building was wired yesterday for your eventual return. Sort of a Sinanju frequency. I don't suppose you'd want to tell me where the van is.''

''Go goose a gorilla.''

''Your cooperation is irrelevant—we will find out what we want to know easily enough.''

Remo remained silent.

''Understand this, Remo, your consciousness may

still be yours, but your body now works for me.''
Holz turned to his assistant.

"The interface van is at the sanitarium in Rye. Get it.'' The man nodded and move toward the door. Holz called after him. "If Smith attempts to stop you, kill him.''

Remo heard the door close behind him.

"It became necessary to import assistance on your unique case,'' Holz said. "You might be curious to see how we're progressing.'' He called downstairs on his office phone and instructed the technical staff to move Remo down to the fourth floor. Holz then went over to the broken office door and pulled it open.

Remo felt his legs kick in automatically. Woodenly. Again he felt the sensation of some outside power forcing its will upon him.

Though he tried to stop it, he felt the interface signal coursing into his brain, seeping down into his limbs. In spite of his determination, he knew it was no use. He followed Holz out the door.

The expression on Holz's face was insufferably smug.

Remo wanted to rip the smile right off his smarmy face. And unbeknownst to Holz, he still had one chance. One thing the man hadn't bargained on. Remo prayed the Master of Sinanju would be able to locate the source of the signal and stop it once and for all.

THEY HAD NEARLY been killed.

Von Breslau seemed to be taking the whole thing in stride, but maybe he didn't understand what a close call it had been. Only Dr. Curt Newton knew that they had made it by the skin of their teeth.

The old Asian had blown into the room like a man possessed.

His hands flailed; his legs pumped. Jaw clenching furiously, he had swooped toward them.

He was halfway to them when his actions began to slow.

The signal had kicked in automatically, as it had been programmed to do, but there was a time lag. The Dynamic Interface System signal hadn't been able to cerebellum lock as quickly as usual. If the mainframes hadn't already been programmed with the information obtained from the younger one, they would never have stopped the Asian.

His speed continued to decrease as he came across the room. In the end, he was like a child's toy with worn-out batteries.

He froze a foot away from Newton.

"What is this sorcery!" the Master of Sinanju demanded. His hazel eyes were sparks of uncomprehending fury.

Newton ignored Chiun. He tried to copy the old doctor's calm demeanor, though his heart pounded at the closeness of Chiun's attack.

He spoke directly to von Breslau.

"You'll be interested to know we've just refined the program to include speech. Before, we were forced to take hold of everything. It took up tons of computer space. Now we're able to be much more selective."

Chiun's eyes were wide in shock as he tried desperately to move his limbs. He couldn't budge them an inch.

The test subject seemed baffled by the strange apparition in the kimono. Newton tapped him on the leg.

"Why don't you take off for now? We'll call you back when we need you."

The man nodded his understanding. He hopped down from the gurney and began buttoning his shirt. He paused a moment, startled. "What—?"

He held his hands out in wonder. The pads of his thumbs and forefingers were covered with a faint white dust. He had crushed one of his plastic buttons to powder.

"A result of the test," Newton said quickly. "Just take it easy on things for the rest of the day. Until we can get back to you."

The man left the room, staring in amazement at his own hands.

Von Breslau had shuffled over to Chiun. He brought his face to within inches of the old Korean. "This one is very old," he said to Newton. He looked even more unhappy than usual.

"An understatement, I'd say," Newton agreed. "His physical reactions are astounding for a man of any age. But they're even more astonishing for someone of his obviously advanced years."

"You have lived a long life," von Breslau said to Chiun.

"Longer than an apricot. Not nearly as long as a mountain." The Master of Sinanju had contained his initial rage. Through a monumental effort, he held himself in check.

"You were Master when Berlin fell?"

Chiun did not speak. His eyes were as cold and barren as the belly of the deepest, iciest sea. His mouth was a razor slit.

"You murdered the chancellor." It was a statement of fact, as well as an accusation.

"If you refer to the strutting little fool with the comical mustache, he ingested poison and shot himself when he heard the Master was coming. Double ignominy for a preening jackanapes. This, of course, after he had bravely taken the lives of a pregnant woman and a dog."

"You lie!"

"He was a coward who sent fools to die for his base cause. His black-booted storm-poopers were devaluing the market for true assassins."

Dr. Erich von Breslau's normally bitter features had slowly churned into a burning fury. "Liar! You are a murderer! And you will stand and watch, filthy

Korean mongrel. You will watch while I wrap my hands around your own lying throat and squeeze the life from you.''

The arms of the Nazi doctor shook with rage as he reached for the unguarded throat of the Master of Sinanju.

Though von Breslau had the determination, it was unlikely he had the strength to follow through on his threat. He never found out. For at the precise moment his palms brushed Chiun's Adam's apple, Lothar Holz entered the lab, Remo in tow.

"Doctor, stop!" Holz raced across the room and grabbed von Breslau's wrists. His hands had just encircled Chiun's throat. Curt Newton, who until that moment was a spectator in the exchange between the pair, joined Holz. Together they pulled von Breslau away from Chiun.

"He will die!" von Breslau barked.

"That is not the plan!" Holz said.

"It is *my* plan!" von Breslau was furious. Spittle sprayed from his mouth as he spoke. His eyes were daggers of hatred aimed at Chiun.

"Curt, please see that this one is transferred down here." Holz nodded to Remo.

Newton reluctantly pulled himself away from von Breslau. He called to the regular interface labs to have the signal controlling Remo switched over to the subordinate mainframe in the current lab.

When Newton was out of earshot, Holz lowered his voice. "Four wants both Sinanju masters."

"Those of Four do not understand," von Breslau said.

"They understand," Holz whispered harshly. "This has been a costly investment. The Americans were not likely to buy into the interface technology anytime in the near future. With the abilities of these men at our disposal, we can recoup our investment a thousandfold. Immediately."

"We don't need them. Your machines can give us what they have. I can make an army like them long after they are gone."

"We don't know that yet. Are you willing to risk the fury of those in command on a single test?"

Von Breslau considered. At long last he nodded. "Agreed. For now," he whispered. To Chiun, he said loudly, "Remember. You live at my convenience, Korean."

"You die at mine," the Master of Sinanju responded levelly.

HOLZ SMILED WARMLY. "Doctor?" he said to Newton. He pointed to Remo. He indicated the floor near Chiun with a nod.

Understanding, the scientist punched a few rapid commands into his computer. The interface signal brought Remo from his place near the door, over to Chiun.

The two men stood side by side, motionless. Neither was able to gain comfort from even a sideward glance at the other. They were blocks of deep-frozen ice.

Holz clapped his hands together warmly. "Imagine. I have the only two living Masters of Sinanju under my control. Yours is a tradition which spreads back, what, thousands of years?"

"You seem to know a fat lot about us," Remo said. His words were thick with loathing.

Holz beamed. "Actually I probably never would have heard of you," he admitted, "if not for my grandfather."

17

Lothar Holz remembered being sickened when his father revealed to him what his family had been during the Second World War.

He was eight years old and attending a private academy in Bonn.

While the public perception was one of danger for unrepentant Nazis still residing in Germany after the war, the reality was quite different. During the 1950s, in the little enclave where Holz spent his formative years, there was safety. The authorities tended to look the other way when Lothar's father and friends were about.

Young Lothar knew some of what had happened. Hushed words. Furtive whispers.

Oftentimes his father would drink to excess. Deep in drunken melancholia, he would curse those forces that had conspired to thwart his dreams. They had crushed all hope of the promised, glorious Reich.

It was only when Lothar had seen pictures of the atrocities committed by his countrymen that he confronted his father. He was a brave boy, in short pants and cuffed felt jacket, standing up to the world-weary drunkard.

He told of the photographs from the book of a boy he had met, the son of an American serviceman who was part of the occupying force in postwar Germany. He told of the half-naked, emaciated men and women standing in the snow. Of the bodies.

He had expected his father to be furious, but instead the elder Holz grew deathly quiet.

Leadenly he sat down on their gaily printed sofa. He beckoned his son to sit next to him.

"You have heard of the so-called atrocities before, have you not?" his father had said softly.

Lothar admitted that he had.

"How long ago did you first hear?"

"I do not remember, Father. All my life."

"And why did you wait until now to question me?"

"The pictures," young Lothar had said desperately. He remembered one of a group of German civilians being led past a row of corpses. They were Jewish women who had died on a forced march. Desiccation had made their faces chillingly deformed. They almost appeared to have been mummified. "The pictures were horrible." Lothar shivered at the recent memory.

"And why was that?"

"Well...these people were dead. Murdered."

His father stroked his chin pensively. "Would it

disturb you to learn that I worked at one of the camps where these *people* were 'murdered,' as you call it?''

He didn't know what to say. His father was admitting to participating in the barbarous acts he had seen depicted in the young American boy's book.

When he saw Lothar was speechless, his father suddenly seemed to change the subject. ''Would you call your mother an evil woman, Lothar?''

Lothar tried to call up an image of his mother. She had died when he was very young. As it was, he had little memory of her, but what he had was all good. She had been loving, nurturing. Everything his father was not.

''My mother was kind,'' Lothar said. When he said it, he found he had a lump in his throat.

''Would you think her any less kind if you found out she was a participant in these events you describe?''

Shock. It could not be.

''My mother would not have done those things.''

''Lothar, you barely knew your mother. I knew her well.''

He didn't tell all, that bitter afternoon, but he told enough.

The rest Lothar learned in years to come.

His mother had been the daughter of a Gestapo officer. Lothar's grandfather was someone who had found favor with Himmler and as a result was posted as representative for the secret police at Kummersdorf, where the V-1 rocket was under development by the Army Weapons Department. Later he was transferred, along with the project.

His daughter was grown by that time—a nurse—and it was her mildly influential father who had gotten her work first at Dachau and later at Buchenwald.

She had found herself special nursing assistant to the camp doctor. Many of her duties involved treating the usual ulcers and headaches of prison guards. Occasionally a fistfight would result in a broken bone or a bloodied nose. But these minor ailments didn't constitute the majority of her work at either camp. She had also participated in "biomedical experimentation."

At the time, she never considered herself a criminal. She was merely someone who was doing a difficult job under trying circumstances. A job that would have been filled by another if not her.

An edict from Berlin had early on sanctioned *sonderbehandlung,* the term that was a directive to kill all Jews. Therefore, any Jew arriving at one of the camps was, in the minds of those in power, already dead. It had been decreed. So, many of those in the medical power structure rationalized their atrocities committed against the Jews by arguing that they were dead the moment they trudged through the gates. Lothar Holz's mother had argued long and passionately that it was impossible for one to murder an individual who was already dead.

This was what she said to her young husband—a camp guard who saw his marriage as an opportunity to move up—many times over.

But the person she had the hardest time convincing, apparently, was herself. She had climbed into a bathtub of warm water one sunny afternoon when Lothar was four. With her she had brought her husband's straight razor.

After that, Lothar and his father were alone. The year was 1951.

And from that day forward, not an hour went by in his young life where Lothar did not remember his mother fondly. But the day his father hinted to him what his mother had been during the war would alter his perceptions of right and wrong forever.

Lothar had received a fine education. English, Spanish and French were all taught at his exclusive school, in addition to his native German. He learned each language fluently. Mathematics was never his forte, nor any of the sciences. But he was persuasive and well liked, by students and instructors alike. However, this early acceptance by his peers was short-lived. Once he had learned the truth about his mother, his grades began to fail.

His father was called, but he didn't seem interested in his son's problems. The elder Holz's drinking had grown worse with each passing day, and though he was still a relatively young man, he looked older and more haggard as his advanced alcoholism ravaged his system.

He died nearly a year to the day he had first told his son the truth about his mother.

At nine years of age, Lothar Holz was an orphan.

He had no other family. The only relative his father had ever spoken of was his father-in-law, but the man had died during the war, a victim of the Russian and American advance in the death throes of the old power system.

He thought he was completely alone.

Lothar was in the small flat where he and his father lived. It was the day after his father's death. There would be a service of some sort, someone had told him, but he didn't wish to attend. Lothar didn't love his father, although he missed his presence in the shabby little apartment. It was a strange feeling for a nine-year-old to have, and with no one to share it with, Lothar had sat in a dusty corner of his father's bedroom and cried for hours.

He was sniffling quietly when he heard a knock at the door.

He assumed it was another woman from the apartment building with a plate of pastries. When he went to answer it, he found a reed-thin old man in a black topcoat and gloves. The man asked if he could come in.

Lothar assumed he was a mortician, such were his gaunt features and pallor. He let him inside.

The man had stepped through the apartment carefully, as if he did not want the grimy carpet to soil the soles of his shoes. He seemed displeased at the stack of empty liquor bottles piled on the floor.

Lothar felt ashamed. He wished he had thought to throw out the bottles. Quickly he tried to pick up a few items of clothing that were draped over the backs of chairs.

"Do not bother with that, Lothar," the old man had said.

He sat down on the sofa, careful to first brush it free of crumbs.

"I'm sorry," Lothar said with a timid half shrug. He felt as if he was apologizing for his entire life.

"Do not apologize," the man said. "Never apologize for that which you cannot control."

Lothar almost said he was sorry again but stopped himself. He nodded his understanding to the man.

"Good." The man sat straight on the battered sofa. His back was as rigid as a board. He spoke without preamble. "Lothar, did you ever wonder where your father got his money?"

"Excuse me, sir?"

"Surely this flat cost your father money? The *rent*, Lothar."

Then Lothar knew. This was the landlord. He knew his father paid someone so that they could continue to live there. His young mind raced. He had no money. His father had died the day before, and this man was going to evict him today.

The old man saw the look of fright and immediately sought to ease his fears. He explained that he and his friends had been helping his father out for quite some time. It was a debt, he said, they owed to their past. And their future.

It made sense. Though his father never seemed to work much, there was always food on the table and clothes on his back. Lothar had never thought of it before, but the money must have been coming from somewhere.

"We are a network of friends," the old man had said. "There are more of us than anyone imagines. We help other friends when we are able. In your case, we weren't as much helping your father, but the grandson of a friend. A great man."

"My grandfather was a member of the Gestapo."

The man seemed surprised. "Your father told you this?"

"I learned some on my own. Some from my father."

The old man smiled. "Then you appreciate his greatness."

"My grandfather was a murderer."

Now there was shock on the visitor's face. "Lothar, you are mistaken."

"I am not," Lothar said. "My grandfather was a

murderer. And my mother, as well." His neck and cheeks grew red as he spoke.

"Is this what the drunkard told you?"

"It is the truth."

The old man shook his head resolutely. He tried to explain to Lothar the old ways. He tried to tell him that, though his father was an aberration, he had come from a great family. His mother and grandfather had served the Fatherland well. As their heir, he had earned the help of the old man and his friends.

The orphaned boy was horrified.

Everything he had, everything he knew, his entire life had been purchased with the blood of those poor dead women in that grainy black-and-white photograph he had seen a year before.

The old man offered to continue assisting Lothar, but he no longer heard him.

Lothar left his father's apartment that night for the last time.

He lived for a time on his own. Scrounging for food, working odd jobs here and there. Some of the Americans stationed nearby felt sorry for him. They gave him food, clothing. In the winter, someone gave him an old pair of service boots. It was never enough. Most times he had barely enough to eat, and more times than he cared to remember he went to sleep hungry.

Not even one year had passed before he sought out the old man.

He was hungry, dirty and frightened. He justified his decision by repeating to himself that, though he didn't agree with what these people had done in the past, he would be foolish to refuse their help in the present.

The old man didn't scold. When his jaundiced eyes settled on Lothar Holz, the old man seemed curiously unsurprised. He smiled warmly at the ragged, emaciated boy.

Lothar returned to school.

He was housed with other boys in similar situations to his own.

For the first time in months, he was able to eat on a regular basis.

Lothar vowed at first to leave as soon as he was able to survive on his own. But that day never came.

As the years went by, his grandfather's friends secured him a position at the German PlattDeutsche. Though he didn't merit advancement, he found himself moving inexorably up the corporate ladder. And why not? The primary stockholders in the company were all somehow involved in the group that had helped him out years before.

This group eventually consolidated its operations in the small village in South America. This was not long before Lothar Holz—with his flawless command of the English language—was sent to the firm's American plant to oversee the development of the Dynamic Interface System.

Lothar never realized he had been victim of the most subtle kind of indoctrination. What he despised in his youth he learned to accept as an adult. He rationalized that there would always be disagreements of opinion in the world and he merely held a different world view from others.

He often argued with his comrades that a different view was not necessarily a superior one. They were always shocked when he said this. It was Lothar's way of holding on to the shreds of his idealistic youth. To harken back to those few brief months when a warm bed and a hot meal did not matter to him. He felt it made him somewhat of a rebel, but the sad truth was that Lothar Holz justified his life the same way his mother had justified her misdeeds back before Lothar had been born.

Lothar Holz had heard the story of the Master of Sinanju during his youth in Bonn. It wasn't something that was public knowledge, but it was known to the men who controlled his group.

The aged Korean was notorious for an act he hadn't even committed. But the cowardly suicide of one man had dispirited his leaders, forcing them underground for half a century. It had been a crushing defeat. And the House of Sinanju was linked inexorably to that defeat.

Now it might be possible to use the same man to create a victory more far-reaching than any previously hoped for—lasting maybe for millennia.

It was all attainable. Right now.

But Lothar Holz was disappointed to find his hopes stifled by bureaucratic inaction.

"YOU MUST LET ME *do* something, Adolf," Holz pleaded into the phone.

"No. You will let the doctor continue his experiments."

"The doctor can complete his experiments with or without them," Holz said, using the same argument von Breslau had used against him an hour earlier. "We have an opportunity here. We should begin to act now."

"I am open to suggestions," Adolf Kluge said. "What is it you wish to do?"

Holz stammered as he searched for words. The truth was, he had nothing concrete in mind.

He had hoped that Kluge would suggest something. And Holz assumed that his experience with the interface technology, coupled with his imprisonment of the men of Sinanju, would make him more valuable to the organization. "Surely something..." he said. "We could go to Berlin."

"And?"

"The government there is never strong. We could foster insurrection. We could even assassinate the new leader."

Kluge laughed. "Insurrection in Germany. Lothar, my friend, there is *always* insurrection in Germany. Or at least the threat of it. You will have to do better than that."

"I do not like this feeling of impotence."

"The scientists are at work, and you feel left out," Kluge said sympathetically. "Do not worry, Lothar. You have done well. There are forces already at work that you do not know of. Having the services of Sinanju at our disposal is valuable to us in many ways. Your success here will not be forgotten by me."

Holz felt his chest swell with pride. Adolf Kluge said his goodbyes and severed the connection.

Kluge had practically promised him a higher posting. It was long overdue. He was stagnating here at his current job.

Today was the beginning of his inexorable climb up the inner command structure. And tomorrow? Well, Kluge wouldn't live forever.

But Holz still wished he could do something with the awesome power at his disposal. It was like having unlimited credit and not being able to spend a dime.

There was a knock at his door. After a second's hesitation, his secretary entered. "The custodial staff promises your door will be repaired by five o'clock, Mr. Holz," she said. She carried with her a stack of envelopes and company correspondence. "You were so busy this morning, you didn't have time to look at your mail." She set the pile on his desk and exited the room.

Holz checked his watch. His assistant wouldn't have arrived at the sanitarium by now. Newton and von Breslau would be busy with their work, with the pair from Sinanju standing like statues in the corner of the fourth-floor lab. Even with his compliment from Kluge, he was beginning once more to feel left out. He needed something to do.

Holz shuffled through the mail halfheartedly. One of the daily New York papers was at the bottom of the pile of envelopes.

He glanced at the headline. Nothing of interest. Besides, there could be nothing more important happening in the world than what was going on in this very building.

He was about to throw the paper in the trash when a minor article caught his attention. It was a sidebar column. A puff piece on United States Secretary of State Helena Eckert. It accompanied a larger story on proposed sanctions against the Middle East country of Lobynia.

He read the column more carefully, an idea evolving even as he scanned down the lines.

He hadn't even gotten halfway through the article when he realized what he would do. It was a brilliant idea. Something that the higher-ups—especially the older ones—would savor for its irony.

In a way, it was fitting.

And most important of all, it was the sort of thing that would advance his career.

He left the newspaper on his desk and hurried downstairs.

To stir up the embers of the past.

18

Running, running…

Smith tried to catch his breath. It came in desperate spurts. The exhaled mist clung to the frigid winter air.

The solid earth beneath his feet suddenly gave way.

Stumbling.

Groping for a handhold, he tumbled roughly down a rocky slope to the beach. He fell, sprawled across the hard-packed sand. The black grit was in his mouth. He spit viciously.

Smith pulled himself to his feet. Too late.

The Nazi captain. He saw the face. Menk was running toward him. His gun was drawn. His cruel features looked more haggard from the exertion.

Menk was upon him.

Smith still wore the stolen greatcoat. It was large, far too big for Smith's lean frame. Hopefully it was concealing. His hands were hidden from Menk, his shoulders stooped. He tried for all the world to look like a broken man. Someone who had tried a last-ditch flight for freedom and had failed.

Menk seemed to revel in Smith's sunken demeanor. He stood, panting on the beach before Smith. In the background, rumbling in the distance, was the faint drone of American warplanes.

"Your Allies are nearly here, Smith," Menk said. It was a taunt.

Smith didn't respond. He stood his ground silently.

"You will not be alive to greet them."

The man had sat calmly by for a week, watching as Smith was being tortured. Occasionally he would offer little hints to increase the level of pain. Now, in defeat, he planned to kill Smith. To Menk, the man before him represented the force that had brought his dreams to a humiliating end. He would kill Smith. But there was one thing that Captain Josef Menk did not realize. He didn't know Smith had a gun.

Menk raised his weapon slowly, for effect. He would make the man before him cower, perhaps beg for his life.

Smith, on the other hand, wasn't one for histrionics. He pulled his own weapon from beneath the long greatcoat and fired.

The look on Menk's face was one of utter shock. His own weapon dropped from his hand. There was nothing melodramatic, nothing unique about the death of Josef Menk. He merely fell to his knees and dropped facedown on the sand.

Smith dropped, as well. Not from a wound, but from exhaustion.

The planes were closer now. Usedom would soon fall to the Allies.

While he gathered his last reserves of strength, vague resolutions began to fill his mind. Smith would facilitate the dismantling of the V-2 rocket program. He would ensure that the German scientists saw the wisdom of using their talents for a better purpose in America.

He left Menk's body for the tide. Slowly he trudged back up to the road. It was over.

So long ago...

BEFORE he had merely been apprehensive. But when Remo didn't call in by noon, Harold W. Smith began to grow more and more distressed.

He couldn't have arrived at PlattDeutsche's Edison complex any later than midmorning. He was, therefore, three hours overdue. Remo had never been the most responsible individual when it came to checking in, but even he would realize the importance of this mission. Perhaps *especially* him.

They had gotten him. There was simply no other explanation.

And if they had Remo, they had Chiun, as well.

Smith had racked his brain to come up with an alternate plan throughout the morning. There was something that had been troubling him for some time. On the surface, it was an inconsequential point.

He didn't deal in trifles, so his mind had stored it away. But it was important. His mind wouldn't let him forget.

Why did the Dynamic Interface System signal not work on him?

They had been able to access his hippocampus easily, but their efforts to physically manipulate him had proved futile. Why?

He wasn't fighting it, surely. If Remo and Chiun couldn't ward off the signals, then he shouldn't have had any hope whatsoever.

Yet, he had. Even in his own office—once when Chiun had arrived the previous day, once as he knelt over Remo—he had felt the tingle at the back of his neck. It was the same sensation he had felt at the bank.

Neither time had he fallen victim to the signal.

He had spent several hours that morning transferring information from the PlattDeutsche van out back to the massive CURE database hidden behind the walls of the basement below. The technology was unquestionably brilliant, and in time he was certain he could crack the sophisticated encoding system of the programmers.

As he downloaded the information, he had no real way of gauging how much of Remo or himself was stored in the company's mobile hard drive. An entire lifetime of knowledge relegated to a few kilobits.

He would have liked to have studied the new information more carefully, but he found himself distracted. As he worked, he continually checked his watch, realizing that as the time grew later and later, it was becoming less and less likely that Remo had succeeded.

Once he was finished, he had returned to his office to wait. As he sat ruminating, the same vexing question that had bothered him for two days surfaced once more.

Why wasn't he affected by the interface signal?

Behind his desk, staring out at the waters of Long Island Sound, Smith's mind wandered.

He thought of Usedom again. Of Captain Menk.

What did those events have to do with the present? Why was he remembering them now?

There were other matters far more pressing. He forced the memories of the island of Usedom and of Captain Menk away.

He thought of the bank. He thought of Lothar Holz.

Holz. Menk.

His brow furrowed.

Yes... Yes, it was possible.

Smith's lemony features grew more intense as he called up an image of Captain Josef Menk in his mind. The face on the beach. The bland look when confronted with mortality.

Yes, he decided. He didn't know how likely it was, but yes, it was possible.

But that was not all. There was more to the bank. What? What?

He tried to picture himself there. He saw it as if he were viewing it on television. The young mortgage officer before him. Holz calling to the crowd. The robbers. The startled looks on the faces of the thieves at the arrival of the bank guards. The sudden movements. Holz glancing at the street outside. The white truck.

Another vehicle beyond...

Smith sat up straight in his chair.

That was the answer.

And he believed he had an explanation for his own apparent immunity to the interface signal.

Smith's analytical mind raced. If they had Remo and Chiun, would they come for the interface van? Quite probably.

It was an old ruse, but it might work.

And if he was right about his own immunity...

If, if, if...

Smith hurriedly patched in his computer to the Pentagon's. He circuitously routed an order from the Chairman of the Joint Chiefs of Staff to Edwards Air Force Base.

When he was done, he shut down his computer

and pulled open his desk drawer. He found a familiar battered cigar box tucked away in the back. In it was a well-oiled automatic and two spare clips. Coiled around the gun was an old leather shoulder holster. This gun was like new, but the well-worn holster was obviously from his CIA days.

Smith slipped the gun, clips and holster into his pockets. Picking up the keys Remo had dropped on his desk earlier that morning, he headed for the door.

At the door, he paused.

He looked around the office for what he realized could be the last time. There was a great risk factor involved. The results of today's events might mean a final end for him, for Remo, for Chiun. For CURE.

Smith was far from an emotional man, and as he looked back inside the room he wondered how normal people said goodbye to a room in which they had served tirelessly for more than thirty years.

Harold W. Smith had no idea.

He felt for the switch beside the door. Certain that the lights were off, he left the office.

No ONE AT THE GATES of Folcroft questioned Holz's assistant.

His cab attracted no attention. It wasn't unusual for a family member to take a taxi to visit a loved one in the sanitarium. No one ever stopped a taxi.

He was surprised to see the white van with the ornately stenciled PlattDeutsche America insignia on the door, parked in the lot beside the building. They had made no attempt to hide it. It was parked right out in the open, clearly visible to the main entrance.

He paid the fare and let the cab go.

Walking as if he belonged there, he crossed over from the main driveway to the parking area.

The broadcast coupling was damaged. He didn't know that was what it was, only that a bare piece of metal hung down from some wires over the cab. Otherwise, everything seemed fine.

He checked the back. The door had been broken off and repaired.

Hastily, it seemed. It was a sloppy welding job. There were furrows that almost looked like finger marks all up and down the sides of the large rear door.

The back handle was bent. He rattled it experimentally. The door was solid. So solid, in fact, it wouldn't open. The fool who had repaired it had welded it to the side panels. At least it wouldn't fall off in traffic.

He shouldn't dawdle. Leaving the rear of the truck, he climbed up into the spacious cab.

He checked the door between the cab and the rear of the van.

That didn't budge, either. It wasn't fused like the other door, but only appeared to be stuck. No matter. Let Holz worry about that in Edison.

The keys weren't in the ignition, but that didn't

matter. He had driven the van several times himself. He pulled a spare set of keys from his pocket and stuck them in the ignition.

The engine turned over on the first try.

The security guard gave him a polite wave as he drove out onto the street. It was the same little half salute the guard gave all the service trucks as they passed through the gates of Folcroft.

Holz's assistant did not wave back.

19

Sir Geoffrey Hyde-Black was out of air freshener.

To the sorts of people who used air freshener, this would seldom be viewed as more than a minor inconvenience. To Sir Geoffrey, it was a disaster far greater than using the Magna Carta for a doily and accidentally flushing the crown jewels down the loo.

Because without his little can of aerosol spray, he would have to smell "them" in all their malodorous glory.

The odors Sir Geoffrey wished to mask were those of the wogs.

This was a disparaging term invented during the British colonial period to refer to Orientals specifically. Through the years, the original meaning had dissipated to the point where it referred to any race or nation deemed primitive. In Sir Geoffrey's case, when he used the term *wog* he was referring to the other members of the United Nations General assembly.

They all, quite frankly, smelled to him like a blood sausage that had gone off. Every last bloody wog.

He longed for the day that he wouldn't have to deal with any of them, but as Her Majesty's chosen ambassador to the United Nations, he hadn't much of a choice.

He only wished the wogs didn't smell so frightfully bad.

It wasn't that Sir Geoffrey was a racist, mind you. Oh my, no.

If he had only thought ill of Third World nations, that would have been racist. They all smelled, of course. That much was certain. And they were most assuredly wogs. If it wasn't the funk of unwashed clothing and bodies, it was the stench of a thousand native spices pouring from endlessly prattling mouths. Mostly chutney.

In the opinion of Ambassador Hyde-Black, the Second World countries didn't fare much better. "Wogs in bad suits," he would say.

And let's face it, the only real Second World country was Russia and the whole population stank as if they'd spent half their lives marinating in the bottom of a vodka bottle.

As far as First World countries were concerned, the only ones that mattered were the United Kingdom and the Americans. And Sir Geoffrey had never quite forgiven the colonists for their 1776 decision. They were, in his humble opinion, wogs to a man. And wogs always smelled.

In the case of the Americans, the collective national odor was one of undercooked beef and over-priced perfume.

So that left Great Britain, alone in the world without an odor.

Of course, that didn't include the East End of London. He refused to go near there without nose plugs and a portable fan. These people, though protected by Her Royal Majesty and equal in the eyes of the Crown, were nonetheless, wogs. As were the British citizens of Liverpool, Wales, Scotland and Northern Ireland.

In fact, you could work in the City, bank on Fleet Street, frequent the haberdasheries on Savile Row and still, in the opinion of Sir Geoffrey Hyde-Black, be a wog.

And a wog, to Ambassador Sir Geoffrey Hyde-Black, always, always, unfailingly and without exception, smelled. It was an immutable fact.

And so when the General Assembly was meeting, Sir Geoffrey always armed himself with as many cans of air freshener as he could carry. He liked to keep an even ratio of cans to wogs. But he invariably exhausted his supply on those long special-censure sessions when one of those bloody mad Arab countries was acting up.

Lobynia was up to some new nonsense, and the world community was meeting at the UN Building to discuss possible sanctions. It should have been an easy matter to resolve, but the Americans had brought back the insufferable Helena Eckert to negotiate. She had been the U.S. ambassador to the UN until her appointment as Secretary of State more than a year ago. As acting ambassador, Eckart had seen fit to offer resistance to a compromise hammered out by the French ambassador. When Eckert had expressed her disapproval, the Arab contingent had become quite agitated, and the stage was set for an afternoon of heated debate.

Sir Geoffrey had just surreptitiously spritzed his last spurt of pine-forest mint onto the sweat-stained caftan of the angry Hamidian delegate and had returned to his briefcase for a fresh supply. He was horrified to find he had no more cans of aerosol freshener left. Sir Geoffrey was faced with the dreadful prospect of having to inhale the unsweetened smells of unshowered, impassioned wogs. As the thought registered in his upper-class mind, the ambassador swooned.

Fortunately for Sir Geoffrey, he needn't have been concerned. The Secretary-General adjourned the meeting for the afternoon.

Delighted at his stroke of luck, Sir Geoffrey hurried from the General Assembly chamber, his monogrammed handkerchief held firmly over his mouth and nose. In the British offices, he ordered up his limousine and took the elevators down nearly thirty stories to the street below.

His man, Parkinson, was waiting near the entrance.

Sir Geoffrey fell into the back of the limo, and the car sped off into Manhattan.

"Problem, sir?" his driver asked. His enunciation had the stodgy, labored cadences of an aristocrat. Sir Geoffrey liked the boy, even if he was a touch woggish.

"It's these people and their ghastly odors, Parkinson." When Sir Geoffrey spoke, it seemed as if his lower lip had been stapled to his uvula. "Remember this always, Parkinson," he said self-importantly, "it is one thing to talk about helping the unwashed masses of the world. It is another thing entirely to have to smell them."

He instructed the chauffeur to drive around the city for a while.

Eventually he had to find a place where he could replenish his supply of air freshener, but first he wanted to purge his mind and lungs of the foul poisons already ingested.

He felt safe in this city, as long as he was in his limousine.

It was the finest, most impregnable high-tech device on wheels this side of a tank. A bomb could go off in the glove box, and in the back seat Sir Geoffrey would still be safe as a babe in his mum's arms.

They stalled in traffic on Forty-second Street. They were parked there, amid a thousand honking wog horns, when the car suddenly hit a bump in the road.

Rather strange, that, Sir Geoffrey thought. How does one hit a pothole when one is parked?

The car rocked as if it had been hit by mortar fire. Sir Geoffrey was thrown roughly around the back seat.

"Good heavens, Parkinson, what was that?"

"I'm not certain, sir."

Sir Geoffrey quickly assessed the situation and employed his great British intellect. "Well, steer around it, then."

"Very good, sir."

The car hopped again.

Parkinson looked genuinely shaken. "This is very confusing, sir. We're not moving. And I didn't seem to see any holes in the road."

Parkinson waited for a response. Sir Geoffrey said not a word.

That was odd. His master generally took a rogue pothole as an opportunity to deride the Americans for their shabby, woglike approach to civil problems.

And, Parkinson noticed, the traffic sounds were suddenly much louder than they had been. Almost as if something was open to the street.

But, of course, Sir Geoffrey would never open a window. He thought the smells of New York City were at least as bad as the rank aromas of his fellow UN delegates.

Must be his hearing. Parkinson made a note to go to a doctor to have his ears checked as soon as possible. And anyway, the traffic had thinned by this time. They were able to move on.

The limo continued driving along Forty-second, both rear doors missing.

The spacious, fragrant back interior of the vehicle was as exposed as a Buckingham Palace scandal.

The back seat where British ambassador to the United Nations, Sir Geoffrey Hyde-Black, had sat was empty.

ARKADY ROKOSSOVSKY was a pirate.

He wasn't the old-fashioned kind of pirate. He had sailed on actual water precisely one time in his life. It was a pleasure boat in the Black Sea, and Arkady had thrown up, feeding the fishes with his half-digested lunch.

No, he wasn't a pirate of the seas, but rather a pirate of technology.

Arkady taped movies illegally. It was a process that, to most Americans, was half hobby, half nuisance. To Arkady, it was a living.

The films he taped he sold to his fellow country-men on his return trips to Moscow. It was quite a successful venture. Movies cost nothing to rent here, so his only real investment was in his two videotape machines. Back home, the tape machines cost a fortune, but those who could afford them could afford to pay top dollar for such great American classics as *Ghoulies* and *Porky's Revenge*.

Arkady made a pretty good buck off of video piracy. It helped supplement his income as Russian ambassador to the United Nations.

In Russia, nothing official paid very well these days. Government service was no longer the easiest way to a posh Moscow apartment, a weekend dacha or a ZIL limousine.

Fortunately America was still the land of opportunity for enterprising Russians. Those lucky enough to be posted at the UN mission had far greater purchasing power than their countrymen back home. And the diplomatic pouch meant that they could cart back duty-free loads of blue jeans, American cigarettes and Mars candy bars. A small payment to the customs officers, a portion to the Moscow police, a stipend to the black market, a cut to select individuals in the foreign-service office, and the rest went to the lucky entrepreneur.

Arkady Rokossovsky felt like a millionaire.

He was pleased when the General Assembly had suspended debate on the Lobynian sanctions. He would be returning to Moscow in another week and he wanted to make certain he brought along with him as many tapes as he could carry.

He left the video store with two full bags.

Arkady balanced the bags in one hand as he searched through his pockets for his car keys. In the days of the old Soviet empire, he would have had his own personal driver, but these days everything was on a much tighter budget. Sometimes he missed the old days.

He was almost at the car when he began to get the feeling he was being watched. It was an odd sensation. One that he hadn't felt in some time.

He had been part of the mission in the old days, back when nearly all of the Soviet diplomatic corps was KGB. In fact, when he first saw the FBI warning at the beginning of a videotaped movie, he thought that the American federal police agency had somehow found a way to watch him through his television set. His belief in an omnipresent state was that ingrained.

But this was different than KGB surveillance. There was a strange thrill of electricity around him. The very air seemed charged.

He was at his car. Arkady, fumbling now, placed his key in the driver's-side door lock.

The pressure around the Russian ambassador suddenly changed. Arkady thought he saw something move out of the corner of his eye.

For an instant, he swore he saw a bony hand with long, tapered fingernails flash before his field of vision. Then he saw nothing.

SECRETARY OF STATE Helena Eckert passed her doorman at the Brewster Building on Park Avenue. Since her appointment to State, she spent very little time here. It was good to be home.

The doorman politely touched the brim of his cap as he held the door open wide. She didn't even acknowledge his presence, pretending instead that the door had mysteriously opened of its own volition.

She was a matronly sixty-year-old woman who used too much makeup and spent too little time applying it. Her lips were smeared with sorry streaks of red, her cheeks caked with blotches of orange rouge and her forehead daubed with bits of shimmery blue where an overzealous application of eyeliner had spilled over. Her hair, tinged blue, looked as though it had been styled at Bellevue.

Helena Eckert didn't care. She prided herself on her ability to apply her own makeup. She never let the servants go near her rapidly aging face. As for her hair? Curlers. It had shocked a lot of people when she first revealed the truth to the *New Yorker* magazine.

She felt so...so bohemian.

Not that she couldn't afford the best hair and face consultants in the world. Helena Eckert was rich.

But she didn't want anyone to hold that against her.

Public perception was so important among the lower orders.

Even after she had graduated from ambassador, she had refused to change her grooming habits. Even after the President himself had weighed in on the subject.

But none of that mattered for now. The Lobynian sanctions had brought her back to her old haunts. She was "ambassador" again. If only temporarily. She insisted while she was in New York that she be addressed as such.

Today, she wore a Perry Ellis raincoat over her Christian Dior blouse and skirt. She felt this proved she had the common touch.

After all, if she wasn't of the people, she never would have been caught dead wearing those rags.

The foyer to her apartment building was mercifully empty and Acting Ambassador Eckert rode up to her penthouse apartment in peace and quiet. Quiet was important to her after the morning she'd spent.

She was a diplomat even though there were those who said behind her back that Helena Eckert wasn't very diplomatic.

Acting Ambassador Helena Eckert didn't care what anyone thought. In spite of what the naysayers said, her work gave her the opportunity to prove her affinity for all persons of all creeds and races.

But those Lobynians were a matter all to themselves.

She didn't understand the issue too clearly. The President had phoned her personally to explain something about oil rights and a sunken boat and missing inspectors, or some such nonsense. She had listened to him for a while before finally stopping him and demanding to know what it was he wanted her to do.

He told her, she thanked him and hung up. Her boss had an unfailing ability to complicate matters.

The elevator stopped one floor below her own, and she got off.

She went over to her private elevator and punched in her personal security code.

It was a wonderful feeling to be home. She wondered if she shouldn't just quit this whole State Department nonsense once and for all. It was really only a lark, after all. But her predecessor had been so utterly dreadful, it was unlikely anyone would let her go back to being just a plain old full-time UN ambassador. They were afraid *he* might come back were she to vacate the post.

Helena decided to forget about the United Nations and the State Department for the time being.

It wasn't even three o'clock in the afternoon, and she was done with that nonsense for the day. She would ride up to her apartment, have the servants draw her a nice hot bath and soak her tired old body until her weary old blood positively boiled.

The elevator opened into the main hall of her apartment. Helena was surprised to find someone standing in the foyer near the great marble staircase. He appeared to be waiting for someone.

"Can I do something for you?" Helena Eckert asked, annoyed by the distraction.

"Lady, run."

The young man seemed positively urgent. His

deep-set eyes were pleading. But he didn't seem to realize something of vital importance. Helena Eckert didn't run.

"What are you doing here?" the ambassador snapped. "I'm going to call the authorities."

He must be with one of the servants. Probably the new Latino maid. Clamidia's friend or no, Acting Ambassador Eckert was not about to be verbally assaulted in her own home.

She had wheeled and was marching on the designer phone on the foyer table when the young man charged.

He seemed to be giving contradictory messages. His body language said one thing; his voice said another.

"Run!"

His advice suddenly seemed quite prudent. Unfortunately Helena Eckert had no time to follow it. The young man with the tortured skull-like eyes was upon her.

His hand slapped down soundly. The telephone was instantly pulverized. Gold and silver plates shattered and skittered across the floor as the inner workings of the device spilled out over the edges of the small table.

Helena Eckert gasped. It was the last sound she would remember making.

The man's other hand flew around and seemed to

flutter before her green contact lenses for a moment. But only for a moment.

The hand descended as if pulled by an invisible line. It made contact with the jowly side of Helena Eckert's neck.

The ambassador slumped to the floor.

Her assailant made a disgusted face. But, he found, his work wasn't finished.

Another signal charged like an electronic stampede through his brain. Against his will, Remo Williams lifted the unconscious woman from her apartment floor.

His face etched in grim lines, he carried Helena Eckert onto the elevator. The silver doors closed on his skeletal visage.

LOTHAR HOLZ SOUNDED thrilled as he talked into the cellular phone.

"All three without a hitch. You're a genius, Curt."

"You're risking a lot, Lothar," Newton replied. "We've never had great luck with the satellite signal. In tests we always got noise on the line eventually. You could have waited for the van."

Holz checked his watch. "The van is back right around now. And we're already through." He stifled a laugh. For the first time, it sounded to Newton like the laugh of a madman. "I couldn't wait another minute for this."

"I'll just feel better once they're hooked back into the office system."

"Don't worry. We'll be leaving in a minute."

"Please get them back here soon, Lothar."

"Just keep monitoring." Holz cut the signal and stuffed the phone back into his jacket pocket. "Will they be out long?" he asked.

Remo and Chiun stood impassively above the prone bodies of the three United Nations delegates. The ambassadors were bound at the wrists and ankles in shiny copper wire.

Remo and Chiun ignored Holz.

"Blast that speech program," the PlattDeutsche vice president said with a chuckle. "You two look like a couple of cigar-store Indians. No matter. Newton will figure out a way to make you answer. Even when you don't want to."

There was a groan from the floor. Holz shifted his attention away from the two men and looked down at the ambassadors.

Helena Eckert's eyelids had fluttered open.

"Where am I?" she asked. She looked around. The floor on which she lay was dirty concrete. High above her were exposed girders. A few feeble white rays filtered in through a single filthy skylight.

As she blinked away the fog, she saw that she was in some kind of warehouse.

Lothar Holz crouched down until his face was a foot above hers.

"You have no idea, madam, but you are going to repay a very old debt."

For the first time in her privileged life, Helena Eckert was scared. The fright registered in her voice. "Is this blackmail? I'll call my brother Rudolph. He'll pay you anything you want."

He touched her gently on her chin. "I already have part of what I want, madam Secretary," he said softly. "The remainder will come from you." He stood up, brushing dirt off his trousers.

"Gentlemen?" he said to Remo and Chiun. He made his confident way toward the warehouse door. A van was backed against the open doorway.

As HOLZ WALKED, the PlattDeutsche satellite tracked his movements.

Dr. Curt Newton, a state away, picked up the information on his computer in Edison and ordered the Dynamic Interface System signal to animate the men from Sinanju. Just as he had for the three kidnappings. The whole procedure took place in under one second.

Remo and Chiun fell in step behind Lothar Holz like dutiful servants.

Holz loaded the two Masters of Sinanju into the back of the waiting van. He had driven it there himself.

They were like mannequins dumped in some dark storage space until further display. Though lights were available, Holz hadn't bothered to switch them on. There were no windows.

The van was the same model as the one that housed the mobile Dynamic Interface System equipment, but the rear of this vehicle was empty save for two benches on either side.

Remo and Chiun sat together on one of the benches.

After a moment, they felt the motion of the wheels beneath them.

"Little Father?" Remo asked. His eyes normally adjusted to the darkness, but Curt Newton obviously hadn't mastered that part of Remo's program. The van was black as a tomb.

"I am still here if that is what you were wondering," Chiun's disembodied voice replied. The all-enveloping darkness made it seem tighter. A plucked violin string.

"What are we going to do?"

"For now we are going to sit."

"I'm serious," Remo pressed. His own voice sounded anxious to him.

"As am I, for at the moment it appears we have no choice."

"That's a pretty damned defeated attitude, isn't it?"

"I am not defeated. I am awaiting an opportunity."

Remo didn't seem convinced. "Great. When do you think that'll be?"

"I will know when it presents itself."

"Hmm," Remo said, nodding. "Wait and see. Isn't that for people without options? I prefer to *do* something."

"Then do this magical whatever-it-is. And when you initiate your daring escape, Remo, do not forget to bring me with you."

"You're not making this easier, Chiun."

"And you are?" In the dark, the old Korean's singsong was annoyed.

Remo sighed. "I guess maybe not," he admitted. "It's just that I went though something like this with the Pythia just a couple of weeks ago. Even as helpless as I felt with that, there seemed to be some hope. A chance I could fight it. We can't do anything here unless Holz's damned machines break down."

"Then that is what we must hope for."

"It seems pretty thin, Little Father."

"It is all we have," Chiun said matter-of-factly.

And in his heart of hearts, Remo knew his teacher was right. One thing was certain. If the interface system *did* go down—if only for a moment—the final switch thrown would be that of Lothar Holz.

The rest of their trip to Edison was tensely quiet.

20

Holz pulled into the PlattDeutsche America parking lot beside the battered interface van. It was the executive lot, and most of the other spots were empty this late in the day. He got out of the cab and went over to the other truck. He eyed the damage to the rear door critically.

As if on cue, Remo and Chiun came around the rear of the van, guided by the interface signal. Their faces were bland reflections of one another.

"Did you do that?" Holz demanded of Remo.

Remo did not respond.

"Your silence is getting very old, very quickly," Holz said impatiently. "This equipment cost a fortune. I hope for your sake it is not damaged." He rattled the handle but found the door was sealed shut. "Splendid. I'm going to have to send this out for repairs," he said with a resigned sigh.

The three of them left the truck and took the rear stairwell up to the lab.

WHEN THEY entered Newton's lab, the first thing Holz noticed was the man on the ceiling. He was crawling like a spider, as if his palms and toes were glue. He slipped across to the wall and climbed rapidly down to the laboratory floor.

Von Breslau stood at the computer terminal near Newton, making little scratch marks in a yellow legal pad. Holz's assistant stood behind the two men. His arms were folded across his chest. His face held the same unreadable expression as always.

"That was incredible!" the man who had just scaled the wall enthused. Holz knew him. His name was David Leib and he was a manager in the sales department. "Did you see that?" Leib asked excitedly. He looked up at the ceiling and then down at the palms of his hands. It was as if he were seeing them for the first time in his life.

Von Breslau fixed his rheumy eyes on Holz. "We have had great success thus far, Lothar," the old man said. He made another mark on his paper.

"I can see that," Holz said, nodding to the incredulous sales manager. "How many test subjects have you used so far?"

"Eight so far, I believe. Eight?" Newton glanced at von Breslau for confirmation.

The old man consulted the yellow legal pad, then nodded.

"Yes, eight," Newton said.

"Have there been any ill effects?"

"None so far," Newton confirmed. Hesitant at

first, he had thrown himself wholeheartedly into the experiments.

"There appear to be no side effects on our subjects," von Breslau said. He was unhappy to have someone answer for him. His lips puckered unpleasantly as he glanced at Curt Newton.

"Then it is obvious to me. Fischer moved too quickly with the first test subject."

"I think that is pretty clear, Lothar. But remember, that's not the only thing to consider. The nervous systems are different. We are still only downloading very basic material. It would take some time for the new systems to adapt. Basically what we have is a new program overriding an old one."

"But it is possible?"

"Hey, they're living proof," Newton said, waving his hand toward Remo and Chiun. "I patched them back into the internal system once you were back on the grounds, by the way."

Holz sloughed the words off as if they were irrelevant. He was watching the sales manager, who had taken to the wall once again. The man climbed effortlessly up and then back down again. The PlattDeutsche vice president's eyes held an envious gleam.

"I think we can bring these tests into a new realm," Holz announced boldly.

"That would be acceptable," von Breslau agreed. His tired eyes strayed to the EKG monitor.

"Hold on, here." Curt Newton jumped in. "I think we should do some more tests. We have no idea what sort of long-term neural side effects there could be to the process."

"That is the problem with scientists, my dear Curt. You people want to test and test and test, while the rest of us are looking for solutions today. And we have one, in your brilliant research. We also have our next volunteer." Holz snapped his fingers. Obediently his assistant stepped away from the two doctors. He hopped up onto the hospital gurney.

"You will step up the process."

"Agreed," von Breslau declared.

"Are you sure?" Newton said. "I mean—" he pitched his voice low so that the sales manager could not hear "—does your assistant realize there are risks?" he asked. He nodded to the blond-haired man.

"He was bred for risk, Doctor. By me." With a minimum of fuss, the old man proceeded to connect the electrodes from Newton's equipment. He worked with the confidence of a man who had been with the Dynamic Interface System program for months. When finished, he stepped over to the computer and proceeded to study the commands Newton gave to the machine. He had done this for the bulk of the day.

For his part, the young man sat on the bench, silent. His eyes were blue stone.

It was all so surreal to Curt Newton. Holz. The infamous Dr. Erich von Breslau. Now this young man's ready acceptance of the danger posed by the Dynamic Interface System.

Newton had become used to the blond man's silent, subservient attitude over the years. He had been with Holz since Newton first arrived at Platt-Deutsche. But Newton was amazed that his pliancy extended to acting as a human guinea pig simply because his employer wished him to do so.

Behind Newton, von Breslau cleared his throat impatiently. He was surprising for a man of his advanced years. He had asked Newton pointed questions concerning the operation of the Dynamic Interface System all afternoon, and the scientist was amazed at the old man's ability to grasp the minutiae of the complex operating system. He remained, however, ill-tempered and impatient.

Taking a deep breath, Curt Newton initiated the procedure that would download the Sinanju information into his latest test subject.

IT WAS AFTER DARK. The waning sunlight had ceased shining through the spaces around the damaged door nearly an hour before.

He used the tiny penlight on his key chain to check the time.

His Timex read 9:18 p.m. It was nearly time.

Harold W. Smith had sat patiently in the back of

the interface van for most of the day. Of course, there was no guarantee that anyone would return for the vehicle. It was logical to assume, though, that if Remo and Chiun had failed, Holz would come back to reclaim his expensive equipment. He would know full well that there was nothing to prevent Smith from giving the PlattDeutsche vice president whatever he wanted.

Smith had opted not to struggle when Holz returned. Using a strategy that dated back to the Trojan War, Smith had stowed away in the rear of the van, waiting. He knew the back door was solid, though it didn't appear to be. Remo had seen to that.

Smith had blocked the door from the cab, hoping that whoever collected the vehicle would assume that it had been damaged in the fight.

Smith's assumption had been a good one. He heard the cab door open at about one-thirty.

There was one tense moment when the handle rattled. Smith held his breath, hoping his barricade would hold. It had. An hour and a half later he was driven safely through the gates of PlattDeutsche America. And he had waited in anxious silence the rest of the afternoon.

He heard Holz arrive about an hour before dusk. From the way he spoke, Smith knew Remo must be with him. But Holz never even checked the cab door. He had left the truck and gone inside the nearest building. After he had disappeared, more silence.

That had been several hours before.

Nine twenty-two. Almost time.

The feeble light from his key chain fell upon the glassy-eyed face of one of the men sent to Folcroft the previous night. The man was dead, as were the others in the back of the truck. Smith had been unable to dispose of them in broad daylight at Folcroft and so had sat in the seat next to the corpses for the past nine hours.

Nine twenty-three.

Smith clicked off the light and replaced his key chain in his pocket. A few rays of yellow, washed-out light spilled into the back of the truck around the spaces in the rear door. Feeling around in the semi-darkness, Smith found the flat metal bar he had propped up against the cab door. It was jammed solidly beneath the door handle, its far end butted up against one of the computer tables.

With the heel of his right hand, he knocked the bar loose. It held for a moment, as if it could not be budged. With a second shove, it popped free. He caught it in his left hand and set it quietly to the floor.

Hoping the door didn't squeak on its hinges, Smith pulled it open. He checked his watch again. 9:25. Five minutes more.

He opened the cab door a crack and glanced around the immediate area. The lot was devoid of cars save for a few stragglers.

Hoping that he had not waited too long, Smith climbed down into the empty parking lot.

"WE'RE GOING TOO FAST." Newton said suddenly.

"His vital signs are perfect," von Breslau countered.

"We didn't download at this rate with any of the others."

"He is different. They were tainted specimens. His physiology is as flawless as is scientifically possible."

Lothar Holz watched the entire procedure delightedly. "The information? He's absorbing it?" He nodded toward the blond man who sat rigidly on the gurney.

"It looks that way," Newton admitted.

"It does not 'look' any way, Doctor. It *is*," said the Nazi doctor. His usually dour expression had given way to one of rare satisfaction.

Newton could only grudgingly agree.

A minute later, von Breslau had the scientist shut down the interface. The flood of information ceased. Holz's assistant showed no reaction.

Muttering happily to himself, von Breslau bustled over to the table and began examining the young man.

Holz turned to Remo and Chiun. "It seems the vaunted men of Sinanju are no longer unique." He indicated his assistant. "In an hour, he has captured your essence. So much for all your years of training, hmm?"

"Release me, thief, and I will test the effectiveness of your device on that one," Chiun said coldly. Von Breslau looked up as Chiun spoke. Sneering at the Master of Sinanju, he continued to administer his tests to the blond-haired man.

Holz smiled broadly. "Aren't you a little concerned?"

Chiun's eyes were as level as a hawk's. And promised far more peril.

"Your servant does not merit Sinanju. Therefore he possesses it not. What you have given him is but a pale reflection of the original glorious light. That light resides in me and my son."

"Are you willing to stake your life on it?"

"I am."

Holz's confident smile broadened. "A fine attempt, Master of Sinanju," he said. "But only a fool would release you. And I, if you had not noticed, am not a fool."

"You're doing a damned good impersonation," Remo offered tightly.

Holz looked at Remo. "I would not be so confident if I were either of you," he said, raising an admonishing finger. He whispered something to Curt Newton. The scientist nodded and punched a few brief instructions into his computer.

Chiun immediately sprang to life. The old man's

back arched, and he flung himself toward the center of the room. He landed flat on the soles of both sandals.

Holz put on his best Western accent. "Dance, pardner," he drawled. He bowed to Newton and the scientist reluctantly began entering commands.

Chiun's pipe-stem legs began stomping the floor of the lab. He twisted his reed-thin arms wildly around, his kimono sleeves flapping like wind socks in a gale. It was like a strange, computer-generated form of the Twist.

Newton chuckled in spite of himself as he watched the sharp contortions of the desperately gyrating old man. Holz clapped his hands and tapped his foot, keeping time with a noiseless band.

Remo watched the entire proceedings stoically, but inside him a hot, roiling pool of anger began to swell. His eyes burned with tears of impotent rage. He knew it was wrong. He knew that Chiun would have told him that it was unprofessional for an assassin to feel such visceral fury. But as he watched the man he had come to love as a father humiliated for sport, he couldn't stop the emotion.

He hated Lothar Holz. And in that moment more than any other since these days of torment had begun, he vowed that he would destroy Holz.

All at once, Chiun stopped his strange cavorting. His twisting arms fell to his sides, and he began to wobble slowly in place. For a moment, Remo thought it was part of their sick show. But all at once, Chiun's legs seemed to roll up inside the skirt of his kimono. Like an aluminum lawn chair, the Master of Sinanju folded in half and fell to the cold laboratory floor. He didn't move again.

Holz stopped clapping. He screwed his face up, angry to have his fun interrupted.

"Why did you stop?" he demanded of Newton.

The scientist was tapping rapidly at his computer keyboard. "I didn't," he said nervously.

Holz looked beyond the Master of Sinanju. He was shocked to find that Remo had dropped to the floor, as well.

"What's going on?" Holz demanded, wheeling.

Newton seemed hopelessly confused. "I have no idea," he replied desperately. "They're both off-line."

Holz eyed Remo and Chiun. The color drained from his face. "So you can't control them?" he hissed.

Newton ignored him. He banged furiously away at the keyboard. "Satellite's gone, too," he announced anxiously.

Chiun lay motionless on the floor. He would not be an immediate problem. But as Holz watched in growing horror, he saw Remo's legs begin to kick feebly. A second later, the young Sinanju Master lifted himself to his elbows.

"Get them back up!" Holz screamed.

"The interface signal is jammed!" Newton cried.
"Reestablish it!"

"I can't!"

Across the room, Remo was pulling himself to his feet. His shoulders and arms twitched spastically as the residual effects of his prolonged exposure to the interface signal began to slowly wear off. He got as far as his knees. But like a toddler taking its first uncertain steps, he fell roughly backward. He immediately began trying again.

Holz's eyes were wild. "What's wrong with the satellite!" he screamed.

"I don't know!"

There was only one option. The men from Sinanju were loose. The life of Lothar Holz was at risk.

It was time to flee. Holz spun to the door. He was shocked by what greeted him.

"NO ONE MOVE." The words came from the laboratory entrance. It was a voice Lothar Holz recognized. He blinked away his disbelief.

Harold W. Smith was framed in the doorway. In his hand was a heavy automatic pistol. He held the gun levelly, near his hip. Smith had positioned himself so that from where he stood he could take out any of the men in the lab.

"Remo?" Smith called evenly. He didn't take his eyes off Holz.

"I'm okay, Smitty," Remo said, voice uncertain.

Chiun's tiny inert form lay nearby.

"The Master of Sinanju?" Smith asked tightly.

"Checking."

Remo couldn't stand. He had been exposed to the radio signal far too long. As quickly as possible—though his every nerve ending protested the punishment—he crawled on hands and knees over to Chiun's prone form. The Master of Sinanju still hadn't moved.

"How—?" Holz didn't have time to get his question out. All at once the building began to shake.

It was like an earthquake.

The computers and mainframe rattled visibly. Clipboards, coffee cups, pens and floppy disks trembled, then tumbled from their perches on tables and computer terminals. A stack of papers fell from a desk near the door and fluttered like autumn leaves to the floor.

Holz was first to see it. Out the high window of the lab, the low black figure seemed to drag through the air. It was so close, he could make it out in spite of the lights of the lab.

It was an odd shape. Silhouetted against the pale blue night sky he spied something that looked like a giant Frisbee balanced atop the back of the massive aircraft.

"A signal jammer!" Newton shouted over the roar of the plane.

THE E-3A SENTRY BANKED north and circled out of sight. But a low, angry rumble could be heard in the distance as the plane circled back around. As it flew, it continued blanketing the area with its broadcast-damping signal.

Remo had to drag himself across the floor to Chiun. His eyes were hot with nervous tears as he rolled the Master of Sinanju over onto his back. Chiun was as still as death. Remo watched impotently. The lips didn't move, nor did the eyes flutter behind their papery lids.

Then all at once, Chiun's narrow chest expanded and deflated. He was breathing. Chiun was still alive.

Remo released his own breath. He had not even realized he was holding it. Above him, the others were talking. Until now, he had shut out their voices.

"I should have killed you immediately," Holz said to Smith.

"A tactical error," Smith agreed, "but not uncommon. Someone else made the same mistake years ago. On the island of Usedom."

A ripple of confusion. "You were on Usedom?" Remo noticed that the tone of Holz's voice had changed.

Smith's voice became brusque. "It's over, Holz," Remo heard Smith say.

Remo didn't even care. Chiun was all right.

"All three of you, move out where I can see you," Smith ordered.

Somehow the thought registered in Remo's mind. Three?

"Smitty, there's—"

He looked up in time to see Holz's assistant attack.

Smith couldn't react. There was no time. The man sprang from out of the shadows beside the door like a panther. His hand flew down toward Smith's arm. It cracked audibly against the barrel of the gun.

A single shot exploded in the room. Curt Newton was caught square in the chest. He toppled backward off his stool, crashing with a fatal thud to the laboratory floor.

Smith's gun rattled off into a corner.

Lothar Holz's response was immediate. "Kill him," he growled.

Smith stood his ground, awaiting the inevitable end.

On the floor, Remo was helpless. He still couldn't move adequately, certainly not quickly enough to help Smith. Desperately Remo searched the area for something, anything he could use against Holz and his accomplices.

The blond man drew back his arm, fingers splayed, in an all too familiar Sinanju move. It was basic but effective. Arms lashed forward in a killer lunge...but they weren't fast enough.

A single projectile rocketed up from the floor of the lab.

The pen tore through the man's shoulder. His

mouth opened in pain, but no sound came out. Where there should have been a scream, there was only gasping silence. Smith dropped down and rolled away from the younger man.

Holz wheeled in the direction from which the pen had come. Remo was already crawling across the floor to where one of the other pens had fallen during the Sentry's first pass.

Holz was lost. Frantic. He barked a command in German to his assistant before racing into the hall. The young man, still bleeding from the shoulder, hustled von Breslau from the lab. Another pen flew after them but, like the first, it missed its mark. It embedded itself up to the PlattDeutsche logo in the door frame.

Smith ran to retrieve his gun. Finding it under a small metal bookcase, he ran out into the hallway, after the fleeing trio.

Several seconds later, Remo heard a single muffled shot accompanied by the squealing of tires. Another noise—this time a distant crash—followed the gunfire. The roar of a truck engine faded into the night.

A minute later Smith returned, panting and shaking his head.

"They got away in the van," he said breathlessly.

"Forget them. Help me with Chiun."

Smith nodded crisply. By now some mobility had returned to Remo's legs. Though he hobbled as

Smith puffed, they managed to get the Master of Sinanju up onto the hospital gurney.

As Remo ministered to Chiun, Smith crouched to check on Newton.

The scientist was wheezing irregularly. A frothy foam of pink encircled his mouth. The wound in his chest had stained the front of his dress shirt a deep crimson.

He was speaking softly, almost moaning. His words were unintelligible as he gasped to get them out. He said the same two syllables over and over.

Smith got down on one knee and tipped his head to Newton's mouth.

Half a minute later, Curt Newton gulped one last, pained lungful of air and then expired. Leaving him, Smith returned to Remo's side.

Remo was massaging the Master of Sinanju's wrists. Chiun's eyes had begun to flutter languidly. The younger Sinanju Master's thin lips were drawn tight.

"What was he saying?" Remo asked, nodding back to Newton.

Smith frowned unhappily. "It sounded like 'Nobel,'" he replied.

21

"You have overstepped your bounds." Over the phone, the voice of Adolf Kluge was as frigid as an Arctic ice storm.

"I only wanted to please," Holz replied.

His superior didn't even acknowledge the statement. "Take what you are able and return to the village immediately. There will be seats reserved for you when you arrive at the airport. Call me from there for further details."

"Herr Kluge, please," Holz begged. "Dr. von Breslau assures me he can operate the equipment."

"You will return to the village immediately," Kluge ordered.

The line went dead.

Holz stared at the receiver for a long time. It felt cold in his grip. Finally, very quietly, he replaced the phone in its silvery cradle. Woodenly he left the small roadside booth and returned to the interface van.

Von Breslau was in the back, along with Holz's assistant. He had bound the shoulder of the blond man with a strip of cloth torn from a bloody lab coat. When Holz reentered the van, the doctor was tapping an impatient index finger on a steel table.

The bodies of Ron Stern and the other technicians were gone.

Holz had dumped them in a shallow ditch by the side of the road late the night before, covering them with handfuls of rotting leaves. The floor of the van was still coated with a thin veneer of dried blood.

"Is he making arrangements?"

Holz was biting the inside of his cheek, deep in concentration.

The doctor had shaken him from his thoughts. *"Nein—"* Holz fell into the language of his youth, but quickly caught himself. "I mean, no. No, we are to stay here and proceed with my plan."

"What?" von Breslau demanded. "Does he realize how dire our situation is?"

"Of course he understands, Doctor. He also understands the importance of our mission." Holz was growing more confident as he spoke. He was here. Kluge was in South America. He still had time to turn this minor setback to his advantage.

Von Breslau shook his head, his naturally dour expression more severe than normal. "I have never known Kluge to be a fool," he said.

"He is not," Holz stated. He spoke in a sharp tone, as if he had taken personal offense.

Von Breslau refused to be taken to task. "What is it we are to do?" he said wearily.

"You will continue your work and thus allow me to complete mine."

"I have told you, Holz, the files have been wiped clean. There is no longer any Sinanju information in these computers. All that is left is the basic programming of the interface system."

"You understand how to use it?"

"Newton outlined the basics of the system yesterday. It has very user-friendly commands."

"That was for my sake," Holz explained impatiently. "I insisted on it." He didn't admit that, in spite of the elementary commands of the Dynamic Interface System design, he still couldn't grasp how to make the machine work. Newton had tried many times to show him the wonderful simplicity of his brainchild, but Holz proved uneducable. He was mildly resentful that a man who was nearly ninety years old had figured it out in less than a day.

"The system might be simple," von Breslau conceded, "but it is worthless without the neural files Newton created."

Holz smiled. "Fortunately for us, Doctor, the late Curt Newton was kind enough to create backup files."

THE FOLCROFT DOCTOR draped his stethoscope around his neck, careful to tuck the diaphragm end into the breast pocket of his white hospital coat.

"There is nothing wrong with this patient," he announced. "In fact, we should all be as healthy when we're his age."

Remo looked greatly relieved.

"Thank you, Doctor," Harold Smith said.

"Not at all. I'd still like to keep him here. Run a few tests on him, if that's okay with you."

"It is not," Chiun sniffed. "The Master of Sinanju will not be prodded like an ox at market."

"That will be all, Doctor," Smith said hurriedly.

The doctor frowned unhappily. He was used to being deferred to when it came to medical judgments. It was a habit, however, the director of Folcroft had never fallen into. His pride as an omnipotent healer wounded, the doctor left the room.

"You had me worried for a minute, Little Father," Remo said.

"And well you should be," Chiun replied. "The vile innerfaze device should have affected you in the same manner as it did I. These fiends were no doubt able to home in on my awesome vibrations, thus impeding my swift return to robust health." He sat on the edge of the hospital bed. His tiny, birdlike feet dangled a foot above the floor.

"It still knocked the wind out of my sails," Remo allowed. He felt silly trying to defend himself for not being more debilitated by the radio signal.

"Actually I imagine the slowness of your recovery had more to do with your lifetime devotion to Sinanju techniques," Smith offered reasonably. "Your training outstrips Remo's by decades. This, coupled with your advanced years, made your system more sensitive to the deleterious side effects of the signal."

Chiun eyed Smith levelly. "I will pretend I did not hear that," he said, voice chilly.

Smith cleared his throat. "Er, yes. In any event, until we have a lead, you will stay here. I will need you close by if I hear from Holz. Master of Sinanju..."

Bowing, the CURE director began to go.

Remo stopped him. "We've got to *do* something, Smitty," Remo stressed.

"For now we have done all we can. I've dismantled the system at the Edison complex and I have destroyed our respective files. There remains no physical link to CURE."

"Except for Holz and his cronies."

"Obviously."

"I should be out looking for them."

Smith shook his head. "Remo, Holz could be anywhere. I have put a description of the van and its license number on the law-enforcement network. If the FBI or some state or local police force discover him, I will hear of it."

"Have you had any luck finding the people he made Chiun and me kidnap?"

Smith admitted he had not. "I have federal authorities looking into it, but PlattDeutsche owns a large number of real-estate holdings in the New York and New Jersey areas. You are certain it was a warehouse?"

"Positive."

"That definitely limits the search parameters. We should have something in regard to that some time soon. Until then, we can only wait. Perhaps you should both use the intervening time to rest."

Though he spoke to both of them, his words were directed to Chiun.

"I do not require rest," the Master of Sinanju huffed.

"You're the one who should go home and grab some shut-eye," Remo suggested to Smith. "You don't look too hot."

"I am fine." The truth was he had not slept more than an hour in the past two days. Smith was exhausted. "Besides," he added, "there is work here that needs my attention. Now, if you will both excuse me…"

Smith tipped his head to Chiun in an informal bow and left the room.

"I can't just sit here like a lump," Remo complained after Smith had gone.

"We will not." The Master of Sinanju hopped down from the bed.

His hand snaked inside the folds of his kimono. A

moment later, it sprang back into view. In his delicate fingers, he clasped a torn sheet of lined yellow paper.

"What's this?" Remo asked suspiciously. He took the paper from Chiun. There were eight names spaced several lines apart. Each was underlined and separated by strings of some sort of text other than English. Even though it was a foreign language, Remo got the impression that everything was written in shorthand.

"It is what passes for language among Huns."

"Did you swipe this from the lab?" Remo demanded.

"It was near me when I awoke. Smith was preoccupied like a deranged tinker with his infernal machines and you were shouting at ambulance attendants. Neither of you seemed interested in a mere scrap of paper."

"So you filched it."

"I do not filch. I acquire," Chiun said with bland amusement. He plucked the list from Remo's fingers. It vanished back inside the folds of his brightly colored kimono. "Come, Remo. We shall visit the thieves in their dens."

One bony hand held aloft in a knot of ivory indignation, the old Korean headed for the door.

22

Leonard Zabik lived in Somerville, New Jersey, in his parent's three-bedroom ranch house. His was the first name on Dr. Erich von Breslau's list.

There was an ambulance parked out front when Remo and Chiun arrived. Its lights were off, its siren quiet.

Remo left his rented car across the street and strolled over to the Zabik home.

Two slow-moving attendants were bringing out a sheet-draped stretcher when Remo and Chiun walked up. The men continued working, used in their jobs to morbid curiosity seekers. Without warning, Chiun pulled the sheet away as the men were lifting the body into the back of the ambulance.

"Hey!" one of the attendants snapped.

Chiun ignored him. "This is the one we seek," he said to Remo.

"Leonard Zabik?" Remo said to the men. He pointed to the body on the stretcher.

"Yeah. What business is it of yours?"

"What happened?" Remo pressed.

The ambulance attendant glanced at his partner. The other man shrugged. "We're not sure. He was dead before we got here. If you want my guess, though, I'd say an overdose."

The man pulled the sheet back over Leonard Zabik's face, and they proceeded to load the body into the back of the ambulance. The doors slammed loudly shut. Both men climbed into the white-and-orange truck and sped away.

"What do you make of that?" Remo asked the Master of Sinanju once the ambulance had gone.

"His body rejected that which it had not earned."

Remo sighed. "I'd better see what happened," he said. He started up the driveway. He was stopped before he had even gotten halfway.

"Yoo-hoo!" The voice came from next door.

A frumpy woman in her early seventies was waving from the front lawn of the house next door. Remo crossed the driveway to a small picket fence, Chiun on his heels.

"Are you with the police or something?" the woman asked.

"Or something," the Master of Sinanju said haughtily.

"I am, he's not," Remo said, indicating Chiun. He thought the lie more plausible that way. It did not seem to matter one way or the other to the woman.

"I'm Gladys Finkle. I live next door. I saw the

whole thing, Officer. That boy went nuts. Absolutely, stark-raving nuts.''

"What do you mean?''

"I go over there some mornings to have coffee with Edna, Leonard's mother. Lovely woman. Anyway, I was there this morning, and she goes in to wake him because he's going to be late for work. He's in the business side of some computer place in Edison. Well he comes ripping out of that room like the house is on fire. I never saw anything like it in my whole life. He's breaking cupboards with his bare hands and chipping Edna's beautiful Formica countertop. I swear he crushed the front of the fridge. Bent the door right in half. He had a wild look in his eye. Almost like he couldn't stop himself. "Finally he just collapsed right there on the kitchen floor.''

"He died just like that?''

"His legs kicked out for a while. And his arms. Like he was doing some kind of judo or something. He was gone before the ambulance drivers got here.''

Remo nodded. The poor guy had been a victim of his body's inability to adapt to the Sinanju information. He probably didn't even know what had happened to him. They had literally reached a dead end.

And if Zabik was dead, the other poor guinea pigs would be soon to follow.

He thanked Mrs. Finkle and started to leave, ready to return to Folcroft and wait for Lothar Holz to show himself.

"The funny thing is I went over this morning to see if everything was okay. I thought I saw an ambulance here in the wee hours."

Remo was anxious to leave. "Really?" He said the word disinterestedly.

"Yeah. There was a big white truck parked in the driveway. My eyes aren't too good anymore. That's why I went to see Edna. I thought something might be wrong."

Remo's curiosity was piqued once more. "Did she say whose truck it was?"

"It was Leonard's boss or something. He took Leonard into the truck for a while and then let him go." The woman scrunched up her jowly face, a thought occurring to her. "Hey, do you think that had something to do with Leonard dying?"

Remo did not hear the question. He and Chiun were already back in their car. The tires sent up plumes of acrid smoke as Remo spun around and headed back down the street.

The next name on the list was Aaron Solon.

AARON SOLON DIDN'T FEEL very well when he awoke that morning.

He spent nearly an hour debating whether or not to waste a sick day but finally, reluctantly, decided to call in.

He found that there was some sort of shake-up going on at PlattDeutsche America. For a minute,

Aaron was worried that the company had been bought up and that his job was gone. He even considered going in after all. But his boss assured him that the problem was internal.

There was something wrong in the R&D section. Nearly everyone with the Dynamic Interface System had vanished. Dr. Curt Newton had been found in a fourth-floor maintenance closet, dead of a gunshot wound.

Aaron felt a little guilty that he was relieved by the news. But in this day of secret mergers and midnight acquisitions, a touch of selfishness was a job requirement. His boss told him to take it easy for the next few days.

Twenty minutes later, Aaron was lying on the living-room sofa. He had just started watching one of the morning talk shows when the palpitations began.

He could feel his heart begin to beat irregularly, almost as if the organ were inflating like an overfull water balloon inside his chest. It felt like it would burst.

His breathing was still good. Centered. It had been that way since he had agreed to undergo the strange test for PlattDeutsche vice president Lothar Holz. He didn't know how he knew the breathing to be right; he only knew it was. And that for the past thirty-seven years he had been breathing completely wrong. Now, though, it was as if every perfect breath his lungs pulled in was causing his heart muscle to expand and contract wildly.

A heart attack.

He grabbed for the phone. It tumbled off the table near the couch. He clawed for it on the rug. The blood pounding from his chest cavity was ringing hollowly inside his ears.

His hand found the phone. He tried to pull it toward him. It wouldn't budge. Only then did he notice that someone was standing on the cord.

He recognized the man. Young. Long blond hair. He had seen him around the office. Behind him was another man. Solon knew him, as well. Lothar Holz.

The two men picked Aaron Solon off the couch and carried him out the kitchen door.

They are taking me to the hospital, Aaron Solon thought. They know they did something wrong with their tests and they're taking me for help.

They carried him up through the cab and into the back of a large white van. The van didn't move.

Five minutes later, the passenger side door opened once more, briefly.

Two figures got out, carrying a large, awkward bundle. The same figures returned a moment later, alone.

Slowly the van drove down the long driveway and out into the street.

"THIS ONE'S GONE, TOO," Remo said grimly.

Aaron Solon lay at the far end of his driveway

behind a pair of trash barrels.

Chiun came out of the kitchen door and squatted to examine the body. He touched the man's forehead experimentally.

"Innerfaze," he announced, tone grave.

"Are you sure?"

"Note the circular marks on his forehead."

Remo squinted. Two round impressions were faintly visible in the flesh at Aaron Solon's temples. They were consistent with the marks made by the rubber suction cups on Holz's temple electrodes.

"We'd better get to the next one on the list." Remo sighed.

As they hurried back to the car, one thought kept passing through Remo's mind.

What was Holz doing?

SIMON WAXMAN'S WIFE was leaving her apartment when Remo arrived.

She was accompanied by her mother-in-law. Simon's father was off handling the funeral arrangements.

Holz had already been there.

The young woman was so distraught Remo didn't detain her.

The same was true for the next four names on the list. All had met with Lothar Holz earlier in the morning; all were dead.

It was afternoon before they reached the final name on the list.

THE APARTMENT COMPLEX where David Leib lived was near Rutgers University in New Brunswick, New Jersey. Remo left his car in a guest spot in the small parking area, and he and Chiun made their way to the string of two-story buildings.

Before they had even gotten near Leib's building, Chiun was sniffing the air like a dog on a scent.

"They have been here already."

The heavy door splintered and fell back inside the small hallway.

They found David Leib on the floor of his bedroom. All around the room was in disarray. The walls were broken, the bed collapsed. A bureau had been split into two neat halves.

Chiun crouched down near the body. "This one still lives," he announced somberly to Remo.

Remo stooped down beside the Master of Sinanju. The pupils of the young man on the floor were pinpricks. His eyes roamed their sockets sightlessly.

"How long ago was Holz here?" Remo asked softly.

Leib shook his head. When he spoke, his voice was distant.

"Hours...hours."

"What did he want?"

The young man nodded. With an effort, he pointed

to his own forehead. Suddenly his limbs shuddered as if charged with electricity.

"The interface system," Remo said to Chiun.

The Master of Sinanju nodded gravely. "He steals back that which was not his to give."

Below them, Leib had another violent spasm. The man who had been so delighted to climb walls the night before had become a wasted shell.

He gasped once, grabbing Chiun by the forearm.

"The breathing," the young man said. "It felt so...so right."

Chiun nodded his understanding.

Leib smiled. A final frantic shudder racked his slender frame before he finally grew still.

Remo noted that, in death Leib had centered himself. His arms and legs were in perfect harmony with the forces of the universe. Chiun gently closed the young man's eyelids.

Slowly Remo stood. "I better call Smith," he said.

"REMO, WHERE HAVE you been?" Smith demanded. His lemony voice seemed distraught.

Remo explained about the list Chiun had found in the PlattDeutsche lab and about the deaths of Holz's test subjects. He also informed Smith of his suspicion that Lothar Holz was retrieving data from the minds of his victims.

"Why did Chiun not show the list to me?"

"I guess he thought it was family business," Remo said.

"It was," Chiun intoned, even of voice.

Smith did not press the issue. "Please return to Folcroft immediately."

Remo glanced at the Master of Sinanju. Chiun was frowning down upon the body of David Leib.

"Why, is something up?" Remo said into the phone.

"They have found one of the missing ambassadors."

23

Wearing grim expressions, the network anchors broke into the afternoon soap operas, each telling the same story.

Arkady Rokossovsky, Russian ambassador to the United Nations, had entered the offices of Schuler Designs on the fifty-seventh floor of the Empire State Building at approximately one o'clock, Eastern standard time.

He was questioned by the firm's receptionist, but Rokossovsky had ignored her.

Rokossovsky had wandered beyond the woman's desk and into the office. Several people asked what he was doing, but he trudged resolutely past them. It was only when he got to the window that someone thought to call security. By then it was too late.

The window panes had been specially devised for high-buildings.

They were triple-enforced plates of high-density polymer. Invisible steel strands crisscrossed the pane. Each window was guaranteed by the manufacturer to withstand a thousand pounds per square inch of pressure. A marketing embellishment, as most people had imagined, but it was understood that the panes could not be shattered by conventional means. It was agreed by all that Arkady Rokossovsky should never have been able to break one.

In a crowded conference room, Rokossovsky kicked out with the heel of his foot. It impacted with the center of a high windowpane.

Against all design specifications, the heavy plastic rattled on its frame, a long, spidery fracture spreading up its middle. Finally the pane cracked apart in a half-dozen huge sections. Broken sheets of simulated glass exploded out onto Fifth Avenue.

Rokossovsky followed them.

Those who witnessed the obvious suicide found it troublesome for more than just the apparent reasons.

To a man, they all said the same thing. Arkady Rokossovsky didn't look or sound like someone who wanted to die. His actions were incongruous with his words. Or at least to his tone.

From the moment he stepped through the office door to the instant he impacted with the sidewalk far below, Rokossovsky could be heard screaming in Russian.

An immigrant who was standing nearby when Rokossovsky hit the ground translated his final words for the networks. Psychologically, it all seemed to fit.

Loosely interpreted, Arkady Rokossovsky had

been pleading for someone to stop the voices inside his head.

HOLZ HAD WANTED Rokossovsky to do a swan dive off of the observation platform at the top of the Empire State Building, but was disappointed to find that the powerful antennae high atop the structure would have interfered with the signal. Reluctantly he had opted for the fifty-seventh floor.

The Dynamic Interface System van had several portable signal boosters tucked away behind the other equipment. Holz had positioned one in a hallway on the twenty-seventh floor. He was worried that the signal strength would not be strong enough even with special enhancement, but any concerns he might have had were dispelled the instant Arkady Rokossovsky splattered like a fat Russian meatball across the pavement of Fifth Avenue.

A crowd had quickly formed around the ambassador's body. The gawkers offered unintentional cover. Holz had slipped back inside the building to retrieve the booster.

When he was gone, Erich von Breslau motioned Holz's assistant to him. Even though they were alone in the back of the white van, he pitched his voice low.

"I have been in contact with the village," von Breslau whispered to the young man. He had left the truck seconds after Holz had gone to place the booster signal, returning not long before the R&D vice president. He had been unable to speak freely until now. "Our Lothar Holz has not been entirely forthright with me."

The blond-haired man was listening, but there was a distracting twitch at the corner of his mouth. It was a nervous tic that had developed late in the morning. It had grown steadily worse as the afternoon wore on.

Von Breslau's expression was dubious as he watched the young man attempt to suppress the twitch.

"He lied to me," von Breslau growled. "He was instructed to return to the village. He disobeyed a direct order. Kluge is furious."

The young man stared at the Nazi doctor. Despite the muscle spasm at the corner of his mouth, his face remained impassive.

"We have the new Sinanju information, collected from you and the other test subjects. I will bring this back to the village." Von Breslau glanced at the door that led into the cab. "Kluge does not want attention drawn to Four. Not yet. When this fool takes us back to where the Britisher and American are being held, you will kill him."

Von Breslau leaned back in his chair, intertwining his fingers over his slight paunch. He had spoken the words as casually as if he had just given the afternoon train schedules.

Holz's assistant of the past eight years did not even raise an eyebrow at the command. He nodded obediently.

Ever so slightly, the corner of his mouth twitched in punctuation.

24

"It was risky for the two of you to go out like that," Smith admonished.

"Sorry," Remo replied across Smith's desk, "but we didn't exactly feel like sitting around for a month twiddling our thumbs."

"It appears that might not be necessary." Smith went on to describe the incident involving the Russian ambassador.

"It sounds like the poor guy was programmed to off himself," Remo said once the CURE director was through.

"I agree," Smith allowed. "And to shatter the window as he did obviously required Sinanju skills."

"Only minor ones, Emperor," Chiun interjected, lest Smith believe his or Remo's skills to be any less valuable. He stood beside Remo in the Spartan office, hands tucked snugly inside his kimono sleeves.

"That is neither here nor there," Smith said. "The point is, Holz has retrieved the Sinanju information from his victims."

Remo shook his head. "It won't do him any good,

Smitty. All the guys we went to were either dead or dying. They can't adapt.''

"Yes, that is true. However, if they slow down the process to take weeks, months or perhaps even years in order to allow the host time to absorb the information, the process might still work. Your skills could conceivably be sold to terrorist nations or organized-crime syndicates. Or for that matter, to any petty criminal.''

"Savages!" Chiun hissed to Remo. "They would be stealing prospective clients away from Sinanju."

Remo steered the conversation back to the problem at hand. "The British and American ambassadors haven't turned up?" he asked.

"Not yet. But we can assume Holz has similar fates planned for each of them. It is clearly his way of paying back the Allied nations for the defeat of Nazi Germany.''

"Have you been able to find out anything about him yet?"

"No, but I have a suspicion," Smith replied, vaguely. His tired eyes stared off distractedly at the distant wall.

Remo snapped his fingers in front of Smith's face. "Earth to Smitty. Care to share it with us?"

Smith's head snapped back. He blinked a few times, hard. "I am sorry," he said, businesslike once more. "The past three days are beginning to take their toll." He took a deep, cleansing breath before responding to Remo's query. "My suspicions concerning Holz are unfounded at the present time. And they are irrelevant to the current investigation."

"If you say so." Remo shrugged.

"I have done some further checking. Though I was unable to locate any concrete information concerning Lothar Holz, I have found something that might be significant." He began tapping his fingers on the edge of his desk. The keyboard buried below the desk's surface lit up obediently beneath his nimble fingers. "You said the warehouse to which he brought the ambassadors was within an hour or so of the Edison facility. That automatically eliminates most of their New York properties."

"I wish I could narrow it down better," Remo said, "but my system was so out of whack I couldn't even tell north from south."

"Alas, the even more powerful signal employed on me dulled my senses, as well, Emperor," Chiun intoned.

"It might not matter," Smith said. "Given the time interval, there are not many places he could have reached by car. There is a warehouse in Jersey City that is owned by PlattDeutsche. It is both convenient to New York City and to Edison. I want you to begin there."

"I hope this isn't just busywork," Remo grumbled.

"It is a start." As he spoke, Smith opened his desk

drawer and removed two small, flat plastic disks. "I want you each to carry one of these."

Smelling a free gift, Chiun bullied his way in front of Remo. He snatched the small item from Smith's hand, examining it carefully.

"A talisman?" Chiun asked cagily.

"Something like that," Smith admitted.

This seemed to satisfy Chiun. The small object disappeared inside the folds of his kimono.

Remo had taken one of the proffered items, as well. He flipped it over in his hand. Small wires extended from the body of the device.

He could feel the faint hum of a battery.

"What is it?" Remo asked, puzzled.

"Possibly nothing," Smith said. "Consider it a good-luck charm."

The words were uncharacteristically cryptic for Harold W. Smith. He turned away from his two operatives and began typing at his computer.

"Come, Remo," Chiun insisted. "With our emperor's talisman in hand, we cannot fail."

Remo glanced skeptically from the small object to the CURE director. Smith looked absolutely exhausted. The strain of the past few days had drained him both physically and emotionally. Remo did not press him.

"Whatever," Remo said. He sounded unconvinced.

Slipping the object into the front pocket of his chinos, he and Chiun headed out the door.

25

Lothar Holz knew he was risking everything. By defying Adolf Kluge, he had made himself a powerful enemy. But even Kluge might change his mind—albeit grudgingly—if Holz was able to turn the situation around. And he was convinced he could do just that.

He knew that those from Sinanju would eventually find this warehouse. It had been a public real-estate transaction made several years before. PlattDeutsche had no reason to keep it secret. They had intended to use it for storage but never had. It would only be a matter of time before Smith uncovered it. He would eventually send his enforcers here.

If Holz could obtain another complete copy of their neural files, either of the young one or the old one, he could claim a resounding victory. As it stood now, he had only been able to reclaim a small fraction of their capabilities.

He planned to download one of them and run before they had a chance to catch him. If he succeeded, even Kluge might come around.

Of course, Kluge had been upset by the abductions. But the old ones in the village would savor the victory. And some of the old ones still had influence.

No, this was the answer. He would return to the village a hero instead of a bumbling clown. And his victory would put him back on the fast track.

Holz drove the white van behind the decrepit warehouse and circled around the building, negotiating the tricky path through the pothole-filled drive. The rear lot was a shambles. Tufts of crabgrass and dandelions pushed up through sections of cracked asphalt.

Wet papers and crushed beer cans were strewed everywhere. At one time, a pile of sand had been dumped toward the rear of the lot, but over the years most of it had washed down over the remaining patches of faded tar. An abandoned car, stripped of doors and tires, lay in one corner, exposed to the elements like the bleached skeleton of some long-dead desert animal.

Holz tucked the interface van beneath the shadow of the abandoned warehouse. Where he parked, the main road was clearly visible around the far rear corner of the building. He turned off the engine.

Almost immediately von Breslau stuck his head through the door into the cab. He squinted at the brightness of the late-afternoon sun.

"Oh." He seemed disappointed to find that they

were back at the dismal warehouse site. Holz got the
impression that the old man had been sleeping.

"Stay alert back there, Doctor," Holz said from
the driver's seat. "We do not know how soon they
will be here."

"Or if at all," von Breslau muttered in German.
He glanced at Holz's blond assistant. The young man
sat silently in the passenger's seat. The bandage on
his shoulder was stained a deep brown.

"They will come," Holz said confidently. He
placed the earpiece for his transceiver into his ear.
They had tested the device earlier to be certain it was
in working order. He had no intention of being
trapped inside the building with Remo and Chiun.
"We will make certain everything inside is ready,
Doctor. Please prepare our present guests for the welcome." He climbed down from the cab.

The instant Holz was not looking, von Breslau
nodded slightly to the young blond man. In spite of
his severe twitching—which had gotten worse on the
trip from New York—Holz's assistant nodded back.

The young man climbed down from the cab. He
trailed his master to the decrepit building.

The old Nazi doctor watched them go through
hooded eyes.

"I will be prepared, Lothar," von Breslau said
quietly. "But I fear you will not be." The old doctor
smiled wickedly and stepped up into the rear of the
van.

REMO AND CHIUN TOOK the Holland Tunnel beneath the Hudson River to Jersey City.

Chiun sat beside Remo in the front seat. He had removed the object Smith had given him and was examining it carefully.

"Stop looking at that thing as if it's going to do something," Remo griped.

"Pray to your gods that Smith's talisman is strong enough to ward off the evils of the innerfaze," Chiun said ominously.

"I wouldn't count on any hocus-pocus to save us," Remo replied tensely. "Smith didn't sound too sure that that whatever-it-is would work. All I can say is we'd better hit hard and fast." His face was grim as they drove out of the tunnel up into the sunlight.

"We will prevail," Chiun insisted as he secreted the strange object away once more.

Remo followed Smith's directions to the letter. They found the building in a bombed-out section of town. An old, faded sign identified the place as the former home of Ingalls Meat Packing Distributors, Inc. The sign at one time had stretched the length of the building.

The place looked familiar to Remo. He did not know if it was because this was the same warehouse he and Chiun had been to the day before or if it merely provoked the same sorry desperation of all abandoned buildings.

They parked in front of the warehouse and headed in the side door.

THE NAZI DOCTOR WATCHED the two men glide into the building. Their shapes were ghostly on the thermal monitor. Four other spectral images registered elsewhere in the building.

Tapping away at the keyboard, von Breslau entered the final elementary commands into two of the shapes. All was ready for the final trap.

He found that the Dynamic Interface System allowed him to operate most men simply. It was a matter of entering the proper commands beforehand. Rokossovsky had been easy to program. But he remembered Newton mentioning the difficulty he had had at first controlling the Sinanju masters. He had needed an entire team to control one man.

That wouldn't matter to von Breslau. He didn't need to manipulate them at first, only to stop them. That, he was told by Newton, was relatively easy.

He saw the spectral outlines of Lothar Holz and his assistant.

Von Breslau would soon send a message ordering the young man to attack Holz. He would wait until Holz was cornered.

That Holz deserved to die wasn't even in question. Any fool who lied to Adolf Kluge had earned death. But his death wouldn't be entirely in vain.

Von Breslau planned to follow through on part of

Lothar Holz's plan. Once the men from Sinanju were frozen like statues, he would download the information from one of them into the computer. Copies of the files would be brought back with him to the village for study and further testing.

But he had one final debt to repay. Before he left, he would enter one last command. He would use the Dynamic Interface System to order the young one to kill the Master of Sinanju.

Tapping his tongue excitedly against his loose dentures, von Breslau watched the two men advance.

IT WAS THE SAME building. Remo had no doubt.

He and Chiun saw the marks on the dirty floor where they had left the three bound ambassadors. Rokossovsky was dead. Sir Geoffrey Hyde-Black and Helena Eckert were gone, as well.

Remo sensed movement to one side of the building. There was a staircase running up to a second floor. The Master of Sinanju indicated the direction with a bony, upturned chin. Remo nodded. He and Chiun made their way toward the stairs.

As they made their stealthy way across the floor, Remo suddenly felt the telltale itchiness at the base of his skull—the controlling signal of the Dynamic Interface System. He glanced at Chiun. The Master of Sinanju was obviously experiencing the same sensation.

But this time, Remo knew that it was different.

The command that until now had allowed the system operators to control their actions was somehow faulty.

This time, they could still move.

Chiun smiled tightly, patting that area of his robe where the strange object from Smith was hidden.

They headed for the stairs.

The rotted staircase ended at a broad landing that overlooked the main warehouse space far below. A single narrow hallway led away from the top step. It ended at a broken, grimy window far away. The hall was flanked on both sides by ancient office doors. Some were broken off their hinges, but most were surprisingly well preserved.

At the entrance to the hallway, Remo hesitated.

There were four occupants. He couldn't tell exactly where two of them were—he could only place them farther down the hall—but the second pair was nearby.

He could also sense that their breathing was too perfect for normal humans. It was almost Sinanju.

Remo turned to warn Chiun of the danger. The instant his guard was down, the first door on the left exploded out into the hallway.

Secretary of State Helena Eckert flew through the air toward Remo, one bare foot tucked up beneath her ample thigh. The other was aimed precisely at Remo's head. He spun to meet her just in time.

Remo caught the ambassador by the ball of her

foot. He flipped her up and over. The mailbox-shaped woman landed on the long balcony with a heavy thump.

Immediately she sprang to her feet, holding her hands out before her in a classic Sinanju attack pose. It was one used by beginners, a throwback to the times when Sinanju masters competed in public contests. Remo could see her fleshy knuckle dimples as she brandished her hands menacingly.

With a hellish growl, the Acting Ambassador lunged at Remo.

BEHIND REMO, Chiun had his own problem to deal with.

The door on the right had sprung open a split second after Acting Ambassador Eckert had flown through the one on the left. From the open doorway, Sir Geoffrey Hyde-Black had launched a rapid series of deadly multiple thrusts against the Master of Sinanju.

Chiun had avoided each of the first half-dozen fists with relative ease. The seventh nearly registered. It was on the eighth that the Master of Sinanju wrapped his delicate hand around the forearm of the British ambassador and yanked the man out into the hallway. Sir Geoffrey crashed into the opposite wall. The water-stained particleboard wall collapsed under his weight, buckling in half. Sir Geoffrey rolled with the wall and sprang back to his feet. He immediately launched another attack against Chiun.

The Master of Sinanju pulled his hand back for a killing blow.

Still battling Helena Eckert, Remo caught the flash of a kimono sleeve from out of the corner of his eye.

"Don't kill him, Little Father!" Remo shouted.

Chiun appeared angry. "Would you suggest I let him kill me?" he asked impatiently.

"Just immobilize him," Remo called.

Helena Eckert's foot lashed out, and Remo ducked away from it.

Chiun let out an angry hiss of air. The British ambassador threw out another malletlike fist. The Master of Sinanju grabbed Sir Geoffrey by the bicep and spun the man around like a top. His hand clamped down on Sir Geoffrey's neck. The man froze stiff as a board. The instant he did so, Chiun heard a groan from behind. When he turned, he saw that Remo had the American ambassador in an identical embrace.

Carrying Helena Eckert like an overfilled bag of groceries, Remo crossed over to Chiun. He had an unhappy expression on his face.

"What do we do with these now, O wise one?" Chiun asked hotly. "For if we let them go, they will be made to attack us once more."

"Wait a minute, Chiun," Remo said in a hushed tone. He cocked an ear to one side, listening down the hall. "Do you hear something funny?"

AT THE REAR of the building, Lothar Holz heard Remo shout to the Master of Sinanju.

His assistant stood nearby. Closer, it seemed, than usual.

The shaking had become almost unbearable. Holz pressed his fingers against the earpiece.

"They're here!" he whispered into the small transceiver. "You were supposed to tell me if they were coming!"

Von Breslau didn't reply. The earpiece remained silent.

Holz glanced around desperately. He had to get out. He couldn't be caught here.

Luckily the rear rooms all opened onto the fire escape. He'd get down to the van. He could not allow these men to capture him.

Quickly he turned toward the rear door. He was just fast enough to see his assistant flash from out of his peripheral vision.

The man's fist moved lightning fast, in a direct line for his face.

He was astonished by what happened next.

Lothar Holz looked on, bewildered, almost a spectator to the actions of his own body. The first Sinanju-enforced blow landed with a squishy thud.

ONE MINUTE BEFORE, von Breslau had been fussing impatiently with the equipment in the van.

He couldn't get a lock on the Sinanju men. He had

tried, but the Dynamic Interface System stubbornly refused to work. He didn't understand the intricacies of the system. If it didn't work, it didn't work. He had gotten some information from the young one. That would have to suffice.

He only wished he had been responsible for the death of the Master of Sinanju. But that could still happen. Even in his lifetime. He had the information that could be used to ultimately destroy the old Korean. In a year, perhaps two...

But first things first. He used the interface system to enter a command into the mind of one of the men in the building. It was to Holz's assistant. He told the man to kill Lothar Holz. Von Breslau waited what he felt was an appropriate amount of time and then cut the signals to both ambassadors. If the blond mute was still in the room when the Sinanju men got there, it was his own fault. And anyway, he was expendable; von Breslau was not.

This task accomplished, the good doctor climbed up into the cab of the mobile interface van and started the engine.

HELENA ECKERT suddenly became slack in Remo's arms. He placed her on the floor and glanced at Chiun. Sir Geoffrey Hyde-Black had gone as limp as a plate of boiled noodles. Chiun dropped the man as if he were diseased. All at once, Remo became aware of an engine roaring from the lot at the rear of the building.

Running to the window at the end of the hall, Remo was just in time to see the rear of the Dynamic Interface System's van clear the side of the building. Its twisted rear door bounced roughly along with the rest of the frame through the potholed driveway, sending up plumes of sandy smoke. A second later, it reached the road. Engine flat out, the truck thundered off.

It was gone.

Remo stood near the door from which he had sensed movement a few moments before. There was nothing now.

He hoped Holz hadn't gotten away again.

Remo pushed open the door. In the middle of the untidy room, a body lay twisted on the floor.

The face was an unrecognizable pulp. It resembled a pile of raw hamburger. The blood-streaked hair was wrenched out by the roots. All that remained were patchy, mottled clumps. The entire head, hands and torso were soaked with blood.

Remo looked more closely. He saw it. The tiny radio earpiece Holz was so fond of wearing. He heard Chiun enter the room behind him.

"His assistant must have killed him," Remo said. "These are Sinanju moves." His nose wrinkled. "Carried to the extreme, though. What a mess." He stood.

It was probably understandable. By now, Holz's assistant would have been experiencing the final side effects of the Sinanju download. He had been in better physical shape than the other test subjects, but he wouldn't be able to hold on to it much longer than the rest. He had already begun experiencing the same savage physical outbursts some of the others had had at the end. His wild, mindless attack was proof. He could no longer stop himself.

The killing blows had been repeated over and over even after Holz must surely have died. It was totally unfocused.

Remo went over to the window. He saw the rusty old fire escape.

He must have escaped out the window. It didn't matter. Wherever he was, the young man would be dead by morning. Remo turned to leave.

Chiun was standing by the bloody body, looking on with a curiously musing expression.

"We'd better get the ambassadors out of here," Remo said with a sigh. "Maybe Smitty can do something to get that programming out of them."

He headed out into the hallway. Chiun didn't move. "You coming?" Remo asked impatiently at the door.

Turning away from the body, Chiun slowly trailed Remo out into the hall. His mouth was a somber frown.

26

Von Breslau registered at the hotel under the name Heinrich Kolb.

No one asked him why he had no luggage. All he carried with him was a large box tucked under one arm and a brown grocery bag that swung from his gnarled hand by its handles. When the bellboy offered to carry the items for him, the elderly man cheerily declined.

Alone in his room, he placed the box on the neatly made bed. He set the bag on the floor.

Kluge had made arrangements for him to leave the country tomorrow.

He had a 9:00 a.m. flight out of JFK.

Von Breslau had spent the better part of the afternoon and early evening copying files from the van computers onto diskettes. What he ended up with filled a container twice as large as a standard shoe box.

This was the box he placed on the bed.

From the bag he took several items—scissors,

brown paper, a marking pen and a roll of packing tape.

He arranged the diskettes snugly in the box, shoving a hotel hand towel in around the cargo to fill up the vacant space. Taking great care, he wrapped and taped the box for shipment. He did not address it. That could wait until morning. When he called down for a cab he would have someone at the front desk mail the package for him.

Von Breslau left the box on the nightstand and undressed for bed.

HE DIDN'T KNOW what time he awoke.

At first he thought he was dreaming. It was a sensation of floating—of gentle hands bearing him softly through the balmy evening air. But all at once, the air turned cold.

He tried to get his bearings.

He saw a green metal door opened behind him. It had no handle.

It was cold here. The wind whipped his sparse hair. Von Breslau shivered in his underwear.

Up, around...

He saw the chimneys. Like something out of his past. Fifty years before. Then they had belched a thick, acrid smoke—the smell of burning flesh weighing heavy in the frigid winter air. The chimneys he saw now were idle.

He floated in close to one, very close. He saw the rough surface of the grimy bricks. Then he was up.

Sure hands guided him to the very top. He saw the New York skyline, dazzlingly white. A sea of lights spreading out brilliantly around him. Then he saw the gaping maw of the chimney. Up close. The blackness slid around his head. He felt the tightness at his bony shoulders. The blood rushed to his head. His arms were pinned to his sides. He was unable to move.

"What is it you want?" he pleaded. His voice echoed in the confines of the chimney. "I can get you money. Gold. Anything."

"Gold is generally an acceptable form of payment."

Von Breslau recognized the voice. The Master of Sinanju. The young one spoke next.

"Gold is pretty good," the voice of Remo agreed.

"I can promise you a fortune. It is guaranteed." Von Breslau tried to move his head. Fragments of black grit jarred loose from the chimney's wall and fell into his eyes. He blinked but could not dislodge the painful flakes.

"What do you think, Little Father?" he heard Remo say.

"It is a tempting offer, admittedly," Chiun said. "But I do not feel it is time yet to do business with the Hun. My memory of the little jester with the funny mustache is too recent. Perhaps in another hundred years or so, my attitude could change.''

Then the younger voice spoke down into the hole. ''Don't go anywhere, we'll get back to you.''

Von Breslau felt the young one slip something around his big toe.

He didn't hear them climb down from the chimney. He only knew they had left when he heard the roof door slam soundly shut.

SIX MONTHS LATER, when a maintenance crew discovered the body stuffed down into the mouth of the chimney, the story would make national news. Public interest in the case would generate an extensive investigation, and it would ultimately be discovered that the deceased was none other than the infamous Dr. Erich von Breslau. With the resulting media firestorm, the hotel would begin to wish they had paid attention to the note left by the killer. Whoever had put the body there had kindly placed a Do Not Disturb sign on the old man's toe.

''YOU MIGHT HAVE done it more neatly,'' Smith chastised.

''I don't want to hear it, Smitty,'' Remo said. ''It felt right.''

The look on Remo's face suggested that Smith not press the issue.

"This is all he had with him?" He had opened the box and removed the diskettes.

"That was it. Oh, here." Remo reached into his pocket and removed the object Smith had given him. He tossed it on the CURE director's desk. "I'm not sure, but I think that little gizmo worked," he said.

Smith allowed himself a rare smile. "I thought it might." He put down the box and picked up the object. He flipped it over in the palm of his hand.

"So what is it?" Remo asked.

"It is a pacemaker. You recall I had one implanted recently. That was why I was in New York earlier this week. To see my doctor. The signal must have somehow interfered with the immobilizing aspect of the Dynamic Interface System signal. If it worked for me, I hoped that it would work for both of you, as well."

"Your talisman was most effective, Emperor," Chiun enthused. "It appears, though Sinanju be your greatest sword, that there are other weapons in your mighty arsenal."

"A pacemaker," Remo said, mildly surprised.

Smith replaced the flat object on his desk and picked up von Breslau's box. He frowned as he turned it over in his hands. "You know, Remo, this looked as though it was packed for shipping," he mused. "I wonder where von Breslau was sending it?"

"He and Holz talked about something called 'Four'," Remo suggested.

Smith nodded. "Yes, you mentioned that to me earlier. I did some checking and I could find no reference to a Four organization in any of the pro- or neo-Nazi literature. It is probably merely a minor splinter group. I would not be concerned."

"Well, if this is all wrapped up, Chiun and I will get going."

"Do not be too hasty," Chiun said, stepping forward. "There is still a minor item."

"What?" Remo knew the answer the instant the word passed his lips. "Oh, Chiun, can't you collect your autograph later?" Remo complained.

"Autograph? Oh, yes. Of course." Smith took a pen and piece of paper from his desk drawer and began writing. "You realize, Master of Sinanju, that due to the need for secrecy in the organization, you may not show this to anyone?" He looked up over the tops of his glasses as he spoke.

Chiun's expression grew concerned. "To no one at all?"

"I am afraid not."

"Therefore selling it is out of the question?"

"I must insist." Smith had finished writing and held the small slip of paper out to Chiun.

The Master of Sinanju looked down his nose at the paper as if Smith were offering him a rotted fish. "I have just remembered that I have many of your autographs already. They grace the contracts you have signed with the House of Sinanju. Long live Emperor Smith.''

When it became clear that Chiun had no intention of taking the sheet of paper, Smith returned it to his desk. ''Well, if this matter is finished, we should all go home and get some rest. It has been a very long week.''

Harold Smith rose from behind his desk. Chiun suddenly held up a staying hand.

''Actually there is another trifling item.''

27

Harold W. Smith trudged wearily up the stairs to his bedroom. He had taken his shoes off at the door and carried them, so as not to wake his wife so late. Only when he entered the room did he remember that Maude had gone out of town to visit their daughter.

She had been telling him for weeks. Like so much of his life that did not revolve around his work, Smith had simply forgotten.

He removed his jacket and tie and lay down atop the bedcovers.

He was so drained he didn't have the energy to put on his pajamas.

He lay there for a few long seconds, in dress shirt and pants, staring at the shadows of the room.

It had been a grueling, grueling week.

He had denied his body sleep for so long, he began to see things in the room around him. Strange black shapes flitted out from the corners as car headlights dragged through the room and across the walls. A patch of darkness seemed to coalesce. It was a bizarre vision. He saw the face of Captain Josef Menk fade up out of the shadows. It was an eerie image in a week of foolish daydreams. His exhausted mind was playing tricks on him.

Suddenly Menk spoke: "You destroyed everything."

Smith was immediately alert. The voice was real. It was in his room. He sat up in bed.

"You did it to yourself," he said crisply.

"No!" It was Lothar Holz who stepped out into the room. "It was you! You started this downward spiral! You ruined my life." His eyes glared hatefully at Smith, and Smith fully saw the family resemblance.

"I refuse to be blamed for your personal failings."

Holz took another step. "At the lab, you spoke of Usedom."

Smith's nod was nearly imperceptible.

"You are the one. You killed Josef Menk."

"I did what I had to do," Smith said coldly.

"You killed my grandfather!"

"Your grandfather was a murderer."

"No! No!" His eyes were wild. "My grandfather was a great man!"

With no warning, Holz lunged for Smith.

At the last minute, a long-nailed hand swiped down from out of the shadows.

It met Holz in the abdomen, knocking him away from Smith. He fell against the wall beneath the window.

The Master of Sinanju stepped out of the shadows, talons raised protectively.

He positioned himself between Smith and Holz. Remo seemed to fade in, as well. He moved away from Chiun, toward Lothar Holz.

Holz stood, shuddering. The spastic contortions his muscles were making made it difficult for him to focus. He saw Remo moving toward him. He braced himself for an attack.

"I would stay back if I were you. I have all your programming," Holz bragged, sneering. He tapped his forehead. "It is all up here."

Remo's face was unchanged. "Then it's time I crashed your system," he said, flatly.

Holz flew at Remo, hands flashing frenetically. He threw everything he had in one assault. Every Sinanju move the computer link had loaded into his mind. Holz went for the complex, but Remo opted for the elementary. When the PlattDeutsche vice president was within arm's reach, the broad side of Remo's hand cracked down against Holz's temple.

Holz felt the pressure in his skull. The new eyes Sinanju had given him were still quick enough to see the hand pull away. The pain in his brain joined the crescendo of agony that had been building in his spine, and in a white-hot moment of pure torture every pain receptor along his entire nervous system fired in perfect, harmonic torment.

The intense, horrific, excruciating anguish he suffered seemed to last an eternity. In reality, it was only a matter of seconds.

Lothar Holz was dead before he hit the floor.

SMITH STEPPED OVER from his bed. "Your suspicion was correct," he said to Chiun. The Master of Sinanju bowed slightly.

"How did you know it wasn't him back at the warehouse?" Remo asked, glancing away from the body.

"Because I use my eyes for seeing," Chiun said blandly. "I do not yet know what it is you do with yours." He clapped his hands. "Come, Remo. Remove this refuse from the emperor's bedchambers. We go." With that, Chiun marched boldly out the door and down the stairs.

Remo stared after him for a few seconds. Finally he turned to Smith. "You'd think I would have wanted them to rewrite his program just a little," he said, grinning broadly.

With a reluctant sigh, he hefted the body of Lothar Holz up onto his shoulders and followed the Master of Sinanju out the door.

Take
2 explosive books
plus a
mystery bonus
FREE

Mail to: Gold Eagle Reader Service
3010 Walden Ave.
P.O. Box 1394
Buffalo, NY 14240-1394

YEAH! Rush me 2 FREE Gold Eagle novels and my FREE mystery bonus. Then send me 4 brand-new novels every other month as they come off the presses. Bill me at the low price of just $16.80* for each shipment. There is NO extra charge for postage and handling! There is no minimum number of books I must buy. I can always cancel at any time simply by returning a shipment at your cost or by returning any shipping statement marked "cancel." Even if I never buy another book from Gold Eagle, the 2 free books and mystery bonus are mine to keep forever. **164 AEN CH7R**

Name _____ (PLEASE PRINT)

Address _____ Apt. No. _____

City _____ State _____ Zip _____

Signature (if under 18, parent or guardian must sign)

* Terms and prices subject to change without notice. Sales tax applicable in N.Y. This offer is limited to one order per household and not valid to present subscribers. Offer not available in Canada.

GE2-98

The Camorra takes on the Mafia on America's streets....

DON PENDLETON's

MACK BOLAN®

BLOOD FEUD

A blood feud erupts between the Camorra and the Mafia, as Antonio Scarlotti takes the Camorra clan into a new era by killing his father. Soon a series of hits against top American Mafia men shocks the country, as families and innocent bystanders are brought into the fray. Brognola entrusts Bolan with the mission of shutting down this turf war and stopping the driving force behind it.

Available in August 1998 at your favorite retail outlet.

GSB61

A preview from hell...

JAMES AXLER
DEATH LANDS®
Dark Emblem

After a relatively easy mat-trans jump, Ryan and his companions find themselves in the company of Dr. Silas Jamaisvous, a seemingly pleasant host who appears to understand the mat-trans systems extremely well.

Seeing signs that local inhabitants have been used as guinea pigs for the scientist's ruthless experiments, the group realizes that they have to stop this line of research before it goes too far....

Follow Remo and Chiun on more of their extraordinary adventures....